Praise for Perilous

by Rich Bullock

"A first-rate thriller that grabs you in Chapter One and doesn't let go."
– James Scott Bell

"His small lake town felt real to me. There was a history. There were people I knew. I believed they were real and I wanted to see how things would work out for them."
– Sally

"Rich Bullock has a unique ability of drawing you into the lives of his characters. My greatest compliment? It takes me three days to read the last chapter because I simply just don't want it to end."
– Roger

"It's a mystery, is riveting, and is hard to put down."
– David

Also by Rich Bullock

SHATTERED GLASS

Rich Bullock

Scripture taken from the New King James Version®. Copyright © 1982 by Thomas Nelson. Used by permission. All rights reserved.

Published by RichWords Press

vCS4/30/17

ISBN: 0692650369
ISBN-13: 978-0692650363

Dedication

To those who put their lives at risk to keep us safe.

SHATTERED GLASS

Prologue

2004

November 4th was the night Lilly Glass's world exploded.

Her sketchbook was spread across her lap, her box of colored pencils sharpened. After glancing again at the open art book from the school library, she used the light brown pencil and drew the first swaying line left to right, then curved it around and down. She compared her outline to the horse in the book. The shape of the back and hindquarters was the same.

Lilly repeated the process several more times, filling the page with flanks, withers, muzzles, knees, and hoofs. But her mind was on the arguing coming from the mobile home's kitchen.

She was wondering if the nightly fight would spill into her tiny room, when a *tap-tap* rattled the cardboard square covering her bedroom window, startling her. There hadn't been real glass in the frame since last summer when Mom's current boyfriend, Jerry, the one arguing in the other room, hurled a beer bottle at the outside of the single-wide in one of his rages.

The cardboard's surface was covered with crayon drawings of horses, a whole herd of red, black, yellow-gold, white, and brown beasts running and prancing. The brown ones were her favorite because they matched the color of her hair.

Lilly peeled back the crinkled duct tape closure and swung the cardboard open. Her friend Tony poked his head in and hitched his chin toward the door of her room.

1

"You okay?"

Lilly followed his gaze to the thin door. Jerry had come home fifteen minutes ago, reeking of beer and perfume. Mom was waiting, fortified by her own bottle, purchased at the Gas-N-Go. The thin walls did nothing to contain their angry confrontation.

"Wanna come out?"

Tony's tanned face withdrew into the night as Lilly climbed onto the low bookcase and swung her legs through the opening. She snatched a gray hooded sweatshirt off the bed before dropping onto a stack of plastic crates. Even though the days were in the 50s and sometimes 60s, the November nights were cold. This morning, thin ice had skimmed the dog bowls outside nearly every trailer.

Although the dogs probably got cold at night, Lilly thought them the lucky ones—they got to spend more time outside than the kids.

She thrust her arms into the soft cotton as they walked the familiar route past the Espinosa's trailer, down the dusty wedge between the Haver's and the Smith's. Lean mutts faced each other across the clearing and raised their heads in silent acknowledgement, used to the traipsing youth. The odor of dog poop blanketed the area, and Lilly was glad to get beyond it and catch the fresh breeze from the desert.

Goose bumps rose on her bare legs as Tony led the way down through the deep drainage gully that bordered the cluster of trailers. Colder air collected in the low area, but a hint of warm breeze tickled her face as they climbed up the other side. The trailer park was outside Mojave, California, five rows of ten concrete pads plopped onto a forlorn field surrounded by nothing.

The hot Santa Ana winds were legendary in Southern California, especially along the coast where they funneled down canyons and fanned raging fires that devoured house after house. The Mojave was famous as the place where the winds originated.

Yay, us.

Distant rumbling and flashing lights of two jets tracked between the stars overhead, banking sharply toward Edwards Air Force Base less than an hour away. Lilly had studied about it in school—Chuck

2

Yeager and all that stuff.

But fast jets weren't part of her world. The parched sandy soil beneath her tennis shoes struggled to grow anything but tumbleweeds, brown grasses, and some low green bushes about two days from croaking. After living here three years, Lilly was sick of the never-ending tan dust that aged every car, mobile home, and bicycle, no matter how new they were. Grit covered everything in her room, including her.

She longed to move back to the San Fernando Valley, but Mom's standard answer was they couldn't afford it. Maybe they could if Mom stopped buying booze and cigarettes.

Near the base of one of the electrical towers that marched like spindly men across the landscape, their friend Bobby hunched in the shelter they'd built before the school year began. Like Lilly, Bobby was twelve, but her thirteenth birthday was coming next month, so she called him her "little brother." Tony was fourteen, a full-on teenager.

"Hey, Bobby," Lilly said as she crawled into the open-sided lean-to made of scrap plywood and a piece of carpet. She sat beside him. He laid his head on her shoulder, and she put her arm around him. "Tough at home?" His slight nod told it all. Every kid in the park had stories, most not too good.

Tony's parents were some of the good ones. His father had a job at the air base. Mr. Baker was a light-skinned African-American, and Tony's mom was white and blond. Tony had his dad's black hair, but his skin was a gorgeous tan all the time. Lilly envied him—in a lot of ways.

Tony used a lighter to ignite a candle stub they kept in a pasta jar, then pulled his travel-size Scrabble game from inside his jacket. He'd gotten it last Christmas. They played at least twice a week, and Lilly's spelling had improved rapidly. At school she searched for words she could use to beat Tony, and even slipped some to Bobby. She and Tony took it easy on the younger boy when they played, but if it was only she and Tony, they went all out. Now Lilly won about half the time, and had totally killed him two days ago with a triple score on Q-U-A-I-L.

After an hour of the game, Bobby left to go home. Tony put away the board and tiles, but asked if Lilly wanted to stay a while. They laid side by side, watching the stars against the black sky. When Lilly shivered, Tony slid closer so they were pressed together, shoulder to ankle. The candle flickered, sucking up the last of the wax.

"We're moving next week," Tony said quietly.

He'd been acting strange for several days. She expected something bad, but not *this* bad. She tried to ask why, ask if he'd take her with him, but her throat had closed up tight.

"My dad got a raise and he wants to move closer to the base."

In spite of Tony's warmth, cold spread through Lilly, stealing her will to face the endless tan days ahead.

The candle sputtered and went out. In the dark, Tony's hand found hers and laced their fingers as if they'd be knit together forever. Tears leaked down the sides of her face into her ears, turning to cold pools in the night air.

Two dogs barked in the distance. They were the lucky ones.

* * *

It was nearly 9:00 when Lilly trudged toward her home. She'd choked out "good-bye" to Tony. She thought he was going to kiss her. He had leaned close, then he separated his fingers from hers and turned right onto his street. Although he said he'd be around for the next few days, his farewell felt like forever. Things would never be the same.

Except for her mom and Jerry. And the endless tan dirt of the Mojave.

At their shelter away from the park, the night was a silent blanket, peaceful and comforting—the best part of the desert. She longed to wrap herself in it again as she passed the other trailers, their windows pulsating with noisy televisions, their aromas of pizza, roasted meat, and coffee leaking into the dark. Some families were happy, content with their lives. In other trailers voices rose, nightly conflicts repeated endlessly with no resolution.

Lilly rounded the front end of the Espinosa's double-wide and paused. Anemic weeds scratched for survival in wide cracks in the two vacant concrete pads that separated this trailer from hers. She was glad the neighbors were far enough away so they wouldn't hear too much of the frequent fights. Dim light shone from some of her trailer's windows, but not her cardboard-covered rectangle.

A warm wind—perhaps the beginning of another Santa Ana—shoved Lilly's sweatshirt hood back and sent her hair snapping around her head as she listened. No arguing voices filled the night. That would make it more difficult to slip inside unnoticed. She sighed. There was no postponing it. Momma would check her room soon, and Lilly had to be in it.

She took two steps, but stopped when a hunched figure came out of the shadow at the far front corner of their trailer. A man. He had something in his hands. What was he doing?

The figure turned away and, staying close to the ground, scuttled like a crab down the dirt lane to a vehicle. Even in the scant light, Lilly recognized the profile of Jerry's old white pickup idling softly. The dome light came on when he climbed inside. Yep, definitely Jerry. Why had he parked down the road instead of by the trailer like usual?

The truck rolled forward in near silence, tires crunching on the gravel. She shook her head. The idiot was driving without headlights. Drunk again.

Lilly hadn't liked him from the first, and she never understood why her mother let him stay. He tried to touch Lilly once while she was at the sink washing dishes. His hand brushed her back, slipped lower. She whipped around, holding a soapy paring knife the way Tony taught her. Jerry dodged to avoid being cut. Her hand never wavered, and Jerry backed away. Although she felt him watching her many times after that, he never touched her again. She kept one of the knives under her pillow every night.

Red brake lights flashed when the truck turned the corner a quarter mile down the road, but he was still driving without lights. Maybe the fool would crash in a ditch. Maybe this time he was gone for good.

Lilly started forward. That's when the world exploded in a blinding ball.

Heat seared her exposed face, and smacked her with a wall of sound that lifted her like a giant scorching hand. She tumbled in the air and slammed into something unforgivingly solid. Bones snapped in her arm and leg, sharp pain joining the burning of her skin. She vaguely registered dropping to the ground where she landed face down.

Burning hair, fabric, and metal singed her nostrils. She coughed and spit out sand as she rolled onto her back. Far up into the night sky, a cloud of orange and black roiled, surging like an angry demon. She stared, fascinated as chunks of burning debris rained down, littering the ground like fire from heaven.

One large square spun toward her, its ragged borders burning and trailing smoke. It landed on one edge only inches away. Before it fell away, she made out melting colored horses.

Flickering yellow reflected off the side of the Espinosa's trailer, but the world, in spite of the violence, was strangely muted. Tony appeared above her, kicking away the burning debris and dropping to his knees.

"Lilly! Can you hear me?" It sounded like he was shouting into a pillow. He brushed the hair from her forehead.

She tried to say his name, tell him that his fingers hurt her skin, but nothing came out.

A man ran up and stomped her flaming cardboard horses, each footfall kicking clouds of dust on her. Other adults elbowed Tony aside and shouted unintelligible questions. She squeezed her eyes shut against the biting pain in her arm and leg, keeping them closed tighter when hands lifted and carried her away from the heat. Away from Tony. Away from Momma.

But Lilly knew Momma was somewhere up in the sky, flying toward heaven in the smoke and orange light, leaving Lilly behind in the world of tan dust.

Chapter 1

Five years later…
July 2010

"Don't do it, Chad!" Lilly Hawthorne yelled.

Chad Holt might as well rip her throat out like he'd done to so many others, because he was going to kill her. Kill them all.

The boat turned and cut toward a massive wake coming off the boat he was chasing. The bow slammed into the wake, lifting and launching them into the air. Below, the powerful motor revved higher as it came free, unable to propel them through air like it did through water. Lilly gripped the handholds tighter, weightlessness briefly lifting her off the seat.

The hull crashed back into the water, sending a sheet of spray into her face. She spit out the warm, salty water, and kicked the beer cooler back across the floor where it belonged. Her sunglasses were somewhere by her feet, but she didn't dare let go to retrieve them. Up front, her best friend Pana Grant squealed as Chad turned parallel to the other craft and accelerated across Santa Monica Bay.

At eighteen, Chad was a couple of months older than Lilly and Pana, and had a half-dozen films to his credit. But being Hollywood's latest teen heartthrob didn't qualify him to drive a boat.

The boat wobbled precariously as Chad jerked right and zoomed alongside the other boat barely ten feet away. It held a matching set of four teenagers—two guys and two girls. Lilly noted their excitement when they recognized Chad, who was grinning madly.

One girl began snapping pictures with her cell phone, and then both girls turned their backs and tried for selfies with Chad laughing and mugging in the background. Pana squealed again as Chad veered to within a couple of feet from the other craft.

In the rear seat across from Lilly, Mickey Cain—relaxed and apparently oblivious to their imminent spectacular crash—twisted the top off a beer bottle and held it out to her. "Want one, Lil?"

She shook her head and watched him shrug and take a long swig. It was at least his fifth. The cooler was the only thing that held his interest since they backed out of the marina slip three hours ago, and she likewise lost interest in him three seconds after the first time he called her "Lil." She hated the nickname, and if he called her that one more time, she was changing it. Or pushing him overboard. She'd blame it on Chad's reckless driving.

Actually, she'd given thought to picking a new name. She knew of six or seven kids at school who changed their names in the past year —anything to catch the attention of talent agents and casting companies. Memorable names could make all the difference in Tinseltown.

She once asked her mother—her birth mother—how she chose the name *Lilly*. Her bio dad was out of the picture by the time of her birth, and Mom was alone in the hospital. She said "Lilly" was the name the other mom in the hospital room chose for *her* baby, and Mom hadn't been able to decide on anything better.

The letdown Lilly felt back then still stung. Shouldn't names mean something? She didn't want to be a copy, a me-too clone of a girl she didn't even know. Since that day, her name never felt truly *hers*.

Even Pana's name had special meaning. Her grandfather worked at Panavision during the development of its first widescreen projection lenses in the 1950s. If anyone had Hollywood in their blood, Pana did, so her name was perfect.

"Hey, Lil," Chad called from the front of the boat, "want to take a turn at the wheel?"

"No thanks," she yelled over the roaring engine. Yep, definitely changing it. But for practicality, she should probably wait until after graduation next year.

The bow bucked as Chad slapped across the choppy water. At least he'd put a dozen feet between them and the other boat. He'd consumed as many beers as Mickey, but so far seemed in control. She momentarily doubted that assessment when he abruptly spun the wheel away from the other boat and carved a tight one-eighty around a marker buoy. The stern of the boat dipped so low that the water rose higher than her head, and she was sure they would be swamped. But Chad accelerated before the green wall caught them, and pointed the bow toward Marina del Rey, leaving the wave and the other boat behind.

"We're not going back so soon, are we?" Pana whined. "It's not even two o'clock."

Chad shot her a grin. "Got an audition at four. I'll make it up to you next week. Are you up for hang gliding?"

Pana turned to Lilly with a big smile and raised brow. Lilly firmly shook her head. A boat ride with these guys was one thing. She was a strong swimmer, and if—when—they capsized, she could make it to shore. But there was no way she was going airborne with Chad Holt or Mickey Cain.

Pana's mother's "people" had set up today's double date, and Lilly only agreed under severe pressure when Pana found out Chad was bringing Mickey. The girl had a "thing" for Chad. Then again, half the girls in the US had a thing for the actor after his new movie, *Blood Moon*, opened nationwide last week.

Lilly had—at her friend's insistence—stood in line with her for nearly four hours at the Chinese Theater in Hollywood so they could catch the first screening. Chad running around shirtless for most of the film had elicited oohs and aahs from the predominantly teen female audience, including Pana, but Lilly thought the director went a little overboard with the tearing out of throats and bloody mouths screaming into the night sky. Rumor was the next film in the series would be more of the same.

"Get me another beer, would you, babe?" Chad asked Pana, and she jumped to retrieve a bottle from the cooler. As she handed him the dripping bottle, she grabbed Chad's arm to steady herself, shamelessly rubbing her body against his.

Pana had a great figure, but she'd confided to Lilly she wanted a boob job for her eighteenth birthday. She was convinced Chad would notice if she was bigger on top. Of *course* he would. So would *every* guy. But that didn't mean she should do it. A number of girls at school got nose jobs and implants last summer before their junior year, and the school hallways resembled lineups for the next Barbie audition. But there were whispers that a couple of the girls experienced some serious complications and side effects. Lilly hoped Pana would reconsider.

But Lilly couldn't come on too strong. Her own mom, Ekaterina Orlov, had her personal plastic-surgeon-to-the-stars on speed dial. However, even though Lilly weighed only one ten and had a chest nearly as flat as a prepubescent boy, there was never a suggestion from her parents that she should get a little "fix up."

A loud belch drew her attention to Mickey. If Lilly had a little more on top, maybe Mickey would have paid her as much attention as he did his beer.

Interest from boys aside, Lilly was clear from day one that part of her role in her new family was to round out the family profile in photo shoots and for the pre-determined paparazzi run-ins. It wasn't to compete with Mom in the looks department. Ekaterina was always the star.

At least that's the way it started. Lilly was surprisingly okay with that, because she also knew her parents chose her, adopted her into their lives. They truly did want *her*.

Nathan Hawthorne and Ekaterina Orlov loved her as much as any self-absorbed Hollywood couple with busy lives were capable of, and Lilly prided herself in subtly growing them into better parents. She bragged to Pana that Mom and Dad were closing in on 100 percent perfect. They absolutely loved each other, which was pretty cool to watch.

Beside her, Mickey casually tossed his empty beer bottle over the side.

"Sheesh, Mickey," she said. "Ever hear of a trash can?"

"What?" His eyes had trouble focusing on her.

Well, that was it: he was officially off the Christmas list. Mom would rip him a new one if she saw him do that. Ekaterina Orlov was an active proponent of the *Heal the Bay* cleanup movement.

The nose of the boat dropped as the craft slowed to the speed limit inside the marina, and after a few minutes of slow cruising, Chad turned into the U-shaped slip. He reversed the engine a little too late and bumped the bow so hard against the padded dock that Pana took a tumble.

"Oops," Chad said with a crooked grin, swaying himself as the boat rocked in the undulating water.

Definitely too much to drink. Good thing one of the patrol boats wasn't near. She didn't want to get in trouble for something dumb Chad did. How could he make it through an audition in only two hours? Or more immediately, drive them home. She wanted to get there in one piece.

* * *

Lilly, Pana, and Mickey waited by the rear hatch while Chad searched for his key fob. When he fumbled it and it rolled under the bumper, Lilly grabbed it.

"Give it," Chad ordered, reaching for the fob.

"I'm driving," she said, hitting the unlock button and opening the rear hatch to distract him. She wasn't trusting her life to someone way over the legal limit. Either that or she was walking, and taking Pana with her.

As the guys loaded in the empty cooler, squealing tires caught Lilly's attention and she turned. An old, white van rounded the corner into their parking aisle and raced toward them.

Thinking it was more crazed fans who recognized Chad, she wasn't surprised when it screeched to a stop behind them. But then the van's doors flew open and four men in ski masks jumped out. Mickey took off running as three of the guys grabbed Chad and began dragging him toward the van's side door. Chad threw an elbow that caught Lilly across the face, knocking her into one of the assailants. Someone stepped on her foot, grinding it into the asphalt as Chad flailed and fought. Pana jumped onto one of the men and punched him in the head.

Terrified of going down and being trampled in the mêlée, Lilly gripped the nearest thing she could. It was one man's mask, and it came free in her hand. His grim face was inches from hers, and she took in the messy blond hair, scruffy beard, acned skin, and distinctive crescent-shaped birthmark on his left cheek.

"Hey," Pana said, "you're the guy from the boat rental place. Barry."

Everything stopped for a second. Someone swore, and another voice shouted, "Take them all."

Hands hurled Lilly into the van on top of Chad, who was sprawled face down on the metal floor and no longer struggling. Before she could shift, Pana crashed on top of them both, followed by one of the men. The weight crushed the wind out of Lilly's lungs and ground her ribs together. The van was already accelerating before the sliding door slammed shut.

"Can't...breathe," she managed, and the worst of the weight lifted as the kidnapper climbed off and clamored into the backseat. Then Pana rolled toward the front of the van. Lilly sucked in air reeking of motor oil, urine, and Chad's sunscreen lotion. She started to elbow herself up off Chad's inert form.

"Don't move," said the same hard voice as before. Barry and another man sat side by side on the rear bench. The van squealed around a series of left and right corners, braked hard, then proceeded at a more sedate speed.

Lilly turned her head so she could see Pana lying half-hidden between her and the front seats. Her eyes widened when her friend slid a small, black semi-automatic pistol from her beach bag. Before Lilly could open her mouth, Pana fired over Lilly. The explosions were deafening, echoing around the metal enclosure as the van suddenly rocked wildly and tires screeched.

Lilly was still watching Pana, when a body landed heavily on her, and something wet splashed on her neck. When she turned, Barry's face was against hers, his beard scratching her face. His eyes were wide open, blank. The other man was slumped sideways in the seat, eyes closed, one hand over his chest. Blood pumped through his fingers and dribbled down his shirt in a glossy cascade.

Behind her, more gunshots blasted. When she turned back toward the front, the man in the passenger seat had come up on his knees and was facing the rear. There were two spidery holes in the windshield inches to the left of his head. Smoke curled lazily from the muzzle of his weapon, which was pointed at Pana.

Lilly tracked its aim. Pana was turned toward Lilly. An ugly, finger-sized hole marred the skin above Pana's right ear, and a growing pool of dark liquid ran across the steel deck toward the unconscious Chad.

Lilly sucked in air, perhaps to scream, but it was cut short by the pungent burning of gunpowder that stung her nose and constricted her throat. She stopped breathing altogether when the gun barrel swung up a few inches until it was aimed right between her eyes. Slowly, she lifted both hands to show him she wasn't armed. Only his mouth and eyes were visible behind the mask, and those eyes shown with furious anger.

Her lungs strained for oxygen. Maybe if she held her breath forever, she wouldn't inhale the coppery scent of death surrounding her.

When the man didn't fire, her gaze shifted back to her friend.

Pana. So alive seconds ago. Tears choked Lilly as she began to comprehend what had happened in less than two minutes. Pana had given her life trying to save them. And almost succeeded. Lilly had never known how brave her friend was.

The driver was pounding the steering wheel and swearing. The other man said something to him as he removed the gun from Pana's limp hand, but Lilly's ears were ringing so loudly she couldn't make out his words. The van roared ahead, but her eyes remained on the man who kept his gun pointed at her.

Chapter 2

Lilly rolled onto her other side on the warehouse's cold, hard concrete, twisting her bonds for the millionth time. After arriving, they had duct-taped her hands and feet. Another strip was pressed across her mouth before they tossed her in a corner of the metal building behind some cardboard boxes.

The cavernous space had only a single overhead fixture on, but through a wide gap in the boxes she could make out the closed roll-up door and part of the van. Two bodies lay on the concrete beside the vehicle's sliding door. Pana's body was still inside, only the soles of her pink flip-flops visible.

Chad sat in a straight-back chair in the center of the room, sagging against the wide bands of tape that held him upright. His whole left side was black with Pana's blood, but the men had washed it off his face.

"I can't believe Barry's dead," the driver said as he paced. They were both still masked, but Lilly recognized his twitchy energy, his inability to remain still. He was high on something.

"Shut up, you fool." The other man sat on a swivel chair pulled up to a battered wooden desk, calmly smoking a thin cigar and fiddling with a cell phone.

"But he was my brother!" the driver shouted, pointing to the van.

The other man tossed his cigar away and picked up his gun. He pulled back the hammer until it clicked, and pointed the gun at the driver. "And you are going to join him if you don't shut up."

The driver froze. "Ernesto, what—"

The desk chair skittered across the concrete as the man lunged and backhanded the driver. He went down hard, then rolled on his back to stare up at the man and gun above him. "I...I'm sorry. I didn't think—"

Ernesto. Lilly memorized the name. The one who killed Pana.

For a moment, Lilly thought Ernesto would pull the trigger. She held her breath, wishing he would do it. One more bad guy down, one to go. But at the same time, she wanted to plug her ears against another death, even if it was one of the bad guys.

Ernesto spat. "You want to shout out our addresses? Social Security numbers too?"

"I..."

Lilly found a rusty edge on the steel wall's support beam and began sawing her taped wrists against it.

"The plan hasn't changed," Ernesto said, standing over the other man.

"What?" The driver rose on his elbows. "But Barry's dead."

"We still have a job to do. Maybe you do not care about the money, but I do."

The driver dropped his head and rubbed the side of his face. Ernesto backed up a couple of steps and motioned with the gun. "Now, get the equipment."

The driver scrambled from the floor and unloaded a large box from the back of the van. In a few minutes, he had a stand-mounted light illuminating Chad. Then he set up a tripod and camera and cabled it to a laptop computer.

Ernesto still wore the full-face ski mask, but now donned dark sunglasses and tied a bandana over his mouth. Gun in hand, he stepped behind Chad, grabbed a fist full of Chad's hair, and pulled his head upright. "Start recording."

The driver adjusted the angle of the tiny video camera, then pushed a button on top. He nodded and stepped back.

"As you can see, we have your son. The two girls are here, unharmed. I will send another message tomorrow with instructions. If you do exactly as told, your son and the girls will be released. If not, well..." He pointed the gun at Chad's head and cocked the hammer. The driver switched off the camera.

In her world religions class at school last year, the teacher tested them on the various core beliefs. One quiz was from the book of Proverbs on what God hates. Lilly had forgotten most of them, but two were *Hands that shed innocent blood,* and *A lying tongue.* Dad said those were the basic plots of most movies. This guy probably matched the other five as well.

And if he was lying about Pana being unharmed, what chance did *she* have? This week's blockbuster success of *Blood Moon* assured Chad's value into the millions. He was already under contract for the next two movies in the series, so he'd be heavily insured.

These guys probably had no idea who she was or, more importantly, who her parents were. Otherwise, they would be making a video with her as the star. They might kill her without ever finding out. If she told them, would that help keep her alive? He'd lied about Pana.

"Check the girl," Ernesto said.

Lilly quickly scooted away from the rusty pillar as footsteps approached, not wanting to give them any reason to think she'd be trouble. As the driver prodded her with his grimy boot, she thought of her friend. Pana surprised the men by fighting back, came close to taking all of them out.

Now it was on Lilly to escape and get help for Chad.

* * *

Lilly woke to a noise behind her. The slightest scrape, like something brushing along the outer wall. She looked through the gap in the boxes. The glint of daylight leaking around the roll-up door had disappeared hours ago. Except for some snoring, the warehouse was quiet.

Her right side was completely numb, and she couldn't believe she had dozed off.

The steel wall at her back radiated cold that sent her into shivers. With jaws clenched to quiet her teeth, she listened for long minutes. Nothing more. Maybe she'd imagined the sound, or maybe it was only a passing rat or mouse.

The cold steel felt like ice cubes through her thin cotton T-shirt, but she scooted back until she was pressed against the wall, searching until she found the rusty rough spot on the vertical post. Using slow, quiet strokes, she rubbed her bonds against the metal.

She went still when the steel door suddenly clattered and began lifting on rollers badly in need of lubrication. A wave of salty, damp air washed across the concrete, preceding several booted men who ducked under the door's rising edge. As she scooted closer to the gap in the boxes, she felt the tape on her wrists give way. Her hands were free.

The door stopped, and a van backed into the opening. The vehicle's rear doors swung open and two more men climbed out cradling assault rifles, the type used in movies to mow down the other side. They took positions on either side of the van doors. Two others began unloading plastic bundles exactly like those on television confiscated by the police in drug busts, and stacking them on an empty wooden pallet.

Lilly massaged feeling back into her wrists as Ernesto came into view and faced off with one of the men. Chad was still tied to the chair, and the way his head lolled, she wondered if they had drugged him.

Ernesto's gaze flicked her direction, and she shrank back from the crack. She could identify these new, unmasked men, and he knew it.

The tape was tight around her ankles, and she picked at it with stiff fingers until finally locating an end. Each eighth-inch of progress felt like it was peeling away her sunburned skin.

The confrontation between the new man and Ernesto escalated into a classic, chest-to-chest, male pissing match, arguing over Chad, the video, the dead bodies. There was so much noise from the other men unloading, she couldn't hear well, but near as she could tell, Ernesto didn't mention another girl. Ernesto's partner was mysteriously scarce, probably hiding behind a crate somewhere.

She peeled one strip of tape free and started on another one. This was the perfect diversion, and she had to make use of it.

The now empty van's engine started, momentarily flooding the air with exhaust as it pulled away. Within thirty seconds, a second van backed into the opening and the whole process began again. Two more armed men, two others unloading the cargo onto pallets.

A couple of guys used stretchy plastic wrap to secure the load on the first pallet, and Lilly used the loud scrunching to get more aggressive with the duct tape. The final strip came loose. She kept an eye on the men as she rubbed the circulation back into her ankles.

The new man arguing with Ernesto was shorter than average, but solidly built, dressed in a tight black T-shirt that exposed bulging, tattooed biceps. Black hair covered his head in a quarter-inch buzz, and he had a red tattoo on the left side of his neck. When the plastic wrapping was completed, their words became clear.

"Not my problem, bro," Tattoo Man replied to something Ernesto said. He raised his hands and turned away in dismissal. "You shouldn't have brought them here. This warehouse is for product." He checked his watch. "The boats will be here in half an hour, and we can't have those guys seeing this. You got ten minutes to clear out."

"But—"

Tattoo Man addressed the men holding the assault rifles. "If they're not gone in ten minutes, shoot them." He laughed like it was the most hilarious thing in the world, then disappeared outside.

The kidnap driver reappeared, and Ernesto ordered him to pack the equipment. Ernesto went to work cutting Chad loose from the chair. They'd be coming for her any second. What would the new men do when they saw her?

Lilly crab-walked along the wall, staying behind the various stacks of boxes and piles of empty pallets. There had to be another door somewhere. She crossed a couple of open gaps, but the men were busy, and there was still only the single light over the work area.

At the corner of the building, she turned right. This area was darker, so she hurried, her bare feet silent on the gritty concrete. Halfway along the wall, a stack of empty pallets was shoved all the way back, blocking her path. The only way past would be to go around—out into the open room. They'd spot her immediately.

She could try to climb over it, get to the other side, but what if there was an endless row of pallets there too?

The barest grinding noise caught her attention, and she watched in amazement as a spinning drill bit the size of a pencil poked an inch through the steel wall inches above her head, then withdrew. Seconds later, it was replaced by a black wand with a reflective glass end. The wand twisted around like something alive, pointing first at the ceiling, then left.

And then right at her.

A camera.

She swore it jerked back in surprise, and she almost smiled despite the circumstances. She raised her finger into the camera's range and pointed toward the men and the center of attention in the room. The camera swiveled, following her direction like something alive.

The video equipment had been packed away, and Ernesto was lifting Chad from the chair. He called the driver to help, and together they carried the limp form to the van. They dumped Chad on top of Pana, then strained to lift the two other bodies in beside him. When finished, Ernesto pointed to where Lilly had been bound and stashed, and the driver headed that way.

She shrank against the building's wall. As soon as he reached the space behind the boxes, he'd find out—

"Hey!" the driver shouted, holding up strips of gray tape. Ernesto came running, gun in hand.

There was no time to climb over the pallet. No time to find another hiding place. She grabbed the camera, twisted so it was pointing at her face, and silently mouthed, *Help me!*

Ernesto rounded the far corner and spotted her squatting by the pallet. He raised his gun as he ran toward her.

Lilly bolted out and around the pallets that hindered her progress. Now in open space, the other men saw her and shouted. She kept moving, looping back to the outside wall and squeezing along another narrow corridor behind stacked materials. She prayed it wouldn't dead-end like the last. Whatever the boxes contained, she feared they wouldn't stop bullets if the men with rifles began shooting.

Violent explosions up front near the roll-up door rocked the building, blinding her with flashes as bright as lightning and compressing the air from her lungs. She dove for scant cover, sliding along the floor behind some large blue plastic drums. Another explosion blew a large hole in the wall directly ahead of her, rattling her eardrums and peppering her bare skin with stinging debris. Ten more feet and she would have been part of the airborne confetti.

The blast was answered with machine guns. There was so much smoke she couldn't see anything around her, but she felt heavy footsteps pounding nearby. Something wet ran into her right eye, and she curled into a ball against the wall, no longer minding its frigid cold.

Rough hands bit into Lilly's arms and hauled her up. At first she thought she'd been rescued, but then she recognized Ernesto's mask.

Chapter 3

"Come, or I'll kill you right here," he said.

She twisted and hit him with her fists. He whacked the side of her head with his pistol, sending her to her knees with dizzying pain. He pulled her up and dragged her through the smoke.

He kept her in front like a shield, letting his gun lead the way. Automatic weapon fire tore the air, and the steel walls rang with each bullet puncture. She expected to be cut down any second. Where were the rescuers, the ones with the camera?

They reached the white van, but instead of putting her in the back with Chad and the bodies, Ernesto circled the front of the vehicle to the passenger side that was away from the worst of the fighting. He opened the front door and roughly pushed her down in the footwell on her back, kicking her legs in as he climbed over her and shut the door. He scrambled into the driver seat and started the engine. She felt the vibration through the rubber mat.

Where was he going to go? The van with the drugs blocked the roll-up door behind them. Ernesto's finger poked something on the sun visor. A red light blinked momentarily. There was another roll-up door!

He gunned the engine. The rear of the van skidded wildly on the smooth concrete floor, crashing into stuff in the warehouse as it began to move. Then they were outside, the windshield above a dark rectangle.

The vehicle bounced over a curb and Lilly's head banged the bottom of the glove compartment. Ernesto twisted the wheel left, then right. She swore the wheels left the ground several times as the van tilted and the engine RPM soared higher and higher. Streetlights zipped by now, flashes of progress across the killer's face as he drove through the night.

Lilly wrapped her arms around her head and twisted around, protecting herself from the seat's hard frame and underside of the dash. Her head throbbed from the pistol slap, and she wanted nothing more than for all movement to cease. The van slowed a little, and she recognized traffic sounds around them. If he stopped for a red light, maybe she could jump out and flag someone down.

Then she heard a siren, far away, but getting louder each second. Ernesto must have heard it too, because he jerked the steering wheel left. The back end of the van slipped sideways and a crunch buckled the inside door panel at her feet and shattered the passenger door window. Glass pellets showered her T-shirt and hair, and littered the rubber floor mat around her.

Ernesto made a hard right, and Lilly winced as glass sliced her legs. Everywhere she braced herself was deadly, and her hands and legs grew slick with blood from dozens of small cuts. She envied Pana, lying only a couple of feet away, oblivious to the pain and chaos. Nausea rose as Lilly's back ground against the sharp beads. She wanted it all to stop.

Suddenly, a brilliant light from overhead turned the inside of the van to daytime, making every piece of lint, broken glass, and gum wrapper stand out in sharp relief. The light followed them no matter which way Ernesto turned, no matter how fast he raced.

Hope rose in Lilly. The good guys had spotted them from the air. L.A. was famous for high-speed chases, and she'd seen enough to know that once a helicopter joined the hunt, bad guys rarely got away. Although many of the chases ended with a spectacular crash, she held onto the fact that she'd been found. Ernesto was no longer all-powerful.

As they roared ahead, the bright light abruptly cut off, and her vision recovered enough to see elongated light strips of an underpass or tunnel streaking by overhead. Ernesto slowed and leaned closer to the windshield, searching for something along the side. The following siren echoed in the enclosed space, sounding as if ten cops were chasing them.

Ernesto stomped the brake pedal and shoved the shift lever into park before the van even quit moving. He disappeared out his door, the inside panel reflecting flashing lights.

Relief flooded Lilly. He was on the run, leaving her behind. She struggled to her knees, preparing to dive through the open driver door. If she kept her hands up, maybe the cops wouldn't shoot.

The door behind her wrenched open with a squeal of protesting metal, and her tormentor dragged her out onto the pavement. Headlights blinded them as the police car screeched to a stop. Its doors flew open and officers crouched behind the cover, their black weapons pointed right at her.

"Police! Down on the ground!"

Lilly jabbed an elbow into Ernesto's stomach, twisting against his grip. She had to get free or the cops would kill her.

Ernesto wrapped his arm tighter, wrestling her in front of him. He answered the officer's command with five shots over her right shoulder as he dragged her backward into an alcove at the side of the tunnel.

Her ears rang from the gunshots. She sucked in rapid breaths, tensing for the return fire that would burn holes through her flesh.

A door behind him creaked open on rusty hinges, and Ernesto pulled her into a concrete hallway lit by a bare overhead bulb. He banged the heavy metal door closed and dropped a thick steel bar across it. Welding burns blackened the crossbar hardware, showing it was a recent add. This was all planned. Ernesto had set this up as an escape route.

Dust and debris littered the hall as he shoved her along. The one good thing was Chad was still in the van. Ernesto didn't have means or time to bring the unconscious boy with them. She was his next best hostage. His *only* hostage. He'd keep her alive until he had no use for her. She had to get away.

The lights—widely spaced with some burned out—revealed little.

The concrete walls were bare of markings, nothing to give her a reference to where they were. After a hundred feet or so, he yanked her down a narrower side tunnel that climbed upward. The air grew warmer with each step, and Lilly fought a hysterical laugh as a brighter light appeared above a door at the end of the tunnel. She doubted this light represented relief and hope.

Using a key from his pocket, Ernesto unlocked the steel door, and they stepped out into the ground floor of a dimly lit, open-air parking garage. Here the night air was warmer and filled with the scent of jasmine in full bloom. She drew in the distinctive fragrance that always reminded her of summer. For a moment, it washed away the blood and death.

But Ernesto wasted no time roughly hauling her to another white van.

They must buy these in bulk.

Or maybe they salvaged this one from the junkyard. It had mismatched wheels, and rust marked every patch of scratched or flaking paint. The rear bumper hung at an angle, and one of the taillights was crudely patched with transparent red tape. Lilly caught a florist company name stenciled on the windowless side as Ernesto dragged her to the rear double doors. He shoved her inside the hollow space, following and forcing her down directly behind the driver's seat. He used an old piece of rope to lash her wrists together and then to an anchor on the bare wall.

Regardless of the floral promise on the exterior sign, the interior reeked like rotten fish, and the walls and floor looked like someone had splashed cans of liquid rust in every direction. She didn't want to think about whether some might be human blood mixed in.

Jagged metal stubs jutted where shelving had been cut and removed. Her ears had mostly stopped ringing, but her body was waking to all the cuts and bruises. The rough steel floor had added more bleeding scrapes, and she wondered if she'd contract tetanus. Which was insane, because the threat of disease was the least of her problems—she'd be lucky to get through the next few hours alive.

Her captor cranked the engine, which coughed, sputtered, and then caught in a shaking, deafening throb right under her butt. As he drove out of the parking structure, exhaust fumes seeped up through the floor and burned her eyes.

From her position behind the seat, she couldn't see Ernesto's face when he pulled off the ski mask and tossed it on the floor. But every once in a while they passed a bright light, and his left profile was reflected in the driver side window. His hair was dark and short, but the thing she noticed immediately was the tattoo on his neck: a red rose, with what appeared to be a sword running through it. It had to be the same as the man he'd argued with at the warehouse. Some kind of brotherhood or organization, but not all friendly with one another.

He had kidnapped Chad to demand a big ransom. While that plan was blown, would he now use her for a smaller payoff? Her parents had money, but she wasn't worth nearly as much as Chad. Maybe the high risk and smaller payoff wouldn't be worth it to him. In that case, she was dead.

His cell phone rang, and he answered it as he drove. *"Si?"*

Like almost every non-Latino student in SoCal, she'd taken Spanish in school. But she'd never been any good at languages, and his rapid, one-sided conversation was too fast to follow. They only word she made out was "donut" in English on a street she didn't know. He made a left at the next corner and accelerated. The fumes cleared a little as fresh air blew through holes in the floor, and she sucked in the cleaner air.

After ten minutes of driving, the van slowed and rocked as they turned into a driveway. Fumes billowed around her once more, this time laced with the unmistakable smell of sugary maple. One of the tall parking lot lights shone down through the windshield, its light sparkling off fish scales on the floor. Lilly gagged on the perverse mix of car exhaust and donuts.

Ernesto got out of the van, but froze in the open doorway when red and white flashing lights lit him up.

Lilly's heart hammered in her chest when she heard, *"Please stay with your vehicle,"* over a loudspeaker.

She could see Ernesto's back where he stood in the doorway. His T-shirt had hiked up, revealing the butt of his gun tucked in his belt. Casually, he adjusted the shirt so the hem fell over the gun. A car door slammed, and she heard footsteps.

"Good evening. May I see your license and registration, please?" a man said. His voice was high pitched, young.

"What's the problem, officer? I'm sure I wasn't speeding," Ernesto said, his voice full of respect.

"Your registration tag is expired. May I see your license and registration?"

"Oh. This is a company van. I don't use it very much, and I guess my partner forgot to put the new sticker on. It's probably buried on his messy desk."

Lilly was torn as to what to do. One peep from her and Ernesto would start shooting. And then the young cop would be dead before he knew what happened, and she would still be Ernesto's prisoner. On the other hand, this was a golden chance, perhaps her only one.

She threw up a quick prayer for God's help, then leaned forward, preparing to bang her head against the thin metal wall at her back.

No. She shut her eyes and rocked back and forth against burning frustration. Even if this was her only hope, she couldn't risk the cop's life.

The officer's radio crackled in a burst of garbled words.

"Just a minute, sir," the cop said, his voice retreating. Then from farther away: "Sir, I've got an emergency call. Be sure to get that current registration tag on your vehicle."

"I will, officer," Ernesto said, all goodwill. "First thing. Good luck at your emergency." Lilly could practically hear the wide grin.

Ernesto evidently decided whoever he'd planned to meet at the donut shop could wait, because he climbed back into the driver's seat and restarted the engine. Soon they were on the streets again in a cloud of exhaust. He made another call in Spanish. She recognized a few street names and *Honda*, but that was it. If she ever got out of this, she vowed to learn the language, even if she had to move to Mexico City.

The junky van rattled and shook, even on the better roads. On the rougher ones, the back end bounced and skittered all over as they rounded corners, throwing Lilly back and forth against the rusty metal. Wetness soaked the back of her T-shirt. She hoped it was sweat.

Since she had no idea where they were going, she tried to think of a plan. Her life was worth nothing to this man, except maybe as ransom. But even if he received a payoff from her parents, he would probably still kill her. This wasn't a *CSI* episode where they always rescued the victim in the nick of time.

Wiggling against the van's side, she found a protruding rough section she could use to saw at the rope.

The rope proved tougher than the duct tape, and the bumping around made it hard to maintain contact with the wall. But if she could get loose, she would bolt through the rear doors, even if it meant jumping into the early morning traffic.

She winced at the image of her skin scraping along the pavement. That was going to hurt, but road rash was better than dead. She doubled her efforts on the binding.

Her head came up when a siren sounded. Close. The inside cab of the van strobed red, blue, and white. Then a second siren joined the first.

She braced her feet, expecting Ernesto to stomp on the gas for a long chase. It would end with the van wrapped around a light post, or T-boned into oblivion by a semi at an intersection, like those YouTube videos from Russian dash cams. Tomorrow's headline: *Kidnapped Teen Killed in High-Speed Chase.* Still, she kept sawing. She had to try.

Ernesto surprised her by slowing, steering to the right, and bringing the van to a stop. He left the engine idling, and heat welled up through the floor as radios crackled outside.

"Police! Show us your hands!"

The rope suddenly slipped from Lilly's wrists. Relief flooded her, but her breath caught as Ernesto retrieved an assault rifle from under his seat.

White light lit up the front cab like daytime, but the windowless back of the van was still in darkness. No one except Ernesto knew she was here. If shooting started…

Ernesto twisted right and squeezed between the front seats, stepping over Lilly without a glance on his way to the back of the van. It wasn't good that he'd let her see his face.

He threw open one rear door and let loose a sweeping machine gun burst.

Before the first brass casings pinged on the van's floor, Lilly scrambled between the seats and curled into a tiny ball in the passenger footwell. The machine gun was deafening, vibrating the door panel, floor, and pounding Lilly's ears. The windshield above her shattered with return fire, showering her with glass pellets. Bullets shredded the upholstery and sent bits of fabric swirling in the bright light. Holes punched through the radio and instrument panel, and white smoke began billowing from under the dash.

Her ears rang with each burst from Ernesto's rifle, and answering bullets thumped and banged the area around her. The passenger seat offered minimal protection. She had to get out.

Keeping her head down, she fumbled blindly with her hand until she found the door handle and wrenched it. The latch released the same time something knocked her arm away. White bone protruded from her flesh. She'd been shot. Cradling her arm across her stomach and ignoring her lurching stomach, Lilly head-butted the door open a few inches.

Before she could think of moving, three successive punches slammed into her chest, hip, and calf, each an exploding bolt of pain that radiated through her body. Even her jaw and teeth hurt.

No matter how hard she fought, she couldn't get enough air into her lungs. It felt like someone was sitting on her chest, and her vision narrowed with the lack of oxygen.

Bullets continued to punch holes around her, ripping gashes in the padded dash and sending upholstery material flying. She'd been hit four times in a couple of seconds. A few *more* seconds and this van would become her stinking, fishy coffin.

With tantalizing fresh air only inches away, she pushed off with her good leg until her head was out the door. The distinctive odor of newly mown grass blew across her face, flushing away the acrid dash smoke and the gunpowder. It reminded her of green pastures and all the drawings she'd made over the years of wild horses running free. Palominos were her new favorites.

And right now, she needed their strength and courage.

After a moment of fighting for breath, she wiggled her shoulders over the threshold, the glass pellets rolling like sharp-edged ball bearings under her back. She shoved her foot against the engine shroud, feeling bones grind together deep within as she slid partway out the door. A few more inches and she'd tumble to—

Ernesto hurled into the driver's seat and yanked the shift lever into gear. He swung his rifle toward her, his finger on the trigger.

Lilly kicked the barrel, knocking it back. It fired into the passenger seat and doorframe. She kept kicking at the gun until he dropped the weapon and stomped the gas pedal.

The acceleration slammed the door against Lilly, trapping her in its vise-like grip. Her useless arm dragged along the asphalt, which rushed by only inches from her face. Ernesto veered left and the spinning tire kicked gravel in her face. She was stuck halfway between captivity and freedom, and now either option would result in death.

Suddenly, Ernesto slowed, and the passenger door whipped forward, releasing Lilly from its grasp. She slipped out the door as a spray of bullets tore through the van. Her last image before she hit the ground was Ernesto jerking as slugs exploded through him and splattered gore across what was left of the windshield.

Then she was outside, flopping onto the pavement and tumbling as the van roared away. She lost count how many times her elbows and knees struck the unyielding surface, but felt every jarring impact.

Finally, everything went still.

Chapter 4

Lilly stared up at wispy high clouds tinged in morning pink. The sky rotated weirdly as her vision spun clockwise, then snapped back, spun and snapped back, again and again. It was like when she and Pana had ridden the teacups at Disneyland last year. They'd used the center wheel to spin the little cup faster and faster until everything had become a swirling blur. And when they staggered off the ride and tried to sit on a bench, they'd slid to the ground in fits of laughter until the world stopped spinning.

The van's engine roared in the distance, followed by a crash and rending of metal. Sirens. More gunshots. He couldn't have survived. She was safe.

The world above her gradually stabilized, but every breath required major effort. A chorus of sirens pierced the dawn, and radios crackled with frantic calls, multiple officers down. Her left arm was twisted and trapped under her back. Something wet ran down her cheek, and when she wiped at it, her hand came away covered in bright red.

"Don't move!" A shadow blocked the sky, and she saw the trembling barrel of another gun pointed at her face.

Lilly coughed out a laugh, spraying more blood that ran back into her mouth. She turned her head and spit it out. Moving was the very last thing on her mind.

Another man came alongside the one with the gun. His hand touched the uniformed officer's arm. "I think this is one of the kidnap victims."

The muzzle moved away.

The new guy dropped to his knees and lifted the hem of her T-shirt, peering at the wound there. He quickly removed his windbreaker and bulletproof vest and tossed them aside. Then he whipped his black T-shirt off and laid it against her wound. He rolled her enough to extract her broken left arm, then wrapped the shirt around her back and bore down on the bleeding holes.

The pressure constricted her chest and stole all but the last narrow inch of her vision. She must have cried out, because he mumbled something about being sorry, then, "Help is on the way."

Her eyes drifted closed, but she opened them when gentle fingers brushed the hair from her eyes. The man was leaning close, no more than a few inches away.

"Stay with me, young lady. I'm Kade Hunt with the FBI. I don't want you to cough, but can you tell me your name?"

She concentrated on his face. How was he old enough for the FBI? He could be in her senior class. His pearl gray eyes were warmed by the rosy morning glow. They were his best feature, or at least the one she noticed most.

The strain of focusing so close became too difficult, and she let her gaze drift to the palm trees above his blond hair. The fronds shushed the world in the warm breeze, and it felt so good to lie still, finally out of the riptide of violence that had nearly dragged her under.

The promise of another hot July day in Southern California didn't banish the lingering cool of the asphalt beneath her. Although it numbed the dozens of glass cuts, it must have been colder than she realized, because she began shivering.

"I need blankets over here!" Agent Gray Eyes yelled over his shoulder and draped his discarded windbreaker over her. The thin cloth at least blocked the breeze.

Another man knelt beside them, unfolding a dark blue blanket that he tucked around her. The man wrapped something around her calf wound, and his hands woke scrapes and cuts temporarily forgotten. The knifing pains tested her resolve to remain conscious.

Still clad only in her bikini and T-shirt, she felt oddly exposed. But there was nothing titillating about the younger man's hands as they roamed her arms, head, even her buttocks—not when they came into view dripping with her blood. His eyes were narrowed in concentration.

Lilly shut out the scene, but the impression of his eyes remained. They became her focus throughout the interminable sirens, blankets, jostling, and questions she couldn't answer. A blood pressure cuff clamped her good arm, followed shortly by a needle prick for an IV. An oxygen mask was fastened over her mouth and nose. She nearly passed out when hands wiggled under her body and lifted.

Maybe she *did* pass out, because the next thing she knew, she was on a gurney being hustled toward a boxy ambulance with flashing lights. Agent Gray Eyes walked beside her, still bare-chested. Pana would be checking him out, sending Lilly covert messages with her eyebrows. Tears stung her eyes at the thought of her lost friend. Had they gotten Pana out of the other van? Or was she still laying there, growing colder?

"You're going to be okay," the agent said, bending close, but his strained smile betrayed the promise. Did he think she was dying?

The gurney bumped over something on the roadway, shooting shockwaves up her broken arm and bringing tears. It seemed like all the strength in her body was draining away with each drop of blood. How much damage could her body take before giving up, shutting down? In the movies, most people died from a single bullet, and she'd been shot four times—at least. Would she even make it to the hospital?

The agent's creased forehead and bunched jaw muscles weren't reassuring. What would it be like to have her life seep away until there was nothing left inside, just a lump of flesh and bone, but no person? Would her spirit go somewhere else?

Her mom believed there was life after death, a heaven for good people, complete with angels and streets of gold. Her dad said he wasn't so sure. Lilly hoped it was true—for Pana's sake.

"Almost there," one of the EMTs said.

Suddenly determined, Lilly fought to remain conscious, utilizing the pain to help. The afterlife wasn't for her right now, even if she might see Pana there. As bad as this world was at times, she had parents, her art, things she wanted to do. She couldn't go out like this.

The agent said something, and she remembered his earlier question. She clutched his arm, and the warmth from his bare skin seeped into her frozen fingers. He'd told her *his* name, Kade something. Now, it was important he know hers—in case she didn't have another chance. At her touch, he leaned closer.

She spoke her name, but it came out a anemic whisper.

His brows knit together, and he bent down until they were cheek to cheek. "Sorry. I couldn't hear you."

Even with the oxygen, every breath was more difficult than the previous one. His morning stubble scratched against her skin as he lifted the edge of the mask.

"My name...Palomino...changing." That simple effort sapped the last of her strength, and her hand slipped off his arm. He tucked her hand in his, remaining at her side as the gurney rattled to a stop and the EMTs folded the wheels. She searched beyond the concern on his face, memorizing the set and shape of his gray eyes, the slightly curved slope of his nose, the single freckle in front of his left earlobe, the blond stubble softening his jawline. If she had her sketchpad...

She coughed and red spray filled the oxygen mask, metallic, and tasting of iron. The EMTs shouted medical terms as the gurney slid into the vehicle. The agent's hand and its warmth was suddenly gone. Uncaring fluorescent lights, as sterile as the van's antiseptic interior, replaced the colored dawn. She wished the agent would climb in with her, hold her hand again, but the doors slammed, shutting him on the outside. Then the siren wailed to life, and her body sagged rearward under the acceleration.

It seemed like Lilly's bones had been replaced with frozen steel bars that speared her from the inside with icy lightning bolts. Her whole body was shaking again, no longer able to tolerate such abuse. The EMT's response was to drape a heated blanket over her and admonish her to hang on. Although the ambulance was tasked to rush her to safety, the turns and side-to-side rolls were hauntingly reminiscent of the rides in Ernesto's white vans. What she really wanted was someone to hang on *to*. In case…

She clung to the comfort that at least one of the last faces she saw in this world, Kade, was no longer a stranger. He knew who she really was.

Chapter 5

Kade Hunt barely refrained from trotting through the darkened hospital lobby. Twenty hours had passed since the shooting, and he still hadn't slept or eaten. Several cups of bad coffee didn't count, and the excessive caffeine probably made him look like a whacko intent on mayhem.

With several cops and innocents in various trauma centers, the medical community was in chaos. It had taken him a frustrating hour to track down the girl's location, especially since he hadn't learned her real name until he stumbled across it in a report. Lilly Hawthorne, not Palomino. Why had she said that?

Kade had initially been called in from the local office as soon as the DEA agents accidentally discovered the kidnapping victims during their preplanned drug warehouse raid.

The third shooting scene had been a bloodbath. Five police officers wounded—one critically—and two civilians injured when stray bullets tore through their passing vehicles. Several other cars, riddled with bullet holes, crashed, sending a half dozen more people to emergency rooms. Three more officers were hit after the girl's escape when they tried to take the perp into custody.

And after all of that, the shooter somehow escaped, but not before forcing another vehicle off the road and into a power pole and bringing down arcing high-voltage wires.

The radio waves were abuzz with an all-out manhunt for the escaped shooter, an unknown number of accomplices, as well as three or four more suspects who fled the drug warehouse. Kade finger-combed his snarled hair and took a calming breath as he approached the information counter. Everyone was on high alert, and he didn't want to spook the woman behind the desk.

"Can you direct me to ICU?" he said, flashing his badge to calm her. She pointed him toward a hallway. His shoes squeaked on the polished floors.

Five others were dead. Television news was painting it as the worst shooting spree since the North Hollywood bank shootout nearly fourteen years ago.

Writing his initial report consumed the previous two hours, every word carefully chosen. City council members and the mayor were already blaming law enforcement for being "heavy handed" and "inconsiderate of public safety."

The dimmed overhead lights bathed the ICU nurses' station in nighttime tranquility, but Kade's insides roiled as he approached and asked the lone nurse if he could see Lilly Hawthorne.

"It's after one o'clock in the morning," she said, as if that were all he needed to know. She was a middle-aged African American, and looked like she could take down half the agents in the L.A. office. Her eyes narrowed. "Are you family?"

Kade presented his ID. "I was first on the scene with her. I…" He took a deep breath. "I just need to know how she's doing."

The nurse pursed her lips, scanning him up and down. Then she glanced at his ID. Her demeanor softened a little.

"Well, the good news is she's young and strong. She lost a lot of blood and was in shock when she arrived. Legally I can't go into specifics with you, but you can talk to her parents, if you'd like. They're in the waiting room down the hall on your right."

Around the corner, Kade spotted the *Family Waiting Room* sign hanging above an open doorway. He stepped inside. Two huddles of adults occupied the rear corners, conversing softly or waiting in silence. He hadn't thought to ask the nurse who the girl's family was.

"Excuse me," he said as every eye focused on him. "I'm looking for Lilly Hawthorne's family?" They all turned toward a woman hidden behind the open door. Kade stepped around and faced her.

She was dressed in plain blue jeans and a snow-white knitted sweater. A Fidel Castro military-style billed cap with silver studs covered jet-black hair pulled back into a low braid. Ordinary style for L.A. But her defined cheekbones, full lips, and large dark eyes distinguished her from every other woman on the planet. Movie star Ekaterina Orlov.

He stood for a moment in shocked silence, realizing he'd missed some critical information probably covered in the briefings. He stepped back and bumped into a man coming into the room.

"You have news about what happened to our daughter?" the man asked, stepping around Kade and taking the woman's hand as she rose.

Kade's weary brain felt like it was misfiring on a few cylinders as he processed the connection.

"I'm Nathan Hawthorne," the man said, evidently recognizing Kade's brain stutter. He extended his hand.

Kade nodded, recovering enough to return the man's firm grip. "I'm Special Agent Kade Hunt with the FBI."

"And this is Lilly's mother, Ekaterina Orlov."

Kade turned to the woman. Her hand was cool and strong. Red-rimmed eyes held both fear and hope.

NateKate—that's how the tabloids referred to this Hollywood power couple. Perhaps *the* Hollywood power couple. Ekaterina commanded some of the highest paying film contracts ever, and Hawthorne had produced several of her films as well as many others. They made a striking pair, and even the mundane hospital waiting room couldn't diminish that.

A few minutes later, they were seated in a conversation area in a dead-end hallway with windows that overlooked the city. Two of Hawthorne's assistants discretely guarded the hall's entrance. The couple told him Police Chief McNamara had come earlier. He explained how Lilly had been kidnapped with the two other teenagers, then gotten caught up in a joint task force drug raid that led to three separate shootouts.

Kade told them the truth: he was the first responder to get to their daughter after the final shooting, and he came tonight not in any official capacity, but simply to find out how she was doing.

While he filled in what details he knew about how the kids ended up in the warehouse during the raid, he didn't touch on the fact that their daughter was hit by friendly fire from the very officers who were trying to rescue her. Perhaps they'd already been informed about that, but if not, that was a message higher-ups would have to deliver when things settled down. Many lawyers would be present.

He also didn't tell them that after only a few minutes of contact, he'd been captivated by their daughter's expressive eyes, striking white hair, and fighting spirit. How he still felt her warm blood leaking through his fingers.

Fortunately, just as Hawthorne began asking for more specifics about the shootings, a police representative arrived to stay with the couple for the next several hours, and Kade dismissed himself.

As he walked to the elevator, he rubbed the spot on his left arm where she'd touched him. Lilly Hawthorne.

Palomino.

He'd forgotten to ask her parents about the name.

* * *

It was after seven o'clock the next evening before Kade made it back to the hospital. Dozens of visitors streamed in and out as he approached the front doors. Some appeared joyful, carrying balloons or stuffed animals; others carried the weight of worry or pending loss.

Before he got inside, his cell phone rang.

"Hi, Mom," he said, taking a seat on a stone planter.

"Kade, are you all packed and ready to leave in the morning?"

For weeks, he'd been looking forward to his transfer to Boston where he would be close to his family again. His parents had sold their family home in Pasadena eighteen months ago and moved with Kade's younger sister, Rowan, to Massachusetts to be near Dad's ailing aunt.

While Dad claimed the snow didn't bother him and had bought into a winter sports center, Kade's mother held a dissenting opinion about the white stuff, especially after last winter. She regularly quizzed Kade about real estate prices in Southern California, and now branded him a traitor for transferring to the East Coast.

"Almost," Kade said. "I'm leaving at six to beat the traffic."

"Your dad's at the center working with a client, but he said to tell you to drive carefully and stop when you need to."

That brought a smile. It sounded more like his mother's caution, rather than Dad's.

He fingered the petals of a one of the plants in the bed behind him while he listened to his mother's voice. Orderly rows of yellow and red flowers out here. Stark contrast to the uncertainty and grief inside the building.

"I bet you're looking forward to your new job," she said. She had to have heard of the shootings, but she didn't ask if he was involved. That was her way of dealing with the danger he sometimes faced.

"I am. It'll be a nice change." He hoped. But the departmental politics there were probably just as nuts.

Still, he felt bad for leaving at such a key time. His coworkers had run the manhunt today while he finished a hundred details, signed papers for HR, and stuffed a few mementos into a box. He was missing the biggest operation in L.A. in years.

"Call us when you get close. I have a new recipe for lasagna I wrangled from an old Italian place in the North End." An hour north of Boston, his parents' home would be an easy getaway for weekends and holidays.

"See you soon, Mom," he said and ended the call. He headed into the hospital and down the aisle leading to ICU.

Evidently his conversation last night with Nathan and Ekaterina scored him some points. The same nurse was on duty tonight. She took him to the window that looked into Lilly's room and stood with him.

"Her condition has been upgraded to serious but stable," the nurse said. "That's a big improvement."

Machines flanked the head of the hospital bed, trailing a tangle of sensor wires and tubes to the diminutive form half-hidden by bandages all the way down her left side. Last night, Nathan and Ekaterina, as they insisted he call them, had recounted some of their daughter's wounds and the surgeries done to repair the damage. According to the doctors, she'd been close to bleeding out on that cold street, and Kade's quick first aid had probably saved her life. She'd been lucky.

Lucky would be if she hadn't been kidnapped in the first place, or if the DEA had rescued her at the warehouse.

Her white hair was washed free of blood and grit, and combed out so it fanned across the pillow. A few tiny cuts marred her cheeks and forehead, her skin still reddened by her day on the water. But the side of her face had turned black and blue from a blow. Kade's fingernails dug into his palms.

"She had surgery to set her arm this morning. The painkillers are letting her sleep so she can heal."

Even severely injured, she was ethereally beautiful. His spirit relaxed as his pulse slowed. It was as if every cell in his body leaned into her gravitational pull.

As excited as he was to see his family again, he sensed an odd hollowness within, as if he were leaving something unfinished.

A buzzer sounded. The nurse patted his shoulder and said, "I'll be back in a minute."

After Lilly's initial recovery would come weeks of the best rehab money could buy. Then back to school.

A smile tugged at Kade's mouth as he shook his head. Sheesh, he was pathetic. A *high school* student, ten years his junior. Guys her own age probably flocked around her, or would when her story got out and she rejoined her class for their senior year. She'd be more famous than the Kardashians. And in this town, with her father as a big-name producer, surely a movie would be forthcoming.

Reluctantly, Kade stepped back, but as he did, Lilly's brows knit together and her back arched. Kade placed his hand on the cool glass. Pain? Or maybe memories?

Before he could react, a nurse entered the room, checked the monitors, and fiddled with one of the IV lines. Within a minute, the worry lines disappeared from Lilly's face, and her body sank into the bed.

Kade breathed again. He'd been ready to sprint into the room, do anything to save her once more.

But others now filled that role. She no longer needed his saving. He hated that the only part of him she would remember would be associated with pain and blood—if she recalled him at all. Trauma victims, especially after anesthesia and pain medication, often blocked out the worst parts of an event. His presence during those few terrifying minutes on the street might fall into that black hole, along with the terror that took her friend's life. Maybe that was for the best.

Her life would go on without him.

His fingertips slipped down the glass to the frame, hung there for a few seconds, then broke free.

He had family and a new adventure waiting in Boston—if he ever got his apartment packed and cleaned. He took one step back, then another, watching to make sure Lilly remained serene. Then he pivoted, walked to the elevator, and stepped inside.

The doors slid shut, their polished stainless surface reflecting his blurry form. So like his new future.

* * *

Percy Maxwell laughed and shook his head as he passed the fourth Target store since leaving the Minneapolis-St. Paul International Airport this evening. Red bullseyes everywhere, as if erected in ignorant testament of his visit. Well, the ignorance would turn to awareness soon enough.

The Twin Cities were also home of the famed Mall of America. He'd only seen pictures, and planned to spend tomorrow afternoon wandering through the stores. Brushing shoulders with so many people after a job, allowed him to share the experience and—yes, he admitted—bask in his power. The fact that none realized death walked among them made it even more enjoyable.

He needed this one tonight. It had been an interminable four weeks since his last work, and he still shuddered from his time in

Illinois. When he'd chosen Irene Collins, he'd had no idea she lived in such a depressing area of the state. A dying little town in a sad county. In a way, he did her a huge favor. They should condemn the whole area.

Percy rolled his shoulders in another attempt to slough off the gritty feeling.

Now the waiting was over. It was time for action. This was July, and July was Minnesota.

He parked his nondescript rental several blocks from his target, in a modest neighborhood built shortly after World War II. Some of the houses were fixed up, but many wore their years in peeling paint, warped vinyl siding, and ragged roofs.

Night provided a bare drop in temperature if not humidity. Percy fanned the tails of his black button-down as he exited the sedan. The nearest streetlight was out—a bonus—but the full moon showed sidewalks heaved up from frozen winters. He chose his foot placement carefully as he walked.

Twelve thirty-eight Windsor Lane was one of the nicer properties, replete with blooming planters, an American flag mounted on one of the craftsman pillars, and red, white, and blue bunting strung along the porch railing—leftover from last week's Fourth of July celebration.

"Patriotic. I expected nothing less," Percy whispered. He paused for a quick check of the street before striding to the gate leading to the backyard.

The lone occupant, Lane Poller, was 83 years old. His wife of over sixty years had succumbed to cancer last year. So sad.

Percy rounded the corner and approached the back door, pulling on thin black gloves as he went. Poller still worked every day in the dry cleaning store he and the missus owned since the late 1950s. Salt of the earth people.

The screen door hinges squeaked as Percy climbed onto the screened porch, but he didn't worry. Poller's hearing was ruined long ago when he manned one of the sixteen-inch gun turrets on the battleship USS *Indiana*. Years in the noisy dry cleaning shop hadn't helped.

The ancient doorknob turned easily in his hand. Mr. Poller was a trusting man. Percy entered the kitchen. Small, and probably not as tidy with Mrs. Poller gone. The countertop microwave door stood open. Spilled food darkened the glass platter, and the room smelled of canned hash.

A few dishes soaked in the chipped white porcelain sink, and boxes of cereal and cookies were lined neatly on the worn countertop. An open two-liter bottle of root beer stood front and center in a sweat puddle.

The dish towel hanging on the oven door was one of the thin ones that tended to push water around rather than absorb it. Not Percy's favorite, but it was better for his purpose tonight. The material was bright white. Did Mr. Poller launder it at his business? That would be so fitting.

Percy twisted the ends of the towel around his gloved hands as he passed through a claustrophobic dining room on his way to the living room.

Poller sat in a wingback chair facing the television, from which Alex Trebek threw out answers, while contestants scrambled for questions. Were they really trying to win money, or was their motivation driven by desperate desire to avoid being embarrassed by the condescending Trebek?

Percy had never cared for the man or the show. Even the contestants were snooty.

Unlike simple Lane Poller.

Percy stood behind the chair, looking down on the old man's bald head. It had lost its blond hair, but that didn't matter. Percy's research showed photographs of a younger version of the man. He fit Percy's target profile: blond.

An ice-filled glass of soda pooled condensation on a coaster on the end table to the man's right. Next to it lay a yellowed newspaper, its three-month-old headline clearly readable:

Businessman Lane Poller

Donates Building for New Youth Center

"No good deed goes unrewarded," Percy said, as he snapped the towel around the old man's neck and pulled.

Trebek read an answer about the day of the week with the most murders. Oddly appropriate as Percy wrenched the towel tighter. The contestants manically mashed their handheld buttons.

The back of the chair gave him the perfect mechanical advantage. He could have taken a much stronger man this way. As it was, Poller gave hardly a struggle. Maybe he was ready to go, ready to meet up with the missus, if he believed that stuff.

It was all over too quickly. Percy let the ends of the towel drop, and stepped back, breathing hard. Not from exertion. No, tonight wasn't a battle like some. Kills were a rush, no matter how weak the victim. He had just ended a man's existence on the planet, in the universe. That was monumental, and not something he took lightly.

He inhaled a deep, cleansing breath, then reached in his pocket and withdrew a single piece of a jigsaw puzzle. He shoved it between the man's right buttock and the chair's worn cushion. Number 19.

On the television, Trebek read about soft drink ingredients, and the contestants jostled for the opportunity to show how smart they were.

Percy smiled, stopping in the kitchen and taking a long swig from the open two-liter.

"Ah." Root beer was his favorite. And none of that tasteless diet junk, either. This was the real stuff. "Thank you, Mr. Poller." He lifted the bottle in salute toward the living room, then exited the way he'd entered, taking the root beer with him.

He downed another long pull in the still-hot night. Stifling before, the warm darkness washed over him like a welcoming breeze. He'd finished another job and ensured new headlines for tomorrow's newspaper.

Someone would find the puzzle piece. The question was, would they know what they'd found? Who would be the one to put the pieces together? So to speak.

Percy chuckled as he sauntered out onto the sidewalk, the bottle dangling from two fingers.

Tomorrow, the mall, but he was already anticipating North Carolina. Number 20.

Chapter 6

Five weeks later…

"Come on, Lilly, three more reps," her physical therapist, James the Merciless, urged. He spent all his free time in the gym and believed everyone else should too. He had no neck.

She paused for a few seconds to get her breath. The gym-like room of the PT office hummed with activity today. Most came due to knee or hip surgery or replacements. Others were recovering from strokes, traumatic brain injury, car accidents, or falls. James said she was the only one who'd been shot.

Salty sweat trickled into her eyes, and she blinked it away as she repositioned her feet on the machine's platform and shoved. Her body slid upward, pulling the cable hooked to the weights. After the two previous sets, her left leg quivered like cooked spaghetti, but it was much stronger than three weeks ago when she'd begun serious rehabilitation. Though the bullet in her leg hadn't broken the bone, it *had* torn out flesh and muscle, requiring two surgeries to tie everything back together. When she first began physical therapy, she swore it was ripping stuff apart inside, but James said it was normal.

Yippee for normal.

She waited a second at the top of her glide, letting her fully extended right leg hold the position. Nothing was normal about any of this. Normal people didn't get kidnapped and shot. Normal people didn't see their friends murdered.

Lilly did another rep, squatting halfway, feeling the burn, then grunting to full extension. Three to go. She swiped the sweat away with her T-shirt sleeve. At least she could shower now after PT. Those first days of dressing changes and sponge baths were the worst. She hated being helpless.

Overall, she was surprised at how quickly her body was healing, at least the bones and outside skin. Even her left lung had bounced back pretty fast, though the gunshot through her chest had made mincemeat of a small portion of it, requiring lobectomy surgery to remove that part. Daily breathing exercises improved her capacity.

The cast on her left arm had come off yesterday, and the skin was still as white as a fish's belly. She'd hardly been able to lift her arm's own weight today in exercises, let alone the five pounder James thrust on her.

"Good job," James said as Lilly finished the last repetition. "That's it for today. See you Wednesday. We'll really get after that arm."

"Oh, joy," she said. "Can't wait." James laughed and steadied her as she climbed off the machine, then headed toward his next victim, a paraplegic man in his forties named Mike who waved at her.

Although Mike had lost use of his legs when his Army unit was hit in Iraq, it hadn't slowed him down. Case in point, his current physical therapy wasn't because of the war injuries. Oh, no. He'd fallen and injured his shoulder at an indoor rock-climbing wall. That was gutsy. His positive outlook and hard work were an encouragement to Lilly, and she returned his wave.

After downing a quart or so from the drinking fountain, she sank onto a bench, leaned against the wall, and closed her eyes.

Today was her anniversary. Five weeks since the shooting. Five weeks since Pana died. Even without physical therapy as a regular reminder, hardly an hour went by without replays running through her head like an out-of-control movie. Often it was merely a snippet: the kidnapping in the parking lot, freezing in the warehouse before the explosions, curled in the van as bullets punctured her body, sliding out on the jagged bits of broken glass.

By far the worst was that single, loud gunshot, followed by Pana's empty, staring eyes—her friend no longer there.

And those were the days. Nights were worse.

Sometimes she imagined being more prepared, able to fight off the attackers like a superhero. She sighed.

"Hey, Lilly. You all right?"

Mike sat in his wheelchair directly in front of her, but she hadn't even noticed his approach. His forearms bulged with muscle, curving the tattoos that patterned his skin. He still wore his hair cut short, military style.

"Sorry. Spaced out there for a second." She scrubbed her face with her hand, shaking off the melancholic malaise and substituting a smile.

Mike's frown said he wasn't buying it. "You've been out for over thirty minutes. I finished my whole session."

Her eyes shot to the wall clock. He was right. She hadn't mentioned these little lapses to her mother, but she had to Mike one day last week.

"Sorry," she said giving a faint smile. "Just living the dream."

He said that's what some of the guys called the flashbacks they experienced when they got back to the states. They, like she, left out the re-living part.

Even her psychologist, good as the woman was, didn't know what it was like to be shot. Mike did. And she'd found him easy to talk to about the trauma, the recurring dreams, the guilt of surviving when her best friend didn't, and the daily effort to keep going.

"Can you come by the gym tomorrow night?" he asked. "Alexandra has a new self-defense class starting. I told her about you."

Mike touted the woman's skills as a trainer, urging Lilly to sign up. The classes were held in the gym where he worked three nights a week as a trainer for others who were wheelchair bound. She hadn't done it yet.

"So, she's good?" Lilly asked.

Mike laughed as if that were the most hilarious thing he'd ever heard. Then he winked at Lilly and leaned forward to whisper, "You can help me figure out if she's former KGB."

He didn't offer more, but Lilly had come to know Mike well enough in the last couple of weeks to trust his judgment. She hated those memories of being helpless. Pana killed two of the kidnappers, so she had undoubtedly had training in defending herself. If Lilly had been similarly prepared, the two of them might have taken out all four men.

"Okay." She nodded, smiling at Mike and confirming it to herself. "Now that my arm is plaster free, I'm ready. Besides, after James the Merciless, it'll be nice to have a woman trainer."

Mike laughed even louder this time.

* * *

"You expect easy because you are injured?" Alexandra Pavlovna taunted, standing over Lilly, hands on hips. "Bad guys not go easy. Get up."

Definitely KGB, Lilly thought. Heavy Russian accent, severely cinched black ponytail, arching eyebrows, sneering red lips. She could play the spy in any movie. Or the assassin.

Lilly moaned and rolled onto her hands and knees for at least the tenth time this evening, mentally debating whether her body could go another round. The other three members in the self-defense class had wisely fled twenty minutes ago, and if Mike hadn't been watching from his wheel chair, she might have joined them. But she was determined to learn everything this woman had to offer.

"Alex," Mike said, rolling forward, "if she dies on her first night, you won't get paid for the rest of the sessions." His T-shirt was drenched in sweat from his own workout, but by the way Alexandra climbed onto his lap and wrapped her arms around his neck, she didn't appear to notice.

"I should go easy on *you* tonight, my Michael?" she cooed, giving him a sexy smile while running a red-painted nail across his cheek and onto his lips. He opened them and bit down gently on her finger.

"Sheesh," Lilly said. "You two should get a room."

Alexandra said without turning, "We have one." She leaned in for a kiss that quickly became passionate and embarrassing.

Oh.

A minute passed, and neither came up for air. Evidently class time was over.

"Well...I'll just be going, then," Lilly said, wobbling to her feet and retrieving her gym bag. "See you tomorrow, Alexandra."

The lip-locked couple gave no indication they'd heard as she slipped out the door.

Her father's SUV idled at the curb.

"How'd it go?" he asked as she climbed in.

"Killer," she said, collapsing against the headrest. Somehow she found the strength to fasten her seatbelt.

* * *

After the third time in two days that Lilly's parents suggested she leave Los Angeles for a while "just in case," she cornered them in her dad's home office.

"All right. What are you not telling me?" Her parents had always been straightforward with each other, and Lilly had picked up the trait.

Her mother was dressed in a silvery Versace white pantsuit. Dad, just back from a soundstage shoot, was in khakis, and wore a black blazer over a white T-shirt.

"The authorities still don't know where this Ernesto is," her dad said. "They think maybe he made it to Mexico. They haven't told us anything else."

"The truth is, we're worried he might come back," her mother said. "We don't want you to—"

"I saw bullets go through him," Lilly said, remembering the blood splattering on the windshield. "He's probably dead somewhere."

Her mother shuddered, but Lilly had become accustomed to the gory images after talking about them during a few sessions with her therapist, and later with Mike. Her world had changed, expanded in unimaginable ways. Bloody shootouts from action movies were her new reality.

Her mother sighed. "We know he had accomplices."

After Lilly had fallen out of the van, Ernesto crashed it a couple of blocks away. Lilly had seen the pictures of the bullet-riddled police cars. Ernesto's friends had carried him to another vehicle and they'd gotten away.

Lilly sat back as her mother talked about the man who had done so much damage, who had killed, wounded, scarred. She'd heard him calling someone on the phone, arranging for help. How many of them were out there?

"So, you think someone's after me? I'm in danger?" She looked at her mother, then shifted quickly to her father. He wasn't as good an actor, so she could read him better—know if he was telling her the truth.

"I've been in touch with an FBI agent about it," he said, holding her eye. "But the bottom line is, no one seems to know. Still, it might be better if you moved away for a while. We have contacts with two good boarding schools on the East Coast that—"

"No," Lilly said, rising and standing before them. "I'm not going."

"Lilly, they aren't prisons," her mother said. "They're very nice schools."

Dad pressed hard too, but Lilly stood her ground. Mom was the emotional sell, her father the logical one.

"Don't I have like a ton of follow-up medical appointments?"

He nodded. "Yes, a few more, but—"

"I don't want to start over with new doctors."

Mom opened her mouth, but Lilly rushed ahead.

"And I'm not quitting my training sessions." Alexandra was a taskmaster, but the woman had a wealth of knowledge that Lilly had only begun to appreciate, let alone absorb. "They're helping more than those expensive therapy sessions."

Ekaterina the actress arched a practiced brow, but Lilly saw a softening in her eyes. She had her.

"Look," Lilly said, standing as tall as her left leg allowed. "We don't have much to go on. Let's wait until the authorities tell us more. I'll be careful. You guys can drive me everywhere I go so I won't be alone."

Her father said, "If there's a threat—"

"Then we'll figure out a new plan," Lilly cut in, watching the wheels turn as her parents looked at each other.

She had come into their lives as a young girl, not a baby. It wasn't a question of love—she had no doubt they loved her as much as she loved them—but she suspected they saw her a little bit as an equal, someone already partially grown who joined their family. And she was almost eighteen now.

"I know it sounds crazy, but for the first time in my life I feel like I'm gaining some control. At least a little bit. You always told me this town is wallowing in peer pressure. Everyone catering to everyone else, few willing to stand for what is right. Going to self-defense training is…well, it's teaching me about standing on my own. It's about attacking life, not letting life attack me, about setting goals and achieving them. Right now, it's what I need most. I can't lose that."

Her father wrapped his arms around her. "And we love that about you. You're a survivor, Lilly. We just want you to be safe."

"The best way to be safe is to be strong," Lilly said, repeating one of Mike's mantras.

"Okay," her father said, stepping back. "We'll do it your way. For now."

Mom stepped in and hugged her, whispering, "Nice soliloquy, daughter of mine."

Lilly chuckled in relief and whispered back, "Learned from the best."

Nothing impressed her parents more than people who thought for themselves, who had goals and a plan. *Her* current goal was physical strength and skill-based self-reliance, and the execution of that plan was through training.

Over the next weeks, her mom and dad kept a close eye on her, making sure one of them was always home. Her days filled, a cycle of medical appointments, physical therapy, gym workouts, and self-defense training with Alexandra. Swimming became a twice-daily habit. And although Southern California tended to hold on to summer well into October, her father was researching a heater and enclosure for their pool.

Getting back into high school was on hold for now. She hadn't missed that much, and all the appointments would shred her class time.

One more minor surgery on her leg repaired a muscle that hadn't properly knit together, and her mom's plastic surgeon used the opportunity to smooth the surface puckering from the bullet entry. The surgery pain was minimal, but it created a new irritating wound that ruined her clothes and bedding if she wasn't careful. She'd had her fill of raw skin and oozing sores.

With all the time in the pool, the last of the road rash scabs had finally sloughed off. Unfortunately, this left white splotches of tender new skin that contrasted with her summer tan, making her look like a patchwork doll. At least the cooler fall weather would lend itself to long sleeves.

Even after the latest surgery, Lilly insisted on lessons with Alexandra five nights a week. As much as the woman taught about physical defense, she also schooled Lilly in the mental game of self-protection, and gave her permission to tag along as a silent observer with new classes or individuals. The redundant lessons quickly changed Lilly's instinctive thought process. Instead of the almost nightly dreams of being helpless, she now visualized her reaction to a threat, how she would move and react using new skills. Of conquering.

"Before you exit building, stop and survey outside," Alexandra drilled into everyone one night. "Are there cars someone hides behind? If nighttime, is lighting good? Do you have keys in hand?"

Lilly repeated it back until she could teach a class herself, complete with Alexandra's thick Russian accent.

"Do not be *oblivious*," Alexandra said, taking pride in the word. "Never, never look at cell phone while walking. If you do, you are saying you do not know what is around. Come. I show you."

Alexandra ushered the group into a small meeting room set up with a DVD player and television. Grainy security camera footage showed both women and men walking through parking lots in broad daylight. In each case they were talking or texting on their phones, completely unaware of a creeper sneaking up behind them.

Some had purses or cell phones snatched by a runner. They were the lucky ones. One man was bludgeoned unconscious while other shoppers walked unaware in the next row over. Lilly shivered when the robber dragged the man behind a white van. She swore to never again take safety for granted.

"Carry pepper spray or stun gun at minimum," Alexandra ordered. "In your hand."

Alexandra asked Lilly to stay behind while the other members of the class filed out, sobered by the reality of the dangers around them. When she got home, she was going to research pepper spray.

"Do you carry a gun?" Alexandra asked.

She shook her head. She was too young to legally carry a handgun. But then so was Pana.

Alexandra said, "I can train you. Mike will too. Think about it."

Maybe she should. Her father could get one for her. He knew music people, and probably every rapper in L.A. had a gun.

"...are second-line defense," Alexandra was saying, as she walked Lilly to the door. "But they can be useful."

Two nights later, Alexandra invited Lilly to help in a new class.

"I will teach you to fight, how to disable attacker," Alexandra told the three new students. "Some moves, if done right, can kill. But again I tell you, that is not first defense. What is?" She leaned toward the women in expectation.

An Asian college student pointed to her head. "My best defensive weapon is right here."

Alexandra gave two sharp claps. "Correct. Use brain. Avoid dangerous situations. Do not go in place where you must fight."

Alexandra paired Lilly with a thirty-something housewife, and they practiced breaking front and back holds, stomping insteps, raking shins, and kneeing the family jewels, while their instructor shouted, "Again. Again." Alexandra even had them gouging out eyeballs on a specially built dummy. While realistically slimy and gross, Lilly got pretty good at it after a dozen tries.

"Come. We go outside," Alexandra ordered.

She led their small group out into the parking lot, down an alley, and into a dark house used for training. She showed in real life how to enter, being cautious, yet confident, not succumbing to fear. "Brave and smart. Brave and smart."

Within the month, the class had graduated, and *brave and smart* had become another one of Lilly's mantras.

Chapter 7

Moving his hand ever so slowly, Kade Hunt brushed away the pesky flies that repeatedly dive-bombed his sweat-filled eyes. Nothing like a Georgia summer. His boss said this one wasn't too bad.

Kade and his partner, Elliott Corey, had been lying in the knoll's foot-high grass overlooking the four homes below for nearly an hour. The houses were situated on one-acre lots, and each had at least one outbuilding. If the telephone tip was correct, one of the structures contained a kidnapper and a missing boy. Any vehicles must have been hidden in garages, so the info about a maroon minivan wasn't helpful right now.

A dozen agents and sheriff's deputies waited half a mile away. Kade and Elliott were the scouting team. Their job was to catch someone outside or at a window.

As the houses lay below them, they had designated the one on the upper left as House A, and proceeded clockwise to B, then down the closest home, C, and then across to the left lower one which they labeled D. Each had at least one outbuilding. Kade was currently focused on House A. They changed every two or three minutes to keep eye fatigue at bay.

"Going to A," Corey announced, signaling time to change.

Kade swung his binoculars to House B on the top right of the grid. He quickly swept across the front windows, then did a check of each side yard. The backyard was on the far side, so mostly blocked by the house, but he had a good view of two rusty storage sheds. He moved back to the front windows and fingered the serrated focus wheel, willing the lenses to sharpen more. Nothing had changed since the last ten times he'd watched this house.

He shook his left leg. Something on tiny feet was crawling below his knee, moving higher inside the pants he'd carefully tucked into boots and wrapped with tape. He couldn't wait to get back to the agency condo and do a full-body tick check. Growing up in California, he'd never appreciated how relatively bug-free his home state was compared to the East Coast. No wonder the pioneers had gone west.

"*People migrated west, but the bugs stayed here,*" his boss often almost bragged, as if battling critters was an honored tradition. Maybe it was, considering how every store sold bug zappers in an amazing array of sizes and power. He'd seen one last week that ran on 220 volts and bragged it could kill small birds. Any day, he fully expected to find one that ran on diesel fuel.

This wasn't anything like he'd imagined assignments in Boston, and it looked like he'd be waiting awhile to find out. He hadn't even unpacked in his new apartment in Bean Town before he was sent to Atlanta as extra manpower on these kidnapping cases. Since he hadn't begun any active assignments in Massachusetts yet, it was fine with him. Of course, that was before he learned about the insect population in the Peach State.

"Movement at A," Corey murmured. "Six o'clock."

Kade slid his binoculars back to the house he'd just left, and focused on the side nearest them, the six o'clock position. The large picture window showed a corner of what was probably a dining room table.

"The guy's on the right," Corey said.

Kade spotted an inch or two of a man's body behind the right edge of the window opening. His partner had a good eye. Then the man poked his head out, scanning the driveway and street.

"Bingo. White guy, blue hoodie," Kade said.

"Don't know if it's our guy," Corey cautioned.

"Who wears a hoodie in this heat?"

"Yeah. Still…"

A boy about ten ran up and put his face against the window. The man quickly grabbed his arm and pulled them both out of view, but not before Kade spotted a silver gun in the man's hand.

"Gun," they both said at the same time.

Kade lowered his head and keyed his mic. He relayed their observations to Special Agent in Charge, John Miller, answering the leader's questions about the lay of the house on the property, blind spots, and placement of sheds and shrubs that could act as cover for the assault.

Within four minutes, Kade spotted five men jump off muffled ATVs and move in a crouched jog through the neighborhood. Typically, the FBI would initiate contact and try to negotiate a release. Not this time. This kidnapper was tied to three recent disappearances in the area, each involving a young boy. Each boy was found dead, killed within twenty-four hours of when he'd been snatched after school ended for the day.

The latest victim, Travis Balmer, was taken at 2:35 yesterday afternoon. Kade checked his watch. Two o'clock. At maximum, Travis Balmer had thirty-five minutes to live. They had to move now.

"Corey, you stay on the glasses and keep us informed of any changes," SAC Miller said into their earpieces. "Hunt, you say you have a line of trees to your left?"

"Yes, sir. Good cover."

Miller ordered him to circle left and approach from that side. There wasn't any way the rest of the team could make it to that area without risk of being spotted.

With a pat on Corey's shoulder, Kade scooted backward until hidden by the knoll, then he scrambled along the hillside.

He smashed his way through berry bushes, poison ivy, and numerous other stinging and probably deadly plants, barely averaging a fast walk for the first two hundred yards. But then the underbrush fell behind, and he broke into a jog.

Coming in from an angle, Kade used a mini barn as cover, then he crawled along a weed-covered wire fence until he got to the left side of the target house. Only the side yard, a weed-choked thirty or forty feet, separated him now. The other team should be in place on the opposite side of the house.

There were two high, frosted windows on this wall. Bathrooms. The back left corner had a sliding glass door that might lead to a rear bedroom or kitchen.

In his earpiece, SAC Miller gave the go order. Kade jumped the fence and made it to the side of the house. Several concussions shook the wall at his back. Flashbangs.

No more than ten feet away on his right, the sliding door opened and a hooded man sprinted out, half carrying a boy against his left side. His right hand held a shiny revolver, and he was headed toward a garden shack about fifty feet away.

"Freeze! FBI!" Kade shouted, aiming his Glock at the fleeing man's back. His finger took up the slack in the trigger until he felt the action engaging and moving. A couple more pounds of trigger pull, and a .40 caliber bullet would rip into the perp's back. He'd never shot anyone, but the kidnapper had to be stopped or Travis would die.

The man turned, but got tangled in the boy's feet, and they crashed to the ground. The man's gun went off, and he dropped it as the boy began screaming.

Kade rushed forward, trying to get a shooting angle clear of the boy who was squirming around half on top of the man.

Beyond the downed pair, another man stepped from behind the garden shed and advanced. Kade assumed it was a member of the team, until he spoke.

"You son of a bitch!" the man shouted. "You killed my boy!"

Kade looked at him now. He was carrying a hunting rifle, and had it aimed at the downed man as he walked forward.

"Drop the weapon!" Kade shouted, but he kept his pistol aimed at the man holding the child. Two more steps right and he'd have a clear shot at the kidnapper. But this new man was sighting down the barrel of his rifle, as if intending to shoot regardless of potentially hitting the kid. Kade brought his weapon around, his front sight a white dot centered on the man's chest.

"Drop the rifle!" Kade shouted at him.

The only response was the man's finger curling around the trigger. He was going to shoot.

Then Kade heard muffled but recognizable pleadings from the boy.

Two team members rounded the back of the house and skidded to a stop, assault rifles panning between the two men.

"Don't shoot!" Kade screamed at everyone.

The rifleman's shoulder hunched tighter into the wooden stock, and his finger whitened on the trigger.

Kade fired, catching the rifleman in the right shoulder, pushing it back. The hunting rifle jerked up and thundered in the humid air, a monstrous assault that dwarfed Kade's comparatively puny pistol. He flinched at a ripping crackle near his left ear.

The shooter dropped the rifle and toppled backward.

"Don't shoot him!" Kade yelled, diving onto the kidnapper and boy. He wrenched the youth aside and grabbed the man's gun hand.

One of the assault team was on the rifleman before he'd fully settled, flipping him face down and securing his wrists with zip ties.

The other team member, a hard looking man of about fifty with YOUNG stitched on his vest, kicked the revolver away and dug his knee into the kidnapper's back while Kade searched for additional weapons. They found none.

"Please," the man pleaded as another Kevlar-clad body snatched up the crying boy and hustled him around the house to safety. "I was just trying to protect him."

"Sure, buddy," Young growled, putting more weight on his knee and wrenching the zip ties tighter than required. "You give psychos a bad name."

Kade fell back on his behind, suddenly dizzy. He'd qualified easily during firearms training, but he'd never fired in the line of duty. Certainly never shot, potentially killed anyone. His hand trembled when he carefully holstered his weapon. It would be needed later for the investigation.

He stared at the man on the ground, who sobbed while Young bound his feet.

"Unfortunately," Kade said, "I think he may be telling the truth."

Young stared at Kade like he'd lost it. Then Young gripped Kade's chin, turning it roughly so he could see Kade's left side. The man swore.

"You got a headache, son?"

Kade felt something wet and hot running down his neck.

Chapter 8

"Ladies and gentlemen, the captain has turned off the seatbelt sign. You are free to move about the cabin. However, we recommend..."

Kade tuned out the rest of the flight attendant's announcement, and reclined his seat. Drowsy as he was, he wanted to stay awake until the captain made his standard announcement when they reached their cruising altitude. It always startled Kade out of his takeoff slumber. He opened his briefcase to get the book he'd brought, and a strip of paper fell out.

FBI Agent Shoots Grieving Father While Protecting Suspected Kidnapper

"Real funny," Kade said, wadding up the photocopy of the newspaper story.

"What's funny?" the man in the next seat asked.

"A coworker's idea of a joke." He leaned against the jet's headrest.

The newspaper headline had been plastered on every flat surface when he returned to his Atlanta office. Someone wasted a ton of copy machine paper.

The good-natured laughs surfaced again at noon when everyone gathered for a cake with "Welcome back, G-Man" lettered on top. The boss, however, was not amused.

Now, before Kade had finished two months of his diverted East Coast assignment to the Atlanta office, he was being exiled to Omaha, Nebraska. His boss said they needed him on the Jigsaw

Puzzle Killer case, but the real reason for Kade's reassignment was the agency wanted him distanced from the local Atlanta media. Even Boston was deemed too close. He had yet to see his mom, dad, and sister.

While the newspaper headline was technically accurate, the reporter—a former police officer who had a past beef with the Feds—knew perfectly well before the story went to press that the suspect with the revolver that they thought was kidnapping young Travis *Balmer* was a man named Clarkson, and it was his son, Travis *Clarkson* who was with him at the house he owned. So Clarkson wasn't a kidnapper, and the boy, Travis Clarkson, wasn't a victim.

Clarkson's wife worked at the school library and usually brought their son home, but she had a doctor's appointment that day, so Clarkson had picked up young Travis. The informant who called in the tip was at the school and overheard Clarkson call his son, Travis, and recognized it as the name of the kidnapped boy. For some reason —maybe simple paranoia, since the whole state was on high alert— she thought Clarkson acted suspicious, and alerted the local FBI. It made no sense at all, now, because Travis Balmer had already been kidnapped and wouldn't have been at the school.

After Clarkson took his son home, he listened to his police scanner and heard the kidnapper was thought to be in his neighborhood. He'd gotten his gun from his safe, and was watching from his house for anyone suspicious on the street. That's when Kade and Elliott spotted him.

When the flashbangs broke through several windows, Clarkson instinctively grabbed his son and ran out the back, where he'd been accosted by Nicholas Spellman, whose son, Jay, had been the first kidnapped victim. Spellman had also heard the activity on a scanner, and loaded his deer rifle.

In those seconds after Clarkson fell and his pistol went off, Kade heard the terrified boy call him, "Daddy." Kade knew then that the man on the ground with a pistol wasn't the kidnapper. The whole incident was a screwed up mess of wrong interpretations.

The FBI shuffled the blame to the informant. The informant

blamed media hysteria. The media blamed the FBI. And Kade was on his way to Omaha.

He gently applied pressure on each side of his head, pressing against the ache. Spellman's slug had carved a channel in the skin above his left ear and glanced off his skull. Half a dozen medical professionals told him how supremely lucky he was. A quarter inch to the left and it would have shattered his skull.

The docs stretched his scalp over the wound and stitched it together. It hurt like a son of a gun, and the pain gave him a humongous headache. In the rush to get out of town, he'd accidentally packed the pain meds in his checked baggage.

Kade looked down the aisle toward the galley where the flight attendants were preparing for beverage service. Could he write off a few drinks as medicinal? Probably not.

"Get on a plane tomorrow," his boss had ordered when *Atlanta in the Morning* TV reported the family of the rifle-wielding father was considering a lawsuit against *"the agent who shot an innocent man."*

Where was the story that Kade protected the innocent father whom Spellman planned to kill right in front of the man's son? The few reporters who posed that question also interviewed "civil rights experts" who speculated Kade should have used nonlethal force first, such as beanbags or a stun gun, or tried to reason with Spellman. Were they nuts? The man was squeezing the trigger! And if anyone filed a lawsuit, it should be Kade suing Spellman for shooting *him*. Of course the bureau would never allow that. Getting shot was part of the job.

"So, are you headed to Omaha?" Kade's seatmate asked.

"I suggested two weeks in Hawaii, but my boss didn't go for it," Kade said, wincing as the sound of his voice echoed around his skull.

The man laughed. "Mine wouldn't either. Then again, I'm the boss."

He introduced himself, but Kade forgot the name as soon as he heard it. Pain had begun radiating down his neck, locking up his back muscles. He'd never had a migraine, but this must be close.

"Hey, buddy, you all right? You're looking a little gray."

"Head injury. Nothing serious. Just need some aspirin," he said, trying to stab the call button. He missed.

"Got something better right here," the man said, reaching into his briefcase and withdrawing a container of the same pain meds packed in Kade's suitcase.

He swallowed two of the offered pills dry and leaned back. "Thanks."

"You're welcome," the man said. "You'll love it in Nebraska. Born and raised there." In his deep, sonorous voice, he described growing up on a farm, driving a tractor at ten years old, swimming in the irrigation pond, and playing hide and seek in barns.

The pills kicked in, or maybe it was the plane's assent and pressure change. As Kade drifted off, his seatmate's voice merged with Kade's FBI boss.

"You'll love it in Omaha. It's a step up from Billings." Billings, Montana, had the reputation of being the place agents were sent to disappear.

Even getting shot, Kade could barely catch a break.

Chapter 9

"Are you sure you don't want me to drive you?" Lilly's mom asked for the tenth time. "I've got to go to Burbank to shoot a commercial, anyway."

"I'll be careful, Mom." Lilly grabbed a banana from the basket on the kitchen counter and tore into it. She'd risen before sunrise and completed a mile swim. The downside to so much exercise was constant hunger. She wrapped two Macadamia nut cookies in a napkin for the drive.

Today was the last day of September, and it was time she faced school. The majority of doctor appointments were behind her, and she'd healed sufficiently. Academics, especially math and science, had never been easy, so getting more behind would only make things worse.

"I wish we'd hear something," Mom said, sipping a cup of coffee.

Lilly didn't have to ask about what. Ernesto hadn't resurfaced. Down deep, she hoped he was dead and rotting somewhere.

She hadn't told her parents, but more than once she thought about skipping this last year of school. Her therapist said it was because Lilly's life experiences were a maturing factor—she had moved beyond her peers. Yeah, murder and death did that.

Her dad walked into the kitchen, frowning when he spotted Lilly's backpack on a barstool. "I still don't think this is a good idea," he said.

"I'm trying to get her to ride with me," Mom said.

"And I'm leaving right now," he said. "I can—"

"I'm driving myself," Lilly cut him off, acutely aware of the teenage defiance in her voice. Her push toward adulthood had slipped a cog or two, but she was determined.

Trying to bend everyone's schedules around her was getting old.

It had taken her a while to figure out her nervousness about driving alone, but her therapist clarified it in one of their sessions. Ernesto had taken away her independence.

During her recovery, others controlled everything from doctor appointments, to medications, to what and when she ate, to when she slept, and when she bathed. She was dependent on them for transportation. Her decision to take self-defense classes was the first major step to regaining control. Driving alone was the second.

But the knowing didn't stop her hands from trembling.

"I have to go," she said, looking between her parents. Resignation and acceptance stared back. They got that this wasn't only about making it to school on time.

She slung her backpack over her shoulder, the weight a dull reminder she wasn't the same as last time she went to school.

"Be careful," Mom said, handing her the wrapped cookies and hugging her.

"Don't let them see you sweat," her dad said.

Lilly backed her Toyota out of the garage and turned onto her street.

She rolled her head on her shoulders. Being solo felt good, freeing, and she quickly relaxed.

The closer she got to the high school, the more she was tempted to turn right or left and go somewhere else. Anywhere. Would another missed day of school matter that much?

But she'd promised she'd drive only to school and back. Dutifully, she parked in the lower student lot and hiked toward the building. She still walked with a limp, and her left arm ached from stuffing a couple of heavy textbooks into her backpack this morning. The scars from the compound fracture and operation were pretty evident. She probably should have worn long sleeves, but it was predicted to be in the upper 80s today, so she'd opted for a T-shirt with half sleeves.

Before she even got to the main entrance, the looks began. Quick widening of eyes in recognition as she passed other students, followed by hissed confidences. Today, more than ever, she felt the giant hole left by Pana. They always met up outside before the first bell, then at lunch break, and later after last class. Even after a full day together at the beach or shopping, they'd text each other late into the night, making plans for the next day.

Today she faced the halls alone.

Lilly's morning classes were characterized by solicitous comments from her teachers: "No rush, dear," as they passed out assignments, or "Take extra time on the test if you need," as if she had been shot in the head and was brain damaged. But at least they meant well.

For the rest of the student body, the facts had somehow been twisted every which way, one rumor hinting Lilly was partly at fault for Chad Holt's injuries. By third period she'd heard a dozen more whispered versions, including one that she'd had sex with the kidnappers as barter for her own life. The whole school was a giant tabloid.

"Good to see you back, Lilly."

She turned from her locker. Three girls she and Pana had hung out with sometimes stood in a semi-circle.

"I'm sorry about the accident," Marcy said.

"And Pana," Jennifer added.

"Have you heard from Chad?" Kristin asked.

They asked how she was feeling. She didn't want to give them a laundry list of her injuries and operations. It wasn't like she was besties with any of them. The conversation quickly waned, and they were outwardly relieved when the warning bell rang. They hurried down the hall.

A couple of other people were brave enough to approach. Both asked about Chad Holt. If Lilly knew anything about his next movie. If she and Chad were dating.

Lilly could face the rumors—she'd never been friends with most of the kids anyway. What Lilly couldn't stomach was how, for the most part, everyone had forgotten Pana. She was old news.

Other than Chad, the conversations were mostly about who had new breast implants or nose jobs, and which party to go to on Friday. Had school been this meaningless last year? It had *seemed* normal then, but now... This was Pana's world, and her friend expertly navigated its shark-infested waters with an ease Lilly could never match.

Her stomach began rumbling during the last morning period. She had to remember she didn't have a stocked refrigerator at her disposal for a mid-morning snack. When the bell for lunch rang, she hurried toward the cafeteria.

From the odors in the room, Lilly identified the menu before she got in line: rubberized skinless chicken drizzled with half a teaspoon of watery, nonfat teriyaki, salt-free green peas, half a peach, and a small carton of milk—2% of course. A government-mandated nutritious lunch, identical to every Monday last year.

She sighed and slid a plastic tray onto the bars of the serving counter. Another student followed suit behind her, and the red trays rattled along like a factory assembly line.

Lilly hated plain milk...always had...but took it without complaint from the woman behind the counter. They got real testy if anyone questioned what they knew was best for you. Some things never changed.

And sometimes, everything changed.

Her new morning swim routine, for one. She was burning a ton more calories than last year, and her stomach growled a demand for real food. She'd need three of these pathetic cafeteria meals to make it through the rest of the day. A Double-Double with grilled onions from In-N-Out sounded about right. Pana would have been down with it.

With another sigh, Lilly carried her inadequate offering into the seating area of the cafeteria and scanned the packed room for a place to sit. The only people who would meet her eye were a trio of girls on the cheer squad who snickered behind their hands as they looked at her.

Seriously? What was this, junior high?

She stood there a minute, stunned by a sudden revelation. She'd heard of light-bulb moments when everything becomes clear. Every movie had one, like when Scarlett O'Hara realizes it's all about keeping Tara. But this was less like a 100 watt and more like a slap up-side the head.

Looking at the three cheerleaders, she realized it was Pana's friendship that made all this palpable. She'd been the bridge, beckoning Lilly into this foreign land of snooty privilege. Now the bridge was gone, swept away in a violent storm. A chasm loomed ahead, and there was no way across.

Those on the other side were born into Hollywood royalty, or at least did a good job of faking it. Special treatment was expected, demanded. The pseudo sophistication, expectation of privilege, the easy offenses—to everyone in the room, that was their normal world.

Lilly, however, was grafted in by her parents' choice.

When Ekaterina Orlov and Nathan Hawthorne had walked into St. Mary's Children's Home in Victorville, California, five years ago and scanned the group of girls, Lilly hadn't known who they were. She had recovered physically from the explosion, but her brown hair had grown back stark white as it was today. Ekaterina's eyes had fixed on her. She remembered trembling as the strange woman sifted her fingers through Lilly's hair and said, "Exquisite."

Then the woman smiled the most beautiful smile Lilly had ever seen. She'd fallen in love with her mother and father that first day. Several visits and a two-inch pile of paperwork later, they'd taken her home for good. They had *chosen* her, taken her into their world. This world.

A group of jocks jostled her from behind. "Sorry," one of them said, not even bothering to look at her. His world was all that was important.

And that said it all. She was like a rock in a stream, they were the water flowing around her. They were aware of her presence, but not connected to her. Nor she to them.

Her therapist was right: the past weeks—living and experiencing such different priorities, witnessing life and death—had irrevocably changed her.

Lilly searched the faces. Probably no one else in this cafeteria was learning how to disable and even kill an opponent. None of them were nearly blown up as a child and had their hair grow back a different color. She was the one thing that wasn't like the others.

If she ever once had, Lilly Hawthorne no longer belonged in their world.

With one final glance at this suddenly alien place, she dumped her balanced diet in the nearest trash can.

Ten minutes later, she had emptied her locker and turned in her textbooks at the school office, informing the flustered secretary she was leaving—permanently. She'd deal with the inevitable phone calls from the principal later.

In her Toyota, Lilly lowered the windows, letting the bone-dry Santa Ana winds tangle her hair as she drove. The air felt alive with possibilities. Real life was more than boob jobs and parties, and she was determined to experience it.

But first, she'd make a stop at In-N-Out.

Chapter 10

"Welcome to Omaha, Special Agent Hunt." A woman who appeared to be around forty years old approached Kade as he finished handing in paperwork and getting a badge waiting for him at Security. "I'm Special Agent Margaret Cartwright. You can call me Maggie."

"Kade," he said, accepting her handshake. It was firm, dry. He detected a subtle attempt at dominance in the way she gripped his hand, squeezing a little too hard and long. The good ole boys network was alive and well in the FBI, requiring female agents to constantly push against barriers.

"This way." She turned and headed rapidly down a corridor, not looking to see if he followed.

As he caught up, he admired the way her high ponytail arced in a perfect question mark. The black mane swished back and forth with each step, brushing well below her shoulder blades. It would have been sexier if it hadn't been cinched so tight, but the way it smoothed her face, she would never need a facelift. High cheekbones hinted at Native American ancestry.

"You'll be working on my team. There are three of us locally—four counting you—plus a consultant."

"Only four agents?"

"A lot of people have been assigned to work the bombings in Dallas and Kansas City. The press doesn't know it yet, but there are other credible solid targets. Several, in fact. Agents are being pulled from all over."

A secretive environmental group known as Rare Earth had begun a anti-development campaign two months ago, targeting big construction projects. Everything from highways, to bridges, to commercial buildings was fair game to the radical group. Kade had hoped to be assigned to one of the teams hunting the group's leaders.

"We have several other resource teams at our disposal, and I have authority to pull more in with justified need." Maggie turned a corner into another long hallway. "You're a bonus because you're a pariah right now."

"Thanks...I think."

She threw him a smile and kept walking.

The good news was his bosses were giving him a chance for redemption. The fact that he was now on this team would play well if the press started digging. Even better if Cartwright's team caught this guy.

"JPK has been active for twenty-one months now. Twenty-one kills, and we only recently determined a partial pattern of how he choses his victims," Maggie said, leading Kade into a conference room with windows facing the interior hall. Six chairs circled the table, which held a laptop and digital projector. She took a chair by the computer.

"He killed ten times before the first hint they were connected. Ten states, ten kills, one each month."

She hit a key to wake up the laptop, and waved toward a credenza that held a coffee carafe, paper cups, and a variety of sweeteners and flavored creamers. Kade fixed a cup while the projector came to life and the letters *JPK* appeared on the wall.

"Why so long to figure that out?" Kade asked, taking the chair opposite hers. He'd heard some of the story through the channels— everyone had since the media caught the scent. But he'd been swamped in his own work. Plus, he wanted the official answer from the team.

"The first nine were investigations by local authorities," Maggie said, "and each had a different MO. Nothing linked them, and I mean nothing."

Kade sipped his coffee. He'd heard that much. "What changed?"

"A tenacious detective in New Mexico. He was convinced a small jigsaw puzzle piece found under the body of his murder victim was a clue, so he combed the databases and emailed law enforcement friends in other cities. He located another open case in Alaska where a puzzle piece was found under the body of a ninety-year-old woman who had been strangled. She was kind of a hoarder, so no one there thought much of the junk under her, but they did document it."

"And the puzzle pieces fit together? Literally?" Kade asked, sipping his coffee.

"Wouldn't that be nice," Maggie said, shaking her head. "But using that information, the detective found three other unsolved murders that had puzzle pieces in evidence. Two of those *did* fit together."

"So he knew there were probably other murders."

"Exactly. That created a firestorm of bulletins to law enforcement agencies all over the country. The result is what we have here." A slide full of puzzle pieces came up.

"Do we know if the pieces are from a single puzzle? I mean besides the two."

Maggie shook her head. "We're looking. But there's no such thing as a jigsaw puzzle database. No one even knows how many puzzles have been sold in the last thirty years—that's our working timeframe on the puzzles based on lab analysis of the cardboard—but certainly tens or hundreds of thousands. We're contacting all the manufacturers, trying to get their sales numbers. One thing, though...these pieces are consistent in size, and fit the standard of most 750- to 1,000-piece puzzles."

She let him do the math. It didn't take a wizard to estimate multi-millions of pieces.

"And we now have twenty-one pieces to compare?" He felt defeated already.

"Actually, we only have sixteen pieces. Two were documented, but are missing from the evidence boxes, and we don't know for sure who three of the victims are. Look at this."

Maggie projected a map of the United States with numbers on each state in the order of the cases. "Alabama was first, Georgia second, Maryland third, New Jersey fourth, South Carolina fifth. Those were all Eastern states. But the sixth state was Wyoming. Then Alaska, Hawaii, back to Massachusetts, and then out to New Mexico where the tenth murder took place. South Dakota, Arizona, Idaho, Michigan, New York, Tennessee, Arkansas, Illinois, Minnesota, North Carolina, and finally, Texas. It gets complicated."

Kade furiously sketched notes on his pad, numbering the states in the order she gave.

"Three of these—New Jersey, Hawaii, and South Dakota—didn't have reported murders. We filled those in after we discovered the pattern. There are undoubtedly victims there, but we don't know who, nor do we have those puzzle pieces."

"There's a pattern?" Kade sure couldn't see it. It looked like the killer bounced around the country at random.

"We listed the states alphabetically. Alabama is the first, Georgia is tenth, Maryland is twentieth."

"Counting by tens," Kade nodded.

"Exactly. Except he started at number one, of course, not zero, so that makes the first batch one state shorter than the rest. And when he ran out of numbers at fifty, he started over with the next one in order from the first group, then the second group, and so on."

Kade stopped taking notes and tried to follow as she changed the slide. It contained a list of the states in alphabetical order. California was highlighted. To its right was a red number 22.

"California is next? What are we doing in Omaha?"

"Well," she rubbed deep creases around her eyes, "we *thought* we had the pattern figured out two months ago, and Iowa or Nebraska were the best guess. And this office covers Iowa."

Kade nodded, trying to relax before the onslaught of data.

"You wouldn't believe how many combinations we tried: the states in alphabetical order, their postal abbreviations, numeric position in the alphabet, the numeric equivalents for letters. We had mathematicians dividing, multiplying, and adding all kinds of combinations. We even tried everything in reverse order. We tracked weather patterns, temperatures, longitude and latitude, the number of national parks, state flowers and birds, number of representatives to Congress, what year the states *became* states. And, of course, we didn't even know if there *was* a pattern. The guy could have been sticking pins in a map, for all we knew.

"But three weeks ago one of our resource consultants came up with this"—she waved at the image—"and everything fits so far." Maggie stood up and tapped the wall. "California is next. And our job is to find the most likely target."

"There are over thirty million people in California," Kade said, sitting back.

"About thirty-five now," Maggie corrected as the conference room door opened.

She introduced the first man, Larry O'Brian, a pudgy young guy who didn't appear to be out of his teens. He came complete with glasses sliding down his nose, a portfolio with papers jutting in all directions, and two laptops that he almost dropped while trying to shake Kade's hand.

"Larry is the consultant I mentioned," Maggie said. "On loan from MIT."

Larry shrugged. "I'm pretty good at math and patterns."

Maggie grunted. "He's a bona fide genius." She turned to the second man. "And this charming…individual, is Special Agent Paulo Estacio." The corner of her mouth twitched.

Estacio was shorter than Kade by a few inches, and had a swarthy complexion topped by curly dark hair going gray. Somewhere around sixty, he had the trim build of someone who either inherited good genes, or worked out regularly. Unlike Larry.

"Paul," Estacio modified as he shook Kade's hand. "Margaret and my mother are the only ones who call me Paulo."

Maggie huffed, then waved at the chairs. "Everyone sit down."

Paul mumbled, "Yes, ma'am," but quietly enough only Kade could hear.

He wondered what the history was between these two, but turned his attention to Larry, who had cabled one of his laptops to the projector and was bringing up multiple spreadsheets. His second laptop was open, and Kade scooted over to get a view. More sheets of numbers and complex formulas filled the screen. Math had never been his strong suit.

Maggie proved herself a natural leader, a confident decider who cut off rabbit trails and kept everyone focused. She'd be the one he'd want watching his six in a firefight. Paul, no less confident, was a thinker, needing more time to analyze before acting. Like Larry, he demonstrated he knew everything there was about JPK.

While Larry came across as a self-deprecating nerd, Kade saw through that to a young man who quietly knew he was smarter in pure knowledge than anyone in the room, yet recognized the wisdom of experience in others. As a consultant, not an agent, he didn't presume to have the same vote in decisions, but he wasn't hesitant to defend his opinions. Kade liked that.

"So, you've heard how we found the order of the states and where they will happen next," Larry said. "The critical knowledge needed now is to find California's specific victim for October. The 1st is only six days away." He hit a key on the laptop and a new slide came up.

"The killings always happen on days that are multiples of three," Larry said, "so the 3rd, 6th, 9th, 12th, 15th, 18th, 21st, 24th, 27th, or 30th. I can't determine any probable order of kill days, as we call them, but that doesn't mean there isn't one. For now, we have to assume it can be any one of those days."

By the time they broke for lunch and headed to the building's cafeteria, Kade was nursing an inferiority complex and a renewed headache, this one not from a bullet.

How did the others view *him*? Generally, he tended to analyze subjectively rather than objectively. This should be a weakness and, in fact, there were classes that taught how to rid agents of exactly that "problem." While he'd not done well in those specific classes, his instinct had served him well in others and in the field, and he'd gained a small reputation.

The fourth member of the team, Benny Philips, was blond, lanky, and proudly from Texas. "Howdy, pardner," he said, sliding his tray onto their table. His handshake felt like years of repairing fences on the open plain, and Kade glanced to see if the man wore a rodeo belt buckle under his regulation clothing.

"Good news, boss lady," Philips said to Maggie, passing her a manila file. "The lab analysis is 90 percent confident that all the puzzle pieces came from the same company, or at least the same manufacturer for multiple puzzle wholesalers or retailers."

"Only ninety?" Kade asked.

Philips cleared his throat. "Don't want to spoil your lunch with details, but some of the pieces were pretty badly contaminated by... stuff leaking onto them. If you know what I mean." He raised a brow.

Kade nodded, no longer quite as interested in lunch.

"We're still trying to figure out how he chooses his victims," Larry said, biting into a heaping Sloppy Joe. "We've got male and female, as young as fifteen and as old as eighty-six, from all backgrounds and occupations, some sick, most healthy. But there are some knowns. One, they are all blond. The second thing is they were all in the news recently for some reason."

"Like celebrities?" Kade asked, picking his way through his barbecue chicken salad. He'd forgotten to ask to hold the cilantro. The chef had chopped it extra fine, making it difficult to separate.

"Not necessarily," Larry continued. "One woman had donated a kidney to the mayor of her city—that was Maryland. Got picked up on the AP wire nationwide. Another was an old man. He was in failing health, and his kids moved him from Texas to Rapid City, South Dakota to live with them."

Kade mulled this over as he used one tang of his fork to free a piece of chicken from the green weed. Across the table, Benny upended a side container of cilantro onto his own salad.

"I don't understand how anyone would want to live in Rapid City," Paul said, setting his tray down next to Larry. "Too cold for me."

This from a man who lived in Nebraska, Kade thought. Not

exactly balmy in the winter.

"Yeah, well his dog that he'd had for a few years was left behind at a neighbor's—the man's kids didn't want to deal with a pet. But the man loved that dog, and evidently the dog loved him. Three weeks after the man arrived at his daughter's home in Rapid City, the dog shows up, skin and bones, and with bleeding paws."

Kade remembered the story because it hit the headlines twice. The reporters said the dog had apparently traveled over a thousand miles. People proclaimed it a miracle, and the mayor of Rapid City presented the dog with a large dog bone shaped like a key to the city. The story earned a tragic retelling when the man was found murdered three months after the dog found him. That was puzzle piece number 11.

"So we're looking for someone in California who's been in the news recently?" Kade asked. "Shouldn't be a problem." That earned a laugh from Paul.

They didn't call it Hollyweird for nothing. Everyone in the city was seeking their fifteen minutes of fame, whether through a heroic act or a life-threatening jackass move caught on a cell phone. And San Francisco wasn't any better.

Because of the entertainment industry, there were probably more reporters in Kade's home state than most of the other states combined, and competition for the best stories was an Olympic event. If it was a slow news day, reporters quoted other reporters about rumors of stories. Anyone could be on the news.

Fortunately, Larry had some ideas on how to ferret out the right story or stories, and had a hand-picked—and FBI vetted—cadre of his students running search software on the supercomputers back at MIT.

"What if the story our killer fixates on doesn't happen until the middle of October?" Kade asked. "We won't have much time to act."

Paul shook his head. "All the stories about the victims take place three months before the murder. So he picks the victim, then acts three months later, not exactly to the day, but within the month. Whatever the story was in California, it already happened sometime in July."

Kade shoved his salad aside, no longer hungry. July was when he had left for Boston. The month of Lilly Hawthorne's kidnapping.

Chapter 11

"You're sure you want to do this?" her father asked for the tenth time.

Lilly nodded, and he slid the plastic clamshell case across his desk.

Ever since she'd come to live with her parents, she'd loved his home office. It wasn't a large room, at least not compared to other rooms in what felt like a mansion to her. About fifteen by twenty feet, one wall was three sets of French doors which opened to a beautiful garden of ferns, hostas, giant agapanthus with flowering purple heads as big as her own, and a trickling fountain. He often kept the doors open, like today, preferring perfumed nature to sterile air conditioning.

Framed movie posters covered much of the opposite wall. Dad loved classic horror and sci-fi, and together they'd watched *Creature From The Black Lagoon*, *Attack Of The 50FT. Woman*, *The Blob*, and even Ed Wood's *Plan 9 from Outer Space*, which was so bad they'd spent the whole time laughing and pitching popcorn at the TV.

Personally, she leaned more toward *Underworld*. Oh, to have a black corseted leather suit like Kate Beckensale wore. That would intimidate any bad guy.

When she bought her own home someday, she wanted a room exactly like this.

Lilly turned her attention to the container, willing her fingers to stop trembling as she released the catches. She sucked in a breath and lifted the plastic lid.

"It's so tiny." No more than four inches long, it appeared made for a child's hand. She tentatively ran her fingers along the polished slide and black grip.

"Yes," her dad agreed, "but it's not a toy."

Everyone in her self-defense classes asked Alexandra about carrying a gun. "*A gun is a tool,*" Alexandra had said, "*something else to keep you safe.*" She'd made it sound no more dangerous than a knife or baseball bat, a benign hunk of metal with some holes drilled in it.

The difference was that a gun had reach. It could stop an attacker yards away, before he got close. But it could also hurt someone a *hundred* feet away. Someone innocent. Knowing about guns was one thing. Having one that was her own that she was going to carry?... that was something entirely different.

"A pistol is only useful for protection if you carry it everywhere, and a big one often gets left at home in a safe. This will fit in a compact clutch or your pocket. No one will know it's there."

The Seecamp .32 caliber pistol lay on a bed of gray egg crate foam. Beside it were three spare magazines.

"Each magazine holds six cartridges," Dad said. "One in the chamber gives you seven total. Always keep one in the chamber when you're carrying it."

"What if it goes off in my pocket?"

"It has a manual safety and a very stiff trigger pull. It will only fire if you intend it to." Then he added, "It's the same as your mother's."

Lilly knew her dad carried a gun, one much larger than this. He was often out in the middle of the night on shoots, and not always in the best areas. But her mother? This was news.

"Check to see if it's loaded," her father ordered, sitting back and crossing his arms.

"I..." Lilly snatched her fingers away from the cool metal. Her eyes darted to his. She'd gone trap shooting with him once, but that was with his old shotguns. She didn't know anything about pistols. "How?"

Dad leaned forward, hands splayed on the desk. No, not her dad now. He'd morphed into Nathan Hawthorne the producer, a man used to being in charge, commanding others to do his bidding, wresting cinematic perfection from a gaggle of disorganized creative types. She'd observed the way his power sucked the oxygen from a set so that everything and everyone focused on him. He was respected, a little feared, and greatly admired. But his voice held kindness over the determination when he spoke.

"That's what you'll learn, beginning tonight. Alexandra knows you'll be bringing this." He picked up the pistol and flicked a lever on the bottom of the grip. The magazine fell onto the foam. Then he pulled back the slide so Lilly could see into the chamber. Empty. His motions were sure and precise. "Alexandra uses an indoor shooting range close to your classroom. Thirty days of training every night and you'll be a master."

Lilly smiled. He always said that. If anyone practiced something for thirty days, they'd be a master. It had worked with her self-defense training. Lilly didn't doubt him on this, either.

"By the way, I've made some calls. Along with your defense training, you'll be starting with some tutors soon."

She slumped in the chair, wishing the whole high school thing were behind her. It seemed so trivial.

Her dad laughed at her. "Buck up, kiddo. You're smart. It'll be over before you know it."

The doorbell rang in the front hall, and her dad rose to get it. She stared at the hunk of machined steel resting on the foam and tried to think of it as a hammer, or perhaps a canister of pepper spray, but neither seemed an appropriate comparison. She closed the lid and laid a few papers on the case when she heard footsteps approaching.

Her father ushered a man into the room. He was medium height, forties, thinning brown hair, and rounding all over. Even his rimless glasses were round. Anybody's dad at a Little League game—save for the navy suit and the bulge of his shoulder holster. She'd been trained to spot that.

"Lilly, this is Special Agent Ron Blake with the FBI."

"Miss Hawthorne," the man acknowledged.

"You caught him?"

He grimaced. "Not exactly." Her father directed Blake to take the chair matching hers. "We have reports—semi-substantiated rumors, really—that Ernesto Viera died of his wounds in a clinic in the hills outside Tijuana, Mexico. But there are other rumors that he's alive."

"Viera," her father said. Although other authorities had given them weekly reports, this was the first time they'd heard a last name for the kidnapper. "You're working to find out for sure whether he's dead?"

"We have other sources nearby," Blake hedged. He shifted in the chair, his glance darting from her father to her and back. Then he cleared his throat. Lilly waited for him to ask for a glass of water, something to delay the other shoe that was about to drop—probably right on her head.

"We didn't know much about the Viera family before about eighteen months ago. They keep an extremely low profile, and that's partly why it took so long to confirm Ernesto's identity. The family business, if you will, goes back three or more generations. These are the current adult children. They've been working almost like silent owners for years, building a base, contacts, and racking up stockpiles of cash. Because they are nowhere as powerful as the big cartels, they've taken a different path to success."

Lilly couldn't figure out if that was some botched attempt at humor. If so, it was overshadowed by the fact that Ernesto could still be alive—and that he had family. She'd never thought of him as human, only a monster that brought death and destruction to all around. She covered her face, listening to the cheerful splashing water from the outdoor fountain.

"From the first, this current Viera family built their business inside the US instead of in Mexico or one of the other Latin American countries. They live here in the southland. Somewhere."

"What kind of business are we talking about?" her father asked, but by the look on his face, he already knew the answer.

"The usual: drugs, prostitution, protection rackets. But their main business is illegals."

"You mean smuggling them in?" Lilly asked.

"Initially," Blake nodded. "But their genius, if you will, has been to keep the cash flowing by charging families for legal documents and forged papers, attorney fees, housing, job contacts, money transfers to family members back home, medical treatment, and a lot more. They are essentially milking their own people in addition to all the rest."

"Can't you arrest them?" Lilly asked.

Blake sighed. "If we knew *where* and *who* they are, we could begin building a case against them, but so far they've succeeded in keeping their identities and location, or locations, secret. Of course, since the kidnapping incident, there is monumental pressure to find out everything about them."

"How many in the family?" Lilly's dad asked.

"Four counting Ernesto. According to DEA, they are all siblings. Two other brothers—we don't know their names yet—and the sister, Magda. Her name comes up more often. She's the oldest, and reputedly the brains of the family business."

Lilly tried to absorb the information. Did the four of them play together as children? Did they like baseball or soccer? Were they old movie fans? None of those pictures formed in her mind.

"So kidnapping is part of their repertoire?" Dad asked.

"That's a little strange," Blake said. "This is the first incident like this that we know of. But it kind of makes sense in a way."

"Explain," her dad demanded.

"Well, in some ways it's California's fault—at least the lawmakers," Blake said, standing so he could pace the length of the room.

Lilly turned in her chair to follow him as he paused and faced the garden.

"You see, the state has been cutting into their business by providing services to illegals without them having to show proof of citizenship. Poof," Blake said, indicating an explosion with his fingers, "no more need for the Vieras to charge for high quality fake IDs. Some of these agencies will accept a photocopy of a driver's license, making it ridiculously simple to make one. Once they sign up with one agency, they can apply for assistance programs at others, getting housing and signing up for utilities. Using utility bills as proof of residence, they can set up bank accounts with automatic money transfers back home, and pass for legal immigrants at jobs. And since marijuana growing is spreading in many counties, there isn't as much demand for imported product, especially when the Vieras have to compete with the big drug boys."

Lilly cut a look to her dad. He sat bouncing his steepled index fingers against his lips. He could be thinking of ways to bring down the Vieras, or how this could be a new screenplay. She wasn't sure which.

"There are so many free clinics now that never check IDs, that the whole Viera network of look-the-other-way doctors and kickbacks is drying up. Now the lawmakers are talking about free college for illegal kids while the rest of us taxpayers pay out the nose for our kids to attend!"

Lilly rose and closed the French doors leading outside. Blake's last part had been loud enough for all the gardeners on the street to hear, most of whom were Hispanic. She wondered if they were gathering pitchforks to storm the castle. She turned to Blake who looked a little surprised at himself.

"Sorry for the soapbox," he said, backing away from the now closed doors. "I... Sorry." He started to go back to the chair, but instead backed up as her dad came around the desk and stood next to Lilly.

"So they're getting into kidnapping to increase cash flow?" Dad asked.

Blake looked at him a moment while regaining his composure. "As you probably know, that's been an increasing danger south of the border for several years. It looks like they're trying it in the US. We hope to know more shortly." He turned toward the exit, then back to them, hesitating, as if he wasn't sure what to say.

Lilly was tempted to clap her hands for his attention before he finally spoke.

"I have to go, but there's one more thing. There's a possibility...

Well, let me just say that, even with their finances down, the Vieras have a lot of money."

"Spit it out, agent," Dad demanded.

Blake looked at Lilly. "You might be in further danger. Especially if Ernesto's dead. Well…even if he's alive, really."

"Why?" Lilly asked. "I was just in the wrong place at the wrong time. I didn't do anything to them."

"Actually, you did," Blake said. "The Vieras operate through intimidation, and their power comes from a reputation of being utterly ruthless. They can't afford for the word to get out that they can be beaten. You survived."

"Bested by a teenager," her dad said.

Blake nodded. "It might be good if your daughter took a long trip somewhere."

With that, he left.

Lilly sank into the chair, her eye catching the side of the black gun case hidden under the papers. Time at the firing range couldn't come soon enough.

Chapter 12

Jigsaw Puzzle Killer Strikes Again!

Percy reread the USA Today headline for the third time, tasting the words as they formed on his tongue. *JPK*. That was a first. He'd wondered what they would call him once they figured out the connection of the murders. Fortunately, the press had gotten wind of the story and come up with the name before the FBI's first press conference. Reporters were creative like that. The FBI? Not so much.

It had a nice ring to it. A *lot* better than Percy Maxwell, Serial Killer. Nope, that didn't work. Nor did any of the names on his fake IDs.

JPK sounded menacing, serious, relentless, unstoppable.

With the first leaks from local authorities comparing cases, his exploits had shown up in a smattering of headlines across the country, but now things were really heating up. It was a good feeling to finally be recognized for his skill, even if they didn't fully know how clever he was.

Percy laughed as he unzipped his travel bag and removed his toiletries. The motel was typical roadside trash, a leftover from the 60s, made of cheap materials back then that hadn't fared well over the decades. The only thing that saved these buildings was the desert climate. The For Sale sign posted in the smelly lobby had faded with age, much like the skeletal man in the yellowed wife-beater who ran the place.

Who would even consider buying a place like this? The parking lot planters held more weeds than anything flowering, and even the weeds were sickly. What had once been a pool surrounded by a patch of grass and low chain-link fence was now a slimy green pit. Unknown numbers of dead things probably rotted at the bottom. Could this seriously be someone's retirement dream? Buy a little place with minimal but steady income, do a bit of maintenance, and settle down to chain-smoke unfiltered Camels and watch a twelve inch TV in a cramped office till you die? Now, *that* was the life, eh?

He shook with an involuntary shiver. The only things that could improve this dump were a fire, a bomb, or a bulldozer.

At the last place he'd stayed—500 miles down the road at the Palms Motel that had not a single palm tree for miles around—he'd seriously considered helping the owner on her way to the ever-after. But she'd been so disgusting a specimen, he hadn't wanted to touch her. And she didn't fit his pattern.

Percy had studied the biographies of killers and gleaned a lot of useful ideas. Everyone knew you couldn't be a serial killer without a pattern. The pattern was everything. Usually it was a modus operandi, an MO, such as using the same weapon each time, or picking victims by looks, or always positioning the body in a certain way. Or maybe all three together. Percy's pattern was so much better it made previous serial killers look like amateurs.

Of course, he'd never planned all this until recently. Who woke up one day and said, "I've made up my mind for a career: Serial Killer"? But in his case he knew exactly when the seed was planted. When he'd been about twelve, he spotted a squirrel running across the road in front of his mother's car, and heard a faint pop as they passed over the spot. He turned, and out the back window a patch of gray and red lay where the living animal had scampered only seconds before.

That started him wondering about life and death. What was it like to truly *end* someone? Take a human being and wipe them from the face of the planet? Perhaps to be there as the light dimmed in their eyes and their chest gave up its last breath?

Alive, then dead—a thin, weak line, so easily crossed. Killers gave people a little shove over the line, that's all.

Then, one boring winter day when he was snowed in at his home in New York, he'd devised a plan: one victim each month in a different state. Ambitious, yes, but by itself too simple. And that's when the complex planning began. JPK's MO.

In some ways, the actual events were a bit of a letdown. He always expected terror on the victim's part. But more often than not, most showed surprise over fear, utter confusion over fighting the sudden onslaught of pain. He didn't believe even one of them had fully comprehended the imminent ceasing of life.

If facing the same ultimate fate, would *he* recognize it? Perhaps—now that he knew the end could be swift and unanticipated.

Afterwards, it really didn't matter if his victims knew they were about to die. He pushed them over that thin line, and they died. Period.

Lots of people killed someone else every day. *His* challenge—JPK's—was to make it something special. Unique. Memorable.

Percy set his laptop on the scarred motel desk. At least this place had free Internet.

His cell phone rang, and he checked the screen. Mother. He waited until the ringing stopped. If he remembered correctly, he was supposed to be in Iceland for three more nights, so it would be five hours later than where she lived in New York. She would assume him long in bed. And, of course, he probably wouldn't have cellular service in Iceland.

If she'd really wanted to reach him anywhere, she would have bought him a satellite phone, but she was too tight for that. Galling, because his mother, Frances Maxwell, was heir to the Maxwell line of steel, concrete, and trucking fortunes, and could purchase anything she wanted. At least she had agreed to finance his world tour so he could learn about different cultures and "find himself." That's what he'd told her. Being frugal with the stipend allowed him to travel freely from state to state. What would she think if she knew he was in a rundown motel off Old Route 66 in Barstow, California?

He double-clicked the computer file named *Travel* and searched his itinerary database of locations, dates, detailed descriptions, and thousands of photos. Yes, today he was supposed to be in Akureyri, Iceland. Only sixty miles from the Arctic Circle, it was the second largest city in the small country, and located near the spectacular Godafoss—Waterfall of the Gods. He'd told her months ago it would be one of his stops. He opened several pictures of the falls, and had to admit it did look amazing. Maybe he'd travel there for real someday.

For now, his mother had to believe he was actually there. She was not a woman easily deceived. But he had an advantage over those with whom she normally conducted business: she *wanted* to believe her only child. He was her hope, her only tenuous thread to immortality. Her biggest disappointment was his failure to give her a grandchild.

Still, he'd be thorough in Photoshopping a few pictures to include his image. She'd never traveled to Iceland, so it shouldn't be too difficult. Plus, the cell phone had a crappy camera, as he'd often reminded her, so the pictures sent were correspondingly poor. He'd dirty up some online stock photos with the editing software and send them to her. Later, when he was due in London, it would be more difficult—she'd traveled there several times. However, with her cancer now so advanced, the pain medications were his assistants in subterfuge.

A few more months at the most.

He set his alarm for 4:30 a.m., when he would return her call and regale her with tales of his adventures, taken straight from travelogues of actual visitors. She'd admonish him to be careful, take no risks. Frances Maxwell had no idea.

He closed the travel database and clicked on his special file. At the encryption prompt, he typed in the required password and watched the spreadsheet load.

Twenty-five columns wide, a hundred rows long, five more tabs of like information. He'd lived within its gridded confines for months, knew the width of each column, the fonts and attributes of each cell, the formulas behind the numbers.

The heading at top had no title. *Murder Plan* had felt gauche when he first created the file, so he'd deleted that and left it blank. But now he had a title.

In cell A1, he typed *JPK*, and sat back rubbing his chin. The sheet still looked plain. It needed graphics. A logo for JPK. A tiny map of the United States? Maybe outlined in blood red. Although decent at tweaking pictures, he'd never been good at creating graphics from scratch.

He opened a browser window and searched for graphic designers in foreign countries. There were dozens who advertised logo creation for a minimal fee. He picked six people on different sites, entered his ideas of what he wanted, then logged out. He'd check it tomorrow. Now it was time to search the news.

He carried the laptop to the bed where he could browse while watching news. The TV remote control was secured to the nightstand with a snarled steel cable. He wrestled with the hopeless mess for a few seconds, then ripped it loose. A chunk of splintered plastic bounced off the other bed then sprang back and dangled off the front of the nightstand, the cable still super-glued to it.

"Stupid people!" he shouted in the direction of the tiny front office while he reinserted one of the batteries that had fallen out. "Do you really think someone will steal your crappy remote?"

Percy punched the power button on the broken controller, and the bulky TV hummed to life displaying a static-laced picture of the KNBC Newsroom in Los Angeles. Smiling, he settled against the headboard. He'd missed the nightly network news show that covered the nation, but local stations often picked up feel-good stories from other affiliates. Right now, he was looking for a good one from Mississippi.

Using a browser window on the laptop, he pulled up his news feed windows, set the filters for Mississippi, and skimmed the headlines while the L.A. channel showed the weather.

So many good stories to choose from. He drummed his fingers as he read. Who to pick? Who to pick?

* * *

Larry's team had compiled a list of 317 possible California

victims. Working around the clock, they'd culled out 102 of those.

"That still leaves 215," Kade said, rising from the conference table and pacing around the end in an effort to remain alert.

"Hey, I'm doing my best," Larry countered.

"Sorry, man." Kade put his hand on the Larry's shoulder. He hadn't meant to lay it all on him.

Kade hadn't even checked into a hotel, instead sleeping behind a row of desks on one of the mats Maggie brought in from a sporting goods store. Even after showering in the locker room off the small gym, he felt gritty and gummy both inside and out, same as he did after a cross-country flight stuck in recycled air.

Needing a break, he exited the building, turned right, and began walking. Gray clouds poked from behind the building, rolling in from the west. Every breath required effort, and he doubted the atmosphere could hold any more moisture.

The J. James Exon Regional FBI Headquarters in Omaha, Nebraska, had the reputation of being very "green" in both the materials it was constructed from, as well as its energy use. But to Kade, its important attribute was that it was big, and provided a long walking path.

A high security fence ringed the perimeter of the entire facility, which also included an annex building, parking garage, and helipad. The barrier separated the compound from the constant hum of traffic on busy roads that bordered three sides of the property. Two manned entry points allowed in only those who were authorized.

But the bad guy they were tracking wasn't trying to gain entrance here in Omaha. He was no doubt already in California, planning his move on an unsuspecting innocent he'd picked out in July.

Kade felt a growing compulsion to get back to his home state. But where would the team go? The killer could be anywhere, from Mendocino to Lone Pine, National City to Eureka. Any place where a person did something nice for someone else, or survived an amazing ordeal, or was the recipient of special recognition. As long as it got reported so JPK could find it.

When he considered it, Larry had done an amazing job of getting down to a few hundred potentials.

Kade and Paul had the task of scrutinizing each of the past case files, listing every possible MO, even if some were only found in one case.

Did JPK repeat using a knife? Yes.

Were the knives the same? No.

Did they grow or decrease in size? Unconfirmed.

Did he alternate between serrated and smooth blades? Three victims weren't enough to determine a pattern.

JPK used a different caliber gun on each of the four victims he shot. Three others were strangled, one with a wire garrote, another with latex-gloved hands, and the latest with a dish towel. Another was bludgeoned with an unknown blunt instrument. Another had a claw hammer beside the split skull. Still another was killed with a garden trowel, of all things.

The murder weapons and methods were so diverse, so seemingly random, they were almost a pattern in themselves. That was highly atypical for an organized serial killer. What was the reason? Or *was* there a reason? Or perhaps the randomness *was* the pattern.

One woman bequeathed her life savings of $137,000 to an animal rescue organization that specialized in reptiles. Three months later, she moved into a private care facility. A week after that, a worker found her deceased with a syringe in her hand. The autopsy and crime lab tests identified a massive amount of neurotoxic snake venom in her system. The syringe, a brand not used at the facility, carried only her finger prints.

Kade shook his head while he scratched the rash on his inner arm. It had developed after his run through the poison ivy in Georgia. A parting gift from the South.

Then his fingers stilled. Snake venom...animal rescue. Could that be a connection for that victim? Animals?

And the man strangled with gloves had latex residue on his neck. Hadn't he been a lab technician? He would have used latex gloves routinely.

Kade began trotting back around the building as his mind

whirled. At least one of the knife victims worked at a machine tool factory. The one who had his skull split by a hammer had worked in a home improvement store. And the owner of a dry cleaning store was strangled with a towel.

Fat rain drops began splattering the concrete, and Kade sprinted toward the building entry. Maggie came through the doors, ponytail whipping back and forth as she looked each way before spotting him.

"I thought of a possibility of why he chooses a murder weapon or method," he said as he ducked under the protection of the entry portico. "Come on," he urged her back inside. "I need to see the murder board."

"No time right now. We're packing for California," she said. "Larry and his team might have an idea to narrow down the potentials list."

A flash of lightning illuminated the lobby, and crashing thunder rolled after them down the hall. Kade hoped it wasn't an ominous portent of the coming days.

Chapter 13

Kade helped carry the final boxes into the building in Inglewood. They had a corner of the second floor, but the rest of the space—most recently used by a drug task force—was unoccupied. Maggie had called in a favor for its use.

It was less than fifteen minutes to LAX. They had to be ready to move any direction in the state. An agency helicopter and crew were on standby for local flights.

Using Kade's idea that the murder weapons were related to the type of work the victim's did, or to the news story itself, Larry's team had compiled a list of murder weapons for each of the new potentials. The list was absurdly long for each person, and really only helped after a killing happened.

Working with a new idea from Larry, his MIT team was also narrowing the list of probable victims. Kade had to admit, the young nerd was a genius.

Maggie was in communication with another team forming in Indiana, the location of November's victim. And a third team was being recruited for Mississippi, which was December's target. No one was even thinking about January in North Dakota.

"Let's get unpacked, pronto," Maggie said as the team members gathered around the cluster of desks and waist-high cubicle dividers. "I ordered Chinese for lunch—should be here in a few minutes. Chop-chop." She clapped her hands, smiling wanly at her own joke. Her ponytail, normally tight and high, drooped, as limp as the rest of the team.

They'd been up half the night packing, and the only sleep was on the uncomfortable plane ride.

Kade's stomach growled as he helped Paul, the eight pretzels in the onboard packet a distant memory. They unrolled two, three-by-five foot printouts and taped them together, making a panorama of the messy murder board from Omaha. Larry had emailed the photos to a local graphics company who had printed the large formats and had them waiting. Kade and Paul taped the prints to a rolling whiteboard, transforming the room from a deserted assemblage of desks to morbid reality.

Along the top was a string of known victims, small pictures with names underneath. October's square had only the month. Kade's job was to ensure no photo, no name of an innocent victim, ever filled that space.

"We'll get him," Paul said, placing his hand on Kade's shoulder. They were closer than ever to making that a reality.

A delivery guy arrived with the food, and the delicious smells almost killed Kade before Maggie gathered them around a conference table littered with the white containers. It was only 10:30 in the morning, but they dove into fried rice, cashew chicken, chow mein, and sweet and sour pork. Kade's stomach continued to growl as he stuffed in the food, skipping the slower chopsticks and using a plastic fork for efficiency.

"What?" he said around a mouthful, as he realized Maggie was laughing at him. So were the others. "So I'm a growing boy. Shoot me."

"All right, everyone," Maggie said, finishing her more modest portion and shoving her empty boxes into a trash can, "let's get to work."

Kade scraped the last bits of chicken out of a carton and began on a remaining half container of chow mein.

Larry grabbed printouts from the printer. "This is the latest analysis from my team in Cambridge." He passed them around. "I haven't had a chance to review it yet, but it looks like we're down to fourteen potentials."

Potentials. Marginally better than *targets* or *future murder victims.* Kade scanned down the rows and columns of names, gender, age, location, employment, reason for inclusion, etc.

Maxine Dollar, F, 53, Pacific Grove, school teacher, administered CPR to a student.

Alonzo Ortega, M, 38, Fresno, farmer, donated building for use by a community food bank.

Nga Nguyen, F, 20, San Jose, law clerk, fought off a serial rapist and identified him to the police. He had previously attacked six women.

Cid Fornay, M, 61, Burbank, entertainment lawyer, rescued an injured dog running loose on the Pasadena Freeway. Caught on camera by a traffic news helicopter.

Mike Deale, M, 40, Ventura, auto mechanic, fixed dozens of cars for free for elderly customers.

The names were becoming familiar, real people who had jobs, families, and homes. They celebrated birthdays, had barbecues, attended church, went to work, all with no idea their names were on a computer printout in a four-story building in Inglewood, a city famous for being home to the L.A. Lakers.

Kade's fork of noodles stopped halfway to his mouth when he scanned the next name on the list.

"What's the matter, Kade?" Benny drawled. "You can't possibly be full."

Kade dropped the fork into the container and pushed it away. His stomach had gone into free fall. "There is a new name," he said quietly.

"Yes," Larry said, clicking through screens and peering at his laptop. "Actually two changes. Marion Fields, 87, in Sacramento is off the list. She passed away last night of natural causes. And—"

"Kade?" Maggie asked, gripping his forearm.

The food, so tasty thirty seconds ago, was an ash-coated brick in his gut.

"Lilly Hawthorne," Kade whispered. *F, 17, Beverly Hills, high school senior, survived kidnapping and shooting.*

Chapter 14

"I go meet new clients," Alexandra said, walking away and leaving Lilly on her butt on the workout mat. "Tomorrow is final exam. Be ready." The office door slammed shut.

"Well, alrighty then," Lilly said. She'd been training with Alexandra for over a month, but never got used to the woman's abruptness.

A squeak sounded, and Lilly turned to find Mike rolling up in his wheelchair. She hadn't seen him in several days.

A slight smile played at the corners of his mouth. "Tough session?"

"Nah," Lilly said, rolling to her hands and knees. She was proud when she got to her feet without groaning. "Where have you been lately?" Her left leg quivered, and she stretched the protesting muscles.

"Oh, just setting up some things for Alex," he said.

Probably for her test tomorrow, but Lilly was too exhausted to probe for details.

"Well, what do you think?" Mike asked, turning his chair and following her to the bench where her bag sat. "KGB?"

"Is there an agency worse than KGB?" Lilly asked, stuffing her water bottle and workout towel into the bag. "The woman is as mysterious as she is unrelenting." Lilly had tried dozens of questions out on her trainer, but all she got was harder sessions.

"She's full of surprises, all right," Mike said, looking at the closed office door.

"So, were you hiding in the corner watching me get whipped?"

"Hey, you're getting better. Remember, you're dealing with a pro."

As in professional spy. Lilly walked toward the front door exit. It was pitch black outside. "Are you leaving too?" She couldn't wait to get home and into the bubbling spa. Maybe she'd sneak a glass of chardonnay from her father's collection and sip it while watching the steam rise to the stars.

He shook his head. "Waiting for Alex. But I'll catch you for your final."

"You'll be here?"

"Wouldn't miss it," he said. "And Lilly...you'll do fine. Trust your training."

It was nice to hear his encouragement. The best she ever got out of Alexandra in recognition of improvement was an occasional wry smile, quickly replaced by a stern, "*Again.*" She'd have to be on her game tomorrow. Alexandra was cryptic about what would be included. Could she pass?

Mike's hint of a smile meant *he* knew what she faced. Nothing good. Tomorrow would be tough. Mike waved goodnight as she walked out into blackness. The door lock clicked behind her, and the bright fluorescents in the training room cut off.

She stood there a minute, letting her eyes adjust. The room had been hot and humid after a day's worth of sweaty bodies. But now a breeze whipped up the deserted street, condensing moisture on her bare arms and hinting at a imminent drop in temperature. It felt good for about three seconds. She pulled on her sweatshirt to avoid stiffening up.

Fog had rolled in with the night, shrouding the warehouse district in gloom.

Situational awareness.

Alexandra stressed it repeatedly. Lilly glanced left. Fifty yards down the street, a group of three men stood in the light spilling from an open doorway, smoking. Non-threatening, but better to avoid them.

She looked right. Two guys, still a good distance away, were walking her direction. Maybe they were meeting up with the guys down the street, but she didn't like the way they swaggered with street gang machismo. Friday night always brought out the best in L.A.

Straight ahead was a narrow alley that cut through two, four-story buildings. It was the quickest path to the next block where her car was parked, but it was a black, unlit chasm. She'd never gone that way, always choosing to walk around the building on her left where there was more light.

Laughter came from the smoking men. One of them turned her way and stared, his flat-billed baseball hat sideways on his head. He probably held his semi-auto sideways too—when he robbed convenience stores.

She could bang on the door behind her. Maybe Mike would hear and come in time, but the men on her right would reach her first. Or...

Get out of the crosshairs. Do not be a target.

The staring man on her left flicked his cigarette away and started toward her.

Move!

Lilly strode across the street and into the alley. Due to the low fog, scant ambient light filtered down from the city sky four stories overhead.

She took a serpentine path through the alley, giving wide berth to the hulking metal trash bins, keeping them in her peripheral vision as she passed, while straining to see what was ahead. But skirting the objects put her closer to recessed doorways, black caverns that dotted the brick walls.

Her eyes darted from cavity to cavity. Everywhere was a potential hiding place.

Her car was in a lighted garage a block down on the far side. Three hundred feet at most. The distance of a football field. She checked behind. No one followed.

It had been late in the afternoon when she'd met Alexandra for training on how to clear a building with multiple floors. Stairs were the most dangerous spots, and they'd rehearsed every conceivable scenario. Then they'd sparred for over an hour.

She shivered as wind rustled trash, masking any footsteps that might be coming.

Anticipate.

Lilly swept her eyes left and right, then checked behind. The silhouette of the man with the baseball hat suddenly stepped into the mouth of the alley behind her and came her way. Lilly quickened her pace, preparing for an all-out sprint if she had to.

A meaty arm came out of nowhere, encircling Lilly and pinning her arms. The man—it had to be, considering his bulk—pulling her backward.

She screamed and struck with her elbow, putting her whole weight into the blow, then dropped straight down when his grip slackened. Once on the ground, she rolled three times. By the time she stopped on her back, she had pepper spray in one hand, her gun in the other. She didn't have to actually see it to know the barrel shook slightly. But she could see his outline well enough not to miss at this distance.

"Stop!" she yelled. "I have a gun, and I'll use it!"

The man took a step forward and slapped the pepper spray away.

Do not hesitate, Alexandra said. *When time comes to act, pull the trigger.*

Lilly aimed high on his chest and pulled the trigger.

Bang! The bullet's flash was bright as fireworks in the night.

The man staggered back a step, but didn't go down. A .32 caliber round packed a wallop, but it wasn't a .45 by any means. Even bigger calibers didn't always stop an attacker. It was a common misconception that one bullet would drop a man.

Lilly debated rolling away. If she got enough distance, especially with him wounded, she could run.

"Ahh!" the man shouted, then stepped forward. "You little bi—"

She pulled the trigger six more times, but nothing happened.

The man slapped the gun away. Lilly heard it clatter against the far wall as he straddled her. His rough hands circled her neck and squeezed.

She bucked with her knees, slapped at his head, and screamed again and again. His grip tightened and her screams choked out as her throat constricted.

Violence of action. Do not hold back. Attack with complete and overwhelming violence.

She tore at the tender backs of his hands, felt the skin ripping free under her nails, growing slick with each pass, but his grip tightened even more. The weight of his body crushed her thighs, and she had visions of lying unconscious while he raped her, then threw her lifeless body into one of the dumpsters.

Total commitment.

His eyes. The reality of permanently blinding him didn't bother her like it had when she'd first practiced with Alexandra. She straightened her fingers and struck.

She was already visualizing pushing him off so she could run, but her fingers slammed against some kind of goggles. Before she could wonder why he wore eye protection, she jammed her index and middle fingers up his nose. They found no resistance in the soft flesh there, and she thrust harder, curling her fingertips, penetrating, digging, twisting.

The animalistic scream startled her in its intensity, but an instant release of weight gave her the opportunity she needed. As he rose, she drove her knee up into his groin and shoved out from under him, rolling away. She ignored the man's cursing, and stumbled to her feet.

Her instinct was to kick him in the head, but she didn't want to get that close.

Always have your keys ready.

Her keys were on a strap around her wrist. She flipped them into her hand. In two steps she was at full sprint, the car's remote ready.

The alley flooded with overhead light, showing every puddle, scrap of paper, broken pallet, but Lilly didn't let the sudden illumination disrupt her concentration.

"Lilly, stop!" A figure in a black jumpsuit stepped out from a cavernous doorway a few steps ahead, palm raised.

Lilly skidded to a stop, her chest heaving, vision narrowed to a point.

The figure pulled off a skull cap, and shook out a waterfall of black hair.

Alexandra. Night vision goggles dangled from her left hand.

"You are safe," Alexandra said stepping closer. "This was a test."

Lilly backed up as Alexandra advanced. A man, also dressed in black like Alexandra, stepped out of the alcove. Lilly put her back to the far wall as he came toward her, but he strode past and went to Lilly's attacker who was leaning against the opposite wall, both hands covering his face.

Lilly sidled a few more feet down the wall, away from her attacker.

A test? Alexandra's words began to sink in.

Then Mike rolled out of the doorway behind Alexandra and stopped beside her. He had night vision goggles on his lap.

Lilly leaned over, resting her hands on her quivering knees and gulping air. This was a stinking test? Her heart might quit any second, and her throat burned from the choking grip. She hoped it wasn't permanently damaged. Her parents would freak when they saw the inevitable bruising.

Pain flared in her left arm where he'd gripped it right on the gunshot wound, and she prodded it gently. She didn't want another surgery.

"Are you injured?" Alexandra asked, coming closer.

"Damn right I'm injured," her attacker shouted from across the way. "That bitch ripped—"

"Enough!" Alexandra turned toward the two men. "Dimitri, take Feral to the hospital."

Feral. As in Feral Dog, the professional wrestler. In the light, Lilly recognized the man's wide face, beefy neck. She'd seen him at the center, sparing with other men. Fitting name.

Dimitri nodded once, and escorted Feral down the alley toward the training studio. The smoking man with the sideways hat had disappeared. Who had *he* been? Another friend of Alexandra's?

Lilly straightened, rubbing her arm. It was tender, but no blood soaked through her long sleeve shirt. She turned on Alexandra.

"What were you thinking? I could have killed him. If my gun hadn't misfired—"

"It did not misfire," Alexandra said, stooping to retrieve the pistol from where it had landed near the brick wall. She examined it, drew a cloth from her coat pocket and wiped away dirt, then brought the gun to Lilly. "We emptied the magazine and inserted one blank in the chamber while you trained. Effective, no?" The woman actually smiled.

Lilly wanted to slap her, but she knew she'd never land the blow. Instead, she took the gun and the offered handful of bullets. Lilly hadn't thought to check it before exiting the building. That was a mistake she'd never make again.

Her attacker's string of swear words faded as he and Dimitri exited the alley mouth and turned down the street.

"I hope I didn't hurt him," Lilly said, not daring to look at the fingers she'd jammed up his nose. She couldn't wait to scrub under her nails. She dug her spare magazine out of her purse. She checked the load indicator holes to make sure it was full while giving Alexandra a glance—never trust a KGB agent—then slapped it home and racked a cartridge into the chamber. She clicked the safety.

Alexandra waved away Lilly's concern as if no consequence. "He is well paid...and careless. Too big ego. He depends on strength, not brains."

Lilly's throat ached from those strong, thick fingers. The guy had arms as big as her thighs. Sometimes strength *did* matter. She ejected the magazine, topped it off with a new cartridge and reinserted it, in case her trainer sprang another "test" before Lilly reached her car.

Alexandra's eyes followed every movement as Lilly readied the gun and returned it to the side pocket of her purse. The movements were second nature to her now, especially after doing it over and over for an hour while blindfolded. Alexandra nodded in approval.

Huge praise indeed.

Mike had run Lilly through scenarios for a week—deserted parking garages, alleys behind houses, several building interiors, both at night and during daytime. The practice paid off tonight.

"Sorry I couldn't warn you," Mike said, rolling forward and smiling, "but she..." He inclined his head toward Alexandra. Alexandra's hand slipped to the nape of his neck, fingertips playing with his hair. "Besides, I knew you'd do great."

Lilly swallowed...or tried to. It felt like a thick rubber band still circled her neck. She resisted the urge to rub at it. Not in front of her instructor. "So, tomorrow—"

Alexandra shook her head. "Tonight was your test. He had training, outweighed you over one hundred pounds, and surprise. Training is not done, but tonight you fought...you won," she said, pointing a finger in Lilly's face. "That is what counts."

For a brief moment, steel glinted in her instructor's dark eyes. Lilly had no doubt that if Alexandra had been her attacker tonight, Lilly would have lost in a heartbeat. How many times had Alexandra "won" in her own past? What events, by force or choice, had shaped this woman, darkened her soul?

In Lilly's case, it took only a single incident to transform her from a mostly typical L.A. high school student to...well, whatever she was now: wary, definitely more pessimistic, yet far more prepared.

Alexandra made it clear in class that training wasn't about overcoming or changing the past—nothing could undo what was done. However, training could change future outcomes, bring safety and hope where disaster would normally reign. There had been a tone of deep regret in her voice, a history she didn't share with others.

While Lilly's greatest regret was Pana's death, she had no desire to regress to what she'd been only a few weeks ago. Even with her still healing wounds, her body was leaner and stronger, and she was more confident than ever before. Prior to training, she would have been another victim lying dead in this alley. But tonight she'd kicked some serious butt. She rolled her shoulders, relishing the trust in her budding abilities.

"So," Mike said, "tell us what you're feeling."

Lilly wasn't sure how to explain the tradeoff of gaining strength at the loss of innocence. Or maybe that was an inevitable part of growing up that came sooner for her rather than later. Her eighteenth birthday was coming a week from Sunday. She would switch from seventeen to eighteen, yet her body sensed she'd already made that transition as well as another five-year jump.

"I feel ready." For what, she wasn't sure, but nothing in her new future was the same as she'd imagined it would be. The trick was to stay positive while preparing for the negative what-ifs—like a mugger in an alley. Paranoia was her new friend.

Lilly prodded her neck, no longer caring what others thought. She was who she was.

"Are you all right?" Alexandra asked, her chin lifting imperiously. Her tone held a hint of challenge.

The sour stench of garbage reminded Lilly of her surroundings, and how tonight could have easily gone to her attacker. What if he'd beaten or choked her unconscious? Broken her bones, crushed her vocal cords? How far would Alexandra have let it go? The look in the Russian's eyes said this wasn't fun and games; it was life and death.

"Never better," Lilly said, maintaining eye contact. She was no match for this woman, but that didn't mean she had to back down.

One of Alexandra's eyebrows quirked slightly, extending the challenge until Mike reached up and squeezed the woman's hand. Alexandra's chin lowered, and her taut face softened. She smiled at Lilly. "Good."

Lilly relaxed too.

Mike was good for Alexandra, bringing essential balance to whatever dark memories lingered from the past.

What would it be like to have a supportive relationship like that? Maybe that was the key to balance in life, conquering the bad things as a team.

Not for the first time, she wondered where Agent Gray Eyes had gone.

* * *

A few days after Lilly's alley test, Mike took her to a closed indoor range where she repeated drill after drill with her pistol as well as other handguns and rifles. Firing, reloading, firing, until she was familiar with bolt actions, lever actions, pumps, and even an illegal but awesome fully automatic assault rifle. Mike wanted her to feel how the weapon climbed with repeated recoil, how the shooter had to hold it down, become its master.

That simple concept changed Lilly's thinking. Weapons—whether knives, guns, or clubs—were devices, tools to be used and controlled. They could kill, yes, but their main role was protection.

"You're not afraid of good shoes or your car, are you?" he asked. "Like a lawn mower or a kitchen mixer, weapons are made for a specific purpose. You can master and have them available to use to your advantage without fearing them."

She nodded, his words sinking in.

"Attack life, Lilly. Don't let it attack *you*."

This was a powerful message from a man in a wheelchair who did rock climbing. His chair didn't hold him back, not in sports nor in pursuing the woman he loved.

After a break, Mike set up a shoot house where she had to move room to room, determining in a split second whether the figures that popped up were innocents or bad guys. By the end of the time, she'd shot twenty-four bad guys and three innocents. He said that was pretty good—for a beginner. She almost clubbed him.

The training was beyond anything she'd likely use in life unless she joined the Navy Seals. She joked to Mike she should be wearing camo and have face paint.

"You train for the worst case," Mike explained, unsmiling. "It's easy to pull back if warranted."

She nodded, trying to grasp the weight of his words.

Then he grinned at her. "Of course, I've always thought women in camo are hot. Alexandra has this little camo crop tee she wears with nothing under—"

"Enough!" Lilly said, laughing. "TMI."

Mike grinned at her embarrassment. "Okay. Let's break for lunch. There's a great food truck that stops a block over. Then it will be time for the next session." He rolled out the exit.

Lilly walked beside him on the sidewalk. "What's the next session?"

"Knife throwing and fighting." Mike stopped and wheeled around. "With Feral."

Lilly's hand flew to her throat. The black and blue had faded to yellow-tan. It still ached, but it probably wasn't nearly as sore as Feral's nose. Plus, she'd kneed him in the crotch. How long did *that* hurt? She wasn't asking Mike. She tried to swallow, but her mouth had suddenly gone dry.

"Relax," Mike said, "it'll be fun."

"This food truck better be really good." It was likely her last meal.

Chapter 15

"Still I cannot believe you left Ernesto there to die," Magda Viera said.

"I didn't. He esca—"

She slapped Tommy hard. He might be three inches taller, but *she* was the power in this family. "You told your men to shoot him—your own brother."

"Ow!" Tommy threw up his hands and moved out of her range. "I was joking. I told you that before."

She dismissed him with a gesture, gratified by the handprint appearing on his cheek. "Your men did not know that. Some of them did not know who he was."

"That's the way you want the business—"

"Shut up, Tommy." Roberto entered the office and closed the thick, soundproof door behind him.

"There is news about Ernesto?" Magda asked, rushing to him. It was the first time since the shooting they had all been together in one room, and the first time to see Roberto in two weeks. For security, they rarely met in person. But this was a special situation.

As ordinary in appearance as Ernesto and Tommy were, Roberto was handsome. His dark pinstriped suit, red tie, and black shoes set him apart from his brothers. And although he never passed the bar exam, he looked like a real lawyer to Magda. Now, his mouth was set in a grim line.

Roberto shook his head. "Nothing's changed." He strode to the credenza's refrigerator and pulled out a bottle of beer. He took a long swig as he dropped into one of the leather side chairs and loosened his tie. "Still in a coma."

"It has been almost three months," Magna said, making her way to her desk and sinking wearily into the chair. "He should be awake by now."

"He may never wake up," Roberto said, his voice devoid of emotion. He took another long swallow. "You know that."

As soon as the clinic doctors had stabilized Ernesto, he was transferred to the best hospital in Monterrey, Mexico, and admitted under a false identity as a victim of a botched kidnapping—which was not far from the truth. With the recent drug violence there, shootings and kidnappings were all too common, so questions were few.

While assured he had top medical care, it was hard to have her baby brother so far away from Los Angeles.

She sighed. After the death of her parents, she had done her best to hold the family together, build the business, and had done so for several years now in spite of Tommy's screw ups, Ernesto's tendency to go off on his own, and Roberto's continual push to be in charge. She straightened her spine and leaned across the desk.

"It is time for retribution. I want the two teenagers dead."

Roberto glanced up. "What for? It was Ernesto's and Tommy's mistakes that led to—"

Magda slammed her hand on the desk. "I do not care. We must not show weakness. Too many on the street know of our…loss. They will think stupid teenagers are able to defeat us. And they will wonder if they can take us down."

"This will only put us more in the crosshairs of the authorities," Roberto said, standing. "Is that what you want?"

"We are well protected—" Magda began.

"By men who can be bought with the highest bid!" Roberto yelled.

"Fifty thousand dollars on the male," Magda said, lowering her voice into her command tone. "And ten thousand on the girl."

"You're crazy, Magda." Roberto paced the length of the room and back to the desk, facing her across it. "All their deaths will do is spur more people to hunt for us."

Magda cut a glance at Tommy. He remained leaning nonchalantly against the bookcase, cleaning his fingernails with a penknife.

"Maybe we shouldn't do the boy." Tommy shrugged when he finally noticed her looking at him. "I liked *Blood Moon*. Hate to see him miss the next film in the series. We could kill him after the last film."

"Tommy, if you get to the girl first, I will personally add another ten thousand. But only to you. Even you should be able to do that job without screwing up."

Tommy frowned, then smiled. Even though he had a quarter share of the business, money still motivated him. She could always twist him to do her bidding.

"You're going to get us all locked up, or worse," Roberto growled, leaning across until he was six inches from her face.

"Then you, mister hotshot attorney, better put together some men who can be trusted to keep us safe. Instead of playing with paperwork, it is time you again got your hands dirty." She straightened, distancing herself from the direct engagement with her brother. He was family, after all, and family was everything.

Roberto stormed to the door, but paused when she called his name.

"I will put out the word," she said. "I want the jobs done by the end of the month. Would that not be a nice Halloween treat?"

"Better than candy," Tommy grinned, snapping his knife closed.

Chapter 16

Percy wiped sweat from his eyes. It was October, but California weather evidently didn't follow the rest of the country. Instead of falling colored leaves, residents sweltered under a heat wave and choked on smoke plumes from two fires in the foothills and mountains to the east. At least it was probably cooler in those higher elevations. Maybe he'd drive up for a visit after this job.

He started the car for the fourth time in an hour, and adjusted the AC vents for maximum flow. But cool air wasn't the aging Honda's strong suit. Probably why the previous owner had traded it in.

His small spotting scope gave an excellent view of the wrought iron gate that led to the house, but tall shrubs marked the driveway entrance, obscuring better views of the structure itself. All he knew was that she had come home an hour ago.

Seeing the house today didn't matter. Percy had already been in the backyard. From there, he knew the room layout well enough.

It was a good day. The media reported that a dedicated FBI team had set up shop in Los Angeles and was hunting for JPK. Though Percy wasn't sure how much of his pattern they'd figured out, it couldn't be coincidence. They knew California was his next state. The game was getting far more interesting.

A glint in his rearview mirror alerted him to a low-slung Jaguar coming down the street. It passed him and pulled up to the gate, idling as it waited for it to swing open. Through the sedan's darkly tinted windows, he made out the profile of a woman, but little else. The gate opened wide enough for the car, and began closing five seconds after the rear bumper cleared the entry.

Another car approached from the opposite direction, its lights on though it wasn't dusk yet. Percy slipped on his wraparound sunglasses, signaled, and pulled away from the curb. As he passed the other car, he noted the security patrol decal on the door. The driver gave him a long stare. If the man was doing his job, he'd make a note of Percy's Honda and its license number. Time to change things up.

It was 6:30 by the time Percy arrived at the independent used car lot he'd researched earlier, and the red sun was setting in a haze of fire smoke. Maybe forty vehicles of all makes and body styles nosed the twin-cable fence that faced the road. Each had optimistic window stickers proclaiming *Low miles! '08!! Certified!!!* Exclamation points were popular, like a shouting preacher bolstering a weak sermon.

Percy wondered who had done the certification. Probably the guy in the white cowboy hat and plaid sport coat who strutted toward the Honda as Percy pulled into a parking space. Seriously, where did anyone find a plaid sport coat? Was there a website? www.cheesycarsalesmanclothing.com?

"Lookin' to trade her in, pardner?" the man said, hitching his belt higher over his bulging gut. He ran fat fingers over the Honda's front fender like a horse trader checking a mare. "Name's Tex," he said, working futilely at the pants again.

Percy almost laughed as he climbed out of the Civic. He avoided the man's outstretched hand by turning to a dark blue Ford Explorer that had *On Sale Today!!!!* in a yellow star faded and ragged by months of sun damage. *Today* evidently meant any day someone showed up with cash. "I need something with more cargo room."

"Well, you come to the right place," Tex said, waddling over to the Explorer and opening the driver door. "This one here's a creampuff if there ever was. Only driven to church and Walmart by a retired librarian. Know'd the lady for years."

Percy climbed inside. Sun-yellowed foam protruded from cracks in the broken-down vinyl seat, and the cruise control buttons on the steering wheel were so worn the symbols were invisible. The paint above the ashtray door had scorch marks, and the odometer indicated 192,127 miles. "She must have been real religious."

"Yes, she was," Tex said, totally missing the irony.

Percy sighed, trying not to breath too deeply of the smoky interior. "Kind of stinks in here." He swiveled to get out.

"Oh, we can fix that right up," Tex said, blocking Percy's exit. He produced an aerosol can labeled *NuCar Odorizer* and let fly a sustained burst in front of Percy.

Coughing, Percy shoved Tex back and climbed out of the Ford, escaping the toxic cloud.

Tex patted the top of the SUV like it was a beloved grandchild. "How 'bout we make a deal and get you on the road in this little honey?"

"Say, Tex, have you ever done anything really nice for anyone recently? Say about three months ago?"

Tex scratched his head, brows furrowed in deep thought, then brightened. "Ju-ly Shriners' Parade count?"

* * *

Tommy Viera sat up straighter when he spotted the red RAV4 zip by him. He recognized her profile from the news photos—twenty grand on mag wheels. She turned into the driveway of the 1920s Tudor home he'd been watching for an hour.

The engine of his twenty-year-old Mercedes effortlessly purred to life under his hand, a testament to exacting German engineering and regular maintenance. Not his car, of course, but that of the poor slob it was stolen from in Texas. A quick paint job and California plates from the junkyard, and his guys had given it a whole new future. Tommy thought of it as *repurposing*.

He shifted into drive and rolled forward until he was even with the wide driveway, slowing to a bare crawl. The house—complete with rock facings, faceted windows, and climbing dark green ivy— was set back from the road a hundred feet or so, half-hidden behind trees and sculpted hedges. It reeked of old money and privilege.

These were the people who crossed the street when they saw him coming toward them. And they should. They thought their wealth gave them protection and power, but *he* was the one with the real power. Life and death.

The girl had parked in one of the four-car garage stalls. She climbed out and gathered a small duffle bag off the passenger seat. Tommy stopped in the middle of the street and watched. She was thin, flat-chested. Not like the girls he went with. A thick black band held her white hair in a low ponytail. Nothing impressive about her. Except this was the girl who had escaped from Ernesto.

She limped toward the door leading into the house, poked the wall-mounted controller, and disappeared behind descending folding panels painted to mimic coach-house doors.

A teenager with a gimp leg? Killing her for Magda was super-easy money.

Tommy pressed the accelerator and drove away, keeping well within the speed limit until he left the exclusive neighborhood and merged onto the Santa Monica freeway.

Thinking back, he had to admit Ernesto had a good idea. Like in Mexico, there were lots of wealthy families in Los Angeles who would part with large sums to get a loved one back. But his brother had screwed up by using idiots as accomplices. Tommy had professionals working for him, loyal men who didn't ask questions and understood who paid the bills. Not like those two brothers, Barry and Jimmy with Ernesto. If they weren't already dead, Tommy would kill the losers himself.

He thought again of the girl. Too bony for his taste, but pretty for an Anglo. Maybe he'd have a little fun with this one before collecting his reward.

A couple of his guys could stake out her school and see where else she went. No way was he letting anyone else take her out first.

Tommy cranked up a hip-hop station, a wide grin spreading on his face. A dumb high school kid still hurting from her injuries? This would be the easiest twenty grand ever. But where was the fun in just snatching her?

He picked up his phone. Time to make a statement.

Chapter 17

October 19

Kade rolled his desk chair back and forth in front of the murder board, trying to mentally squint, blur out the extraneous detail and see something obvious, but the only thing this case revealed was his headache. He rubbed his eyes. That didn't help either.

No matter which potential he tried to concentrate on, his chair always rolled to a stop before the eight-by-ten with Lilly Hawthorne's driver's license photo. She stared back, an innocent, grinning younger version of the girl he'd tended to on the street. He closed his eyes.

He'd never heard so many sirens, high and low, pulsing and steady, each with its own unique voice that shattered the hope of a new day.

Her blood was hot on his hands, wet and rapidly cooling in the morning air until his fingers should have stuck together. Only the new flow kept them free.

Every shift of pressure elicited a moan that tightened like a band around his chest, until he fought for each breath.

"Kade."

If only he could draw the pain out of her body, force the life liquid back inside. But he was helpless, aching as the light dimmed in her eyes.

My…name. Palomino.

"Kade."

Someone was shaking his shoulder.

"Sorry," he said, coming awake and realizing Paul was standing beside him. He rubbed his face, then jerked his hands away, turning them over and checking for blood between his fingers. It had seemed real.

"Everything all right?" Paul asked, giving him a strange look.

"Yeah," Kade said, dropping his hands. "Just tired. What do you need?"

Paul held up his phone. "Text from Maggie."

Kade automatically patted his pockets, but remembered he'd left his own phone on his desk.

"There's a victim."

Kade's eyes shot to the murder board, scanning the photos and settling on the one that mattered most. "Which one?"

Paul squeezed his shoulder. "Not one of those. A man in Sacramento."

"He's not on the list but he fits the profile?" Kade asked, standing and giving himself a couple of mental slaps to wake up. Other than the sun coming in the windows, he had no idea what time it was. How long had it been since he'd last slept?

"Down to the puzzle piece found with the body," Paul said. "Maggie is on her way back from a meeting. She'll pick you up in ten. Your flight leaves in an hour."

Kade glanced at the board again. That meant these fourteen people were out of danger. Lilly Hawthorne was safe.

* * *

JPK Strikes Again!

Sacramento police and the FBI are searching for the person or persons responsible for the death of Herman "Tex" Owens, 55, owner of Tex's Best Used Cars and Trucks on Avenue K, sometime last night. According to a source inside the department, the evidence preliminarily points to the Jigsaw Puzzle Killer, a serial murderer who has left a trail of bodies across at least twenty-one states. This could be number twenty-two.

Percy reread the piece, struggling to control his grin as he savored both the story and his Caramel Macchiato. The article was well written. He should send a compliment to the reporter. Her email address was printed at the end of the two columns.

A worker found Owens at 9:10 this morning, pinned under an automobile lift in the mechanics bay behind the dealership offices. Police aren't releasing further details of Owens's death, but they say they are following up every lead.

In the Starbucks, crowded with two dozen or more people, at least four others were reading the same newspaper story. Percy wanted to shout out that he was right here!

A twenty-something mother took the chair opposite, directing her preschoolers, a boy and a girl, to share the other chair. Percy relaxed into a full smile. The mom smiled back before passing out snacks to her children, unaware she sat one chair away from a cold-blooded killer. A *serial* killer. *The* serial killer others were reading about right now.

That got Percy to wondering. He'd been in tons of coffee shops over the years. How many times had someone sat next to him who had also taken another's life? Probably never. Murder—except for those stupid gang members who shot each other in inner city turf wars—was relatively rare. That's what made it special, why so many were paid to find the killer. To find *him*.

He held back a laugh. Such a great game. What could be more exciting than sitting among these ignorant, self-absorbed people, knowing he could follow a man outside and plunge a knife into his internal organs before he climbed into his car? Or track a woman home and hang her from a backyard tree when she went out searching for the wayward kitty? Or slip a little chopped monkshood into a bagged salad mix labeled, *Pre-washed, Ready for Consumption.* The opportunities were positively endless!

This time he did laugh, and the mom shot him a grin, thinking he was amused by her children who were now squabbling over who got which color gummy bear.

More thirsty coffee addicts shuttled through the door, seeking all things seasonally pumpkin flavored, cluelessly unaware a killer watched and imagined their deaths.

Chapter 18

Kade roused when the engine noise decreased, and he sensed the nose of the aircraft angling downward.

Since there were so many flights to Sacramento, Maggie had chosen to go commercial instead of charter. They'd been lucky to find a row at the back of the plane with no one in the middle seat. She was at the window, using both her own and the center tray tables for her laptop and stacks of stapled printouts. Kade preferred the aisle anyway, and took every opportunity to stretch out his legs.

The flight attendant announced their imminent arrival at Sacramento International Airport, and gave the familiar instructions for tray tables, seat backs, and seat belts. With the twitchy moves of someone hopped up on caffeine, Maggie stowed her laptop and papers in a carry-on and toed it under the seat in front of her.

Kade felt a little guilty for napping while she worked on the short flight, but he and Benny had spent most of the night correlating and eliminating possible connections with the past victims. They had to figure out exactly why JPK picked certain people to kill on certain days. For every detail they eliminated, Larry or his team back at MIT thought up two new ones. Kade ferreted out birthdays, baptisms, anniversaries, school graduations, recent deaths of family members, and even local parades. Benny Philips found two victims treated by the same dentist in different states. But with more digging he traced what appeared to be a simple family move for the dentist. Two other potentials were related to past presidents. A little after 4:30 this morning, Kade's mind had dissolved into oatmeal.

Twenty feet before the aircraft rolled to a stop, passengers ignored the flight attendant's instructions and shot to their feet, wrenching massive suitcases from the overburdened bins and packing the aisle. They shuffled for position in preparation for a mad rush through the terminal. Kade stayed in his seat, not anxious to stand up only to wait five more minutes until everyone ahead of them moved.

He'd lost track of the current time and day, but he knew the daily routines of twenty-one people over the last twenty-one months in twenty-one states. Now it looked like they would change that number to twenty-two.

How many more? Would the killer stop at 50? If they didn't catch him, could Kade survive over two more years of senseless death?

"Move it, Hunt," Maggie said, nudging him in the shoulder. He looked up to find all the passengers in front of them moving up the aisle.

The walk to the airport exit woke him up.

* * *

"This Hummer was on the lift when it came down on Tex, and these suckers are heavy." The police detective pointed out the black vehicle raised several feet in the air as Maggie and Kade followed him into the service bay of Tex's Best Used Cars. On the concrete under one of the lift arms, a dark red splotch stood out from the surrounding grease and oil. "Squashed Tex's chest right down to his spine. Had to raise the Hummer so the coroner could take the body."

Maggie quizzed him about who found the body and when, asked about estimated time of death, and why they contacted the FBI.

"Well, it was the puzzle pieces," the detective said.

Kade couldn't remember the man's name. Carlisle or Carson or something. "Wait. You said *pieces*?"

"Sure. Three of them. They're right over here." The detective led them to a portable table set up against the wall. A clear plastic bag held three puzzle pieces. They were locked together. The edge of one was darkened by what looked like blood.

"We were only told about one piece," Maggie said, mirroring Kade's thinking.

The detective shook his head, instantly defensive. "We told the local FBI office there were three pieces. They must have screwed up the message."

Maggie paced around the garage. Kade knew what she was thinking before she verbalized it. "This doesn't fit the pattern of JPK."

Their phones dinged at the same time, and Kade checked his display. Larry had sent his findings about Tex Owens: *Fifty-five years old, male, unmarried, owner of a car dealership. Twenty-seven-year member of Ben Ali Shrine in Sacramento. Drove one of the little motorized cars in a parade in July. No other news mentions.*

A deep furrow creased Maggie's forehead when she looked up from reading on her phone. "That's two anomalies," she said. "Three pieces instead of one, and his parade participation doesn't seem like enough notability."

"Not compared to past victims and our other potentials," Kade agreed. "But the method of death fits my theory of something to do with the victim's work or activity."

Maggie asked about surveillance video. There was none. "How about a record of appointments?"

"Not really. According to the other salesman, he'd just meet people as they came on the lot."

"Detective?" A uniformed officer stood with an elderly man wearing a chartreuse sports coat and a lime green cowboy hat.

Kade shook his head. That could only be the other salesman. The officer introduced him as Elroy Lake, the only other full time employee.

"Mr. Lake, here, says there is a vehicle missing from the lot. A Ford Explorer."

The detective left to get a full description of the SUV and put out an APB to all agencies.

"This doesn't feel right, Kade," Maggie said. "Could this be a copycat?"

Kade had already thought of that. It was only a matter of time before one or more sickos decided to get in on the action. But while a puzzle piece under the body was now common knowledge, the order of which state was next on JPK's list was not. "What are the odds of a copycat picking the right state?"

"Larry can calculate that for us." She pulled out her phone.

"Agents?" the detective called from the bay door. He was holding up his phone. "Looks like you have another victim."

* * *

Percy's phone rang, and he checked the display. Mother.

"Nothing like her to spoil the day," he mumbled, rising.

"Sorry?" the Starbucks mom across from him asked.

He ignored her and stalked outside the noisy shop.

"Hello, Mother," he said, seeking a shady spot in the parking lot.

"Mr. Maxwell, this is Miss Nichols, Mrs. Maxwell's personal assistant."

The condescension dripped through the phone line, and Percy resisted wiping his ear. Eve Nichols always announced herself and her position, as if he might forget who she was.

More often than not, it was she who answered when Percy called. This was unusual, for he couldn't remember a time when she'd initiated a call to him. Probably that was because she took every opportunity to make it clear she couldn't stand Percy. Well, the feeling was mutual. As soon as his mother passed, he'd fire the old biddy.

"What can I do for you, Eve?" He always used her first name because it rankled her. Small pleasures.

"Are you enjoying Norway, Mr. Maxwell?"

"I…" For a moment, Percy was caught off guard. "Yes, of course. I'm staying north of Oslo."

"You must be close to Holmenkollen. Lovely views. I visited there once."

"Perhaps," Percy said vaguely. Had she truly traveled to Norway? If so, he didn't want to get into a discussion of specifics. He had no idea where or what Holmenkollen was, or even *if* there was such a place. He should have looked at the map. Whenever he spoke with Eve, she always asked about where he was, what he had seen. He

124

suspected she doubted his trip was legitimate, and he made a mental note to spend more time studying his destinations. "With the Norwegian language and all, I'm finding the names of places particularly confusing."

"I do hope you made it to the Kon-Tiki Museum."

"It's on my list," Percy said, relaxing. At least he'd read up on Thor Heyerdahl, the Norwegian explorer who had sailed the Pacific Ocean in 1947. The man had constructed a raft entirely of balsa wood and natural materials to prove South Americans could have settled the Polynesian Islands. Heyerdahl was one of Norway's heroes, and the museum was located at Oslo's harbor.

"The Ra II is quite amazing," she said. "How long was his journey again?"

Percy had no idea how long Heyerdahl spent on the water, but then how would he know if he hadn't been to the museum yet? Ignoring the question, Percy did some mental calculations. It was 3:00 p.m. in New York, where Eve was, and 9:00 p.m. in Oslo. "Please get to the point, Eve. I have dinner plans."

"I thought Norwegians by custom ate earlier in the evening?"

"Why are you calling, Eve?"

An expressive harrumph filled the phone line. "I'm afraid you'll have to cut your time short, Mr. Maxwell. Mrs. Maxwell has been transported to the hospital, and the doctors are not optimistic." She prattled on for another minute about declining blood oxygen levels, high or low readings from liver, kidneys, and other organs.

Percy was only half listening, running through all the things he'd have to wrap up. The flight time from Oslo to New York was about 8 hours. But going the way *he'd* be traveling—Sacramento to New York —was less than 5 hours. That left three hours difference to get everything done. Impossible.

He wished he'd told her he had changed his itinerary and was stuck in Hungary, or someplace equally remote from which it would take longer to travel home. Of course he could always throw in excuses of flights being full, missed flights, or other delays, but Eve might check. A missed flight was probably best.

She broke into his calculations. "Should I arrange for a car to meet you at LAX?"

"Los Angeles?" His mother lived in New York.

Eve's sigh communicated disdain and impatience. "As I just explained, Mr. Maxwell, Mrs. Maxwell was visiting her cousin in Los Angeles. She's been taken to Cedars-Sinai."

Percy relaxed a little. This was even better. He'd have several hours to complete his work here, then catch a flight to L.A.

"A car, Mr. Maxwell?" The impatience radiated from the phone.

"No," he said. "I'll rent a car or take a cab."

"It's not an imposition for me—"

"I said I'd take care of it, Mrs. Nichols."

"The corporate board will want you to—"

"Leave the board to me," Percy said, wiping perspiration on his sleeve. "Now, I have to make travel arrangements, so if there is nothing else…"

"Very well, Mr. Maxwell," Eve said. "We'll see you in a few hours." The line went dead.

Firing was too good for Eve Nichols.

Chapter 19

It was after 4:30 when Maggie steered their rental onto the street in an affluent Sacramento neighborhood. A variety of mature trees lined the boulevard. These weren't new McMansions rising in modest neighborhoods where land was cheap from the real estate crash. No, these were older, stately homes, roots solidly fixed into the bedrock of large lots. Wrought iron fences circled many properties, some built with ornate designs and crests. Even in the midst of the California drought, the lawns here appeared healthy and recently trimmed.

However, what would have been a beautiful street to stroll after the sun went down was marred by yellow crime scene tape, crisscrossing through the bars of one of the fences and drooping across the driveway entrance.

Kade noted several spectators across the road, huddled in small groups, no doubt discussing the violence that had broken through their protections, shattered their sanctuary. At their feet, little dogs sniffed each other and tied their leashes in knots.

Maggie parked by the curb. When they ducked under the yellow tape, Special Agent Ana Escobar met them. The agent was short and stocky, mid-thirties, and no-nonsense. Kade liked her immediately. She led them into the house through the open garage.

"The victims were found about two hours ago by the hired cook who came to prepare for a small dinner party—about twenty guests."

Kade was thinking twenty was a pretty big crowd in his circles as he followed Maggie and Escobar through a rear door and around to a flagstone patio.

"Someone spent a fortune on landscaping," Maggie murmured as they descended a series of curved, shallow steps.

Kade had come to the same conclusion. The backyard was far more elaborate than the front. The expanse was divided by rock planters the size of small cars, spaced strategically to add height and dimension to the mostly level lot. On the left of the stairs, an artificial stream followed the gentle slope, gurgling over rocks as it flowed to an irregular pond filled with water plants and large koi. The fish were nosed into the bank by the stairs, mouths gaping in anticipation of one of the passersby feeding them.

"How did the cook find the bodies out here?" Maggie asked, as Ana turned right at the bottom of the steps and led them to a swimming pool nearly hidden by shrubbery.

"She noticed right away that the French doors were wide open," Ana said. "There was water all over the hardwood floor, and a wet trail led down the steps and right to the pool gate." Ana opened the gate and motioned for them to proceed.

"So she followed the trail?" Kade asked.

"And the music." Ana pointed to an outdoor fireplace located near a comfortable looking seating area shaded by a pergola. "It was turned up so loud that the cook feared the neighbors would complain, so she investigated."

A giant flatscreen TV was mounted above the fireplace, and an open cabinet built into the stone on the right held a DVD player, amplifier, and radio receiver. Man, this would be the ultimate Super Bowl house. He could picture several good buddies, a few beers, chips, dip, and the game on the big screen.

Kade turned slowly, surveying the pool and entertainment area. There was no chalk outline, no crime lab techs, no detectives. Except for the three of them, the pool area was deserted. "So where were the bodies?"

Ana pointed to the blank television screen. "Right there."

"Explain," Maggie said, rubbing her forehead.

Ana opened the gate again, talking as she led them back toward the house. "The owners have a sophisticated security system, complete with several cameras mounted both inside and outside. Using the TV remote control, anyone watching any television can view one or all of the cameras in full or split-screen mode." Ana stopped at the top of the patio and turned to them. "I wanted you to see the pool first so you'd have a feel for the whole situation. The TV at the pool was playing the feed from the formal dining room."

Kade realized his mouth was open. He shut it and followed Ana into the house and then through another doorway.

This room was buzzing with activity, all of it concentrated on the massive table that ran the length of the room. Two bodies, a man and a woman who both appeared to be in their sixties, lay facedown, head to head, at the center of the table. They were fully clothed, their arms were at their sides, palms up, and each had a small red apple in their mouth like pigs on a platter.

"The camera is up there in the corner," Ana said, pointing to the nearer end of the room.

Kade and Maggie tracked her hand, then turned back. The table was prepared for dining, complete with silverware, multiple plates and glasses, candles, and white cloth napkins folded in the shape of swans. A few settings had been moved to a sideboard.

"Look at the champagne," Maggie said, pointing out two bottles on each end of the table. "Now that one." A lone bottle sat between the man and woman. The cork was missing, and two glasses were filled with amber liquid and placed alongside the bottle.

"This is bizarre," Kade said. "None of the other crime scenes have been close to this elaborate."

Maggie nodded, then turned to Ana. "Why call us? Do you think this is related to JPK?"

Ana gestured at a man on the opposite side of the table, and he came around to join them. He was carrying a white, square box that could have been used for a cake. "Liam, these are Special Agents Cartwright and Hunt. Can you show them what we found?"

Liam removed the lid and extended the box so they could see.

Inside were dozens of coasters for placing under drinks. Each was about four inches square, had a narrow wood edging, and each was filled with jigsaw puzzle pieces. A single center puzzle piece of several of the coasters was missing.

"Although we haven't taken the bodies," Liam said, "we rolled them to check for wounds. Each had six puzzle pieces under them." Liam held up a plastic bag containing twelve disconnected pieces. "Curiously, none of these pieces match the ones missing from the coasters."

Maggie looked sharply at Ana. "Who are these people? What do they do?"

Ana stepped aside so Kade and Maggie had an unobstructed view of the bodies. "Meet Mr. and Mrs. Peter Nape, founders of Pickwick Toy and Puzzle Company."

Maggie sagged onto a nearby side chair.

"You okay?" Kade said. If there'd been another chair handy, he'd have sat too.

His boss nodded, but it was clear the momentum that had carried her through the flight and car dealership had fizzled. She needed rest, and he wondered how long it would be before either of them got any.

She looked up at him. "Did we fall down a rabbit hole?"

* * *

Percy laughed half the flight to L.A. He was loving this! Two scenes and three victims. That should keep those FeeBees going in circles for a while.

He had parked the SUV at the Sacramento airport long term lot, backing it in and removing the front license plate. The back sported a new plate after Percy did a three-way rotation with two other cars. It might keep the police and FBI busy for a couple more hours.

He reclined the airplane seat and celebrated with a white wine. It was almost too easy. Maybe he should send the FBI scattering again with another scene in one of the outlying areas of Los Angeles, say Apple Valley, the home of cowboy couple Roy Rogers and Dale Evans? They were both long dead now, but Percy could come up with something western related.

He'd never needed diversions before. They were a lot of extra work, but were kind of fun.

Sadly, Eve Nichols would be calling him every five minutes if he didn't show up at the hospital soon after his supposed flight from Norway was scheduled to land. Talk about a buzz kill. There would be no time for more diversions.

In some ways, he felt closer to some of his victims than his own flesh and blood. His father had died when Percy was two, and Mother had shipped Percy off to boarding school when he was five so she could spend her time in New York society, trying in vain to land another significant fortune as a husband. Percy recognized early on it was easier if her son was not around.

Summer breaks were filled by endless camps, training him in knot tying, sharpening knives, archery, shooting, survival, computers, martial arts, and even acting and stage makeup—all things that came in very handy in his current activities.

On those occasions where he had the opportunity to watch the life drain from his victim's eyes, the experience was heightened by the adrenaline of violence, the exhilaration of watching their heart stutter and stop while his kept beating, the titillating fear of discovery.

Would it be the same when his mother finally died? He'd have to wait and see, but it sounded like that would come soon.

"Would you like another glass of wine, Mr. Elliott?"

Percy almost didn't respond to the name he'd used to book the flight. He smiled at the flight attendant. "No, thank you. One is my limit."

Unless it came to puzzle pieces.

Chapter 20

"I'm sorry to inform you of this, but we have knowledge of a credible and specific threat on your life."

No need to sugar-coat it, Lilly thought, just spit it out.

FBI Special Agent Ron Blake had arrived right in the middle of a rare family dinner where they were all together in the dining room. He insisted it was urgent, and made his announcement over their cooling chicken piccata and rice pilaf.

"A confidential informant working with the police came forward yesterday with the information. Fifty thousand dollars on Chad Holt's life. Ten thousand on yours, Miss Hawthorne."

"So this is like on TV, when someone orders a hit?" Lilly said. She slid the plate away. It no longer looked appetizing.

"It's, ah…" the man cleared his throat, "sort of like that. But as far as we know, no one person has been contracted to do the job. It's more like a general reward for anyone who succeeds."

Ten thousand dollars. She was only worth one fifth what Chad was? She began to laugh at the difference, imagining it as a math question on the SAT: *If Chad is worth $50,000 dead, and Lilly is worth only $10,000 dead, what percentage of Chad's life is Lilly's life worth? - Show all work.*

Side by side, was one life more valuable than another? The whole situation was surreal, cloaked in swirling fog that obscured both danger and the path to safety.

"Lilly," Mom said, "do you need to go lie down?"

Lilly saw that Blake was looking uncomfortable, like he might call the crew in white coats any minute. She took a long drink of water and willed herself to calm down.

Dad leaned forward in his chair, his face set in Nathan Hawthorne Producer mode. Lilly sensed he was going to take over the situation, direct its path like one of his productions. But *she* wanted control of her life.

"Why?" she directed at the agent. "I don't understand what they want with me. Chad was the original target. He was the one with the mega movie-deal."

"It appears the motivation has switched to revenge."

"For escaping a kidnapper?" her father asked.

Agent Blake shook his head. "For his death. Ernesto Viera died this morning at a hospital in Monterey, Mexico. The local police knew we were looking for him."

"So they want me dead in retaliation? Why not go after the cops? They're the ones that shot him."

The agent gave a resigned nod. "These people are criminals, and most are not known for logic. And, unfortunately, you're the easier target."

Unfortunately.

"We've learned that the two remaining brothers are Roberto and Tommy, both ruthless in their own ways. But it's the sister, Magda, who issued the order. The family has a lot of resources."

Blake turned to Lilly's dad. "Now that we have credible information on the threat, we think it's time to get Lilly out of the area for a while."

"I'll be leaving day after tomorrow to film on location in New York," her mother said to Blake. To Lilly, she said, "Sweetheart, you can come with me, help out on the set."

Heat rose through Lilly's core. She was just getting her life back. And now...

Her father nodded, agreeing with the plan.

"For how long?" Lilly asked. "Is there an expiration on a hit? Six months? A year?" She was standing now, both hands on the table as she stared across at Blake. "Will it ever be safe to come home?"

The agent cleared his throat, glancing between her and her parents. "Unfortunately, there is no way to know. Perhaps a few months. A year or two would be better."

Unfortunately.

Agent Blake excused himself after assuring them he'd be in touch as soon as he received any more information.

Lilly was still contemplating the forty grand difference in the value of her life verses Chad's. No doubt a different FBI agent was meeting with Chad's family right now, giving them the same message. But he was filming his new movie, *Blood Moon - Dark Circle*, in various locations around the world. Each week's shooting plans were advertised on the movie's website to generate buzz. Keeping Chad safe would tax a team of people.

Her mom enveloped her in a tight hug. "We'll get through this, Lilly. Don't be afraid."

The strange thing was, she *wasn't* afraid. She still felt confident, strong, prepared. Just because the Viera family wanted her dead, didn't mean it would happen. Down deep, she wrestled with whether she was being overconfident in her new abilities.

Still, the main part of Alexandra's training was avoiding the fight altogether. It would be stupid to stay in L.A. and be an easy target.

Chapter 21

October 20

Lilly had tossed a few clothes in her open suitcases, jeans and T-shirts mostly, but that was it. This felt like a strange combination of a trip and a move. She'd need warm clothes if she stayed in New York through the winter. Those would fill a couple suitcases by themselves. And what about her art tools? Should she pack and take them now, or should she wait and see? There were large sketch pads, boxes of colored pencils, paints, pallets, a folding easel, and a lot more.

Her mother's standard answer was they could buy more of whatever Lilly needed after they got to New York. But even though she was part of a family that had no money worries, she couldn't divest herself entirely of her first thirteen years. The lessons of *make do* and *don't waste* were impossible to unlearn, especially after eating canned beans and Ramen for weeks on end, even for breakfast.

With a sigh, Lilly pulled one of the suitcases over and began wedging in her drawing supplies. No matter how long the trip, she wanted them at hand.

"Lil-ly!" her mother singsonged from somewhere in the house.

"Wha-at?" Lilly singsonged back, knowing there would be no answer. Even though the house had an intercom and Mom knew how to use it, by ignoring the technology, it forced everyone to get up and go looking for Ekaterina.

"Diva time," Lilly mumbled, getting to her feet and starting the search. She found her mom in the kitchen, assembling a salad the size of a teacup. The price of stardom.

"There's been a change of plans. I have to stay here a few more days for some live interviews on November 2nd. Which works out perfectly, because Leonardo DiCaprio is hosting a Halloween Party, and now I won't miss it. All the right people will be there, so I have to attend. You could come too, you know, make some contacts. Who knows? You might be considered for an upcoming project."

"I'm supposed to go into hiding, Mom," Lilly said, sliding onto a barstool. "Getting involved in a movie seems like the opposite."

Her mother pursed her lips. "Yes, I suppose it does. But at least you could meet interesting people. I worry about you being by yourself so much. Wear a mask. No one will know you're out and about."

Her parents were opposites in the party and schmooze departments. Mom loved not only the attention the gatherings brought to her, but also the excitement generated by talented people packed into a room. She came home energized, brimming with new ideas. Dad, though he often accompanied her, barely tolerated Hollywood parties. Five minutes and he was ready to leave.

Pana would have drooled all over herself to be invited to DiCaprio's party. Lilly could hear the squeal now. Hollywood celebs had been in her blood.

Lilly pulled the cookie jar over and looked inside. Oatmeal raisin. She took one and nibbled the edge.

A few of the industry people Lilly had met over the years were pretty down-to-earth, especially some of the middle-aged men. They had learned that hard work and craft made the star, not being seen coming out of the trendy restaurant of the week. The women though... Whew. As Pana used to say, *"Plastic looks; plastic explosive,"* then *"Boom!"* they'd both shout in unison and laugh. It was their inside joke on the weirdness of the society they lived in. Then Pana started measuring for fake boobs.

Lilly sighed. She missed her friend.

"Well," her mother said, "either way, we're going to have to increase the security. Unless you want to go to New York early— accompanied by a security detail of course."

"I'd rather stay here and leave with you. I want as much time with Alexandra as possible—"

"Lilly, I don't—"

"We'll have fun on the flight together, Mom," Lilly rushed ahead, knowing that was what her mother really wanted to hear. "And my new tutors will be starting as soon as we get to New York. With luck, I can test out of my classes in a couple of months." At least she'd convinced her dad to delay the tutoring until New York.

Her mother narrowed her gaze at Lilly. Being her mother's daughter, Lilly struck what she hoped was the right balance of innocence and determination. It must have worked.

"We'll talk to your father when he gets home."

"Mom?" Lilly waited until she had her mother's full attention, which always took a minute. Her mother looked up, and Lilly took a breath. "I'm thinking of changing my name."

Ekaterina the actress raised a brow, a move Lilly had seen her practice a hundred times in her dressing mirror. Lilly still hadn't mastered it.

"Not that I'm opposed, mind you, but what brought this on?"

Her parents had sat down with her a week after they'd brought her home and asked if she'd like to change her name, for a *"fresh start in your new life."* That was five years ago. She thought again of how her biological mother simply copied the woman in the next hospital delivery bed who named her daughter *Lilly.*

Lilly looked across the breakfast counter at her new mother, the one who loved and cared for her. Yes, she could be a little distracted at times with her busy schedule. But Ekaterina took her to movie sets and proudly introduced her as *"my daughter."*

"With all that's happened, I guess I... I don't feel like who I was. I'm not that person any longer. Does that make sense?"

Mom gave her an appraising look. "I'll call our legal firm. I'm sure they have contacts in New York. Perhaps we can change it there so it won't be on any court records here in L.A."

* * *

"Can we see your security system?" Fin Silvan asked Lilly's dad.

Lilly trailed behind her dad and the two security men from Omron International as they walked through the backyard toward the utility room that, in addition to the security panel, held the heating and air conditioning, water heater, and other mechanical systems for the house.

Fin and his partner, Doug, were burly and thick necked. They were the kind whose hands always joined at the belt buckle when standing at ease, because there was no way their thick arms could cross their massive chests.

Lilly fought the urge to flex her own biceps. She'd been working out with weights every day, and while her arms had better muscle definition than before, no one would mistake her for a body builder. Did these guys live at the gym?

Fin was a Nordic blond and reminded her of a younger cousin of Jean-Claude Van Damme except about ten times more serious. Doug had softer, brown hair, with a no less imposing demeanor.

She bit back a laugh, expecting them any minute to flex and say, "We want to pump you up!"

Fin and Doug, not Hans and Franz, she repeated silently. This could take some work.

"It's a good system," her dad said as they huddled around the main controller talking tech. "We updated it last year with state-of-the-art cameras."

The men would be her escorts whenever she left home—or *the premises,* as they referred to it. As much as they resembled stereotypical hired muscle, they seemed intelligent, listening intently as Dad—in full producer mode—discussed the scheduling needs and showed them around the property.

Now that Lilly had worked with Alexandra, she was interested to know the men's assessment of the house and grounds, and how they planned to keep her safe.

"The system is certainly adequate for your home, Mr. Hawthorne," Fin agreed. "Of course with your current threat, security away from the premises is every bit as important."

She listened closely as the men, both former military, recounted their training and experience to her father. Fin handed him a thick brochure with photos of black SUVs.

"All our vehicles are armored, and our drivers are all professionally trained in threat detection and evasive maneuvers," Fin said.

She was a little miffed that they continued to address only her dad, but that would change the minute they all got in one of those black SUVs to take her to Alexandra's.

Lilly sighed. Her days of driving solo were over. She wondered if she could coax these guys into the drive-thru at In-N-Out?

Chapter 22

Tommy could be a patient man if it paid, but every hour he delayed was an opportunity for someone else to sneak in and take out the girl first, rob him of twenty grand. Of course others would only get the $10,000 Magda had advertised, but plenty of guys would do it for that, even with the security risks. Most of them were idiots who would fail, making it even harder for Tommy to get close to her. So he had to move first and decisively. He lifted his binoculars.

From his roof position on the two-story house across the street from the girl's, he had a perfect view. One guard at the gate carried some kind of mini automatic rifle slung under his coat. Another man patrolled somewhere in the backyard. And two new ones had recently arrived in a black Mercedes SUV. Tommy couldn't help grinning. Twenty more goons couldn't save Lilly Hawthorne.

Something moved at the edge of his field of vision.

There. White hair. She was walking with the new guards toward the Mercedes parked in front of the garage. Tommy had seen enough cartel vehicles in Mexico to recognize the thick glass and reinforced tires. Armored. He wondered if he should rethink the explosive charge?

The men swept the area with their eyes as she climbed into the backseat with a gym bag. Once she was inside and completely obscured by the dark tint on the windows, the men climbed in the front and the engine started. The vehicle exited the front gate and turned right, accelerating rapidly down the street.

"Time to go to work," he said, sliding down the roof a few feet.

Once out of sight, he crab-walked to the waiting ladder and descended to the back patio.

It was difficult to get close enough for observation in this neighborhood. Every house had alarm systems and cameras. He'd bribed an alarm company employee—well, threatened to dismember the man's missing wife and children if you wanted to get technical—to disable this home's security system. The occupants were away on a cruise and had thoughtfully alerted their alarm company about their travel plans. Perfect.

Now, if he could just depend on Ari to do his part. An engine caught his ear, and he listened as it slowed, then got closer. Like all expensive homes, the garages were hidden from the street, accessed by a driveway alongside the house that led to a rear courtyard.

Tommy came around the corner and spotted Ari climbing out of a white van with the name of the security company for this house on its side. Magda had ordered large magnetic signs for every security company and most utilities, plus a variety of bogus but authentic-sounding companies, like Ultra-Tek Landscaping, Phoenix Pest Control, and Best Electric. Each one had a phone number and website. Slap a set sign on a white van and ninety-nine percent of people wouldn't look twice.

"Hey, Tommy," Ari said, climbing out of the van.

"You got the equipment?" Tommy asked. He waited as Ari opened the rear doors.

"Three sets, like you ordered. Triggered by remote control up to a quarter mile."

"And you know how to aim them?" Tommy ran his hands over the olive drab steel tubes.

"As long as you've got the range, I'll level and adjust them. But without a forward observer and multiple shots, it's always a bit of a guess," Ari said, then noticed the look in Tommy's eyes. Ari fiddled with the knobs on one device. "I can get close enough."

Ari had served in his country's military, been shot down in a helicopter and left for dead. Spent seven months in captivity. He had no love for authorities—or anyone else for that matter. A promise of two grand plus expenses was all it took—that and knowing he'd be on Tommy's short list if he screwed up.

"Okay," Tommy said, handing over the targeting he had measured from the rooftop. Laser rangefinders were handy tools. He swung his leg over a big Honda motorcycle that had belonged to Ernesto and pulled on his helmet. "We haven't got a lot of time. Get them set up and get out of here. I'll call you as soon as I'm in position."

"Understood."

Tommy fired the engine. Motorcycles were perfect for neighborhood work like this. Unless it was some screaming street rocket or a Harley, no one paid much attention. The license plate was small enough that most people couldn't read it, and the helmet's dark visor eliminated any description of the rider.

He drove out of the driveway and turned left on the street, the same direction the SUV had taken.

* * *

Percy drove down the street toward the Hawthorne house, but was forced to slow as a motorcycle pulled out of a driveway on the opposite side of the street and passed him head on. The distraction was fortunate, for when he looked left again, he spotted a man standing back from the Hawthorne entrance, half-hidden by shrubs. A guard. This was new.

Percy had observed the house from the backyard before flying up to Sacramento. He knew the property, especially in the dark. They never closed the blinds on the rear of the house. Today, he'd simply wanted another look.

Before the guard could become suspicious, Percy accelerated to the corner and turned right to get out of sight. In spite of the air conditioning, sweat trickled down his neck.

Why the security guard? Had the FBI somehow figured out she was his target? He shook his head. It wasn't possible. Even if they knew he picked targets from three months prior, there were hundreds, thousands of people in California who matched that requirement. Even old Tex had fit close enough.

And the toy company couple. Genius! The FBI would be running in circles trying to figure out their connection. The extra puzzle pieces would keep them spinning too—until they found the girl's body with a single piece. Then they'd know he'd beaten them again.

Percy pulled to the curb and parked behind a gardener's truck and trailer. The tailgate was down, and the sound of a lawnmower drifted in the quiet of the day. He rolled down the window and breathed in fresh-cut grass.

Something had put the girl's family on edge. The goon by the gate was going to make this more difficult than he first thought. Of course, one could think of it as a greater challenge too.

A clatter startled him, and he sat up straight. A Mexican gardener had shoved his lawnmower up the trailer gate, and was situating it for travel. Another man—could be the first's brother—was tying the corners of a large burlap square bulging with grass clippings. No messy mulching in this neighborhood. Percy wouldn't be surprised if they vacuumed the lawns after mowing to suck up every wayward blade.

Well, the neighborhood wouldn't be so pristine when he got through with it. People would be loath to walk their poodles after dark.

Chapter 23

It wasn't that Lilly wasn't used to being chauffeured around at times. Mom and Dad often hired cars when they were in unfamiliar cities, or when they needed the drive time for memorizing lines or studying financials. But riding in the backseat with two bodyguards in the front only reinforced the feeling that she was "the package" to be safely delivered. She could have been a briefcase for all the conversation she got out of the two men. Her life now was a thriller when she longed for a romantic comedy.

Lilly reached to open the door as soon as the SUV pulled up to Alexandra's studio. The sooner she got out of here—

"Please wait until we secure the area, ma'am," Doug said, extending his arm between the seats like she was a toddler needing restraint.

Lilly choked down a laugh, but couldn't restrain her smile as the two men climbed out and stood behind their doors while their eyes searched the alley and roofs. As serious as this all was, she couldn't help feel she'd been dropped into a Mission Impossible movie. Tom Cruise could show up any minute. Maybe he'd be her sparring partner? He was in pretty good shape. Could she take him?

Doug, apparently satisfied, opened her door and stood back, using his body and the vehicle door as a short alley to the building. The door of Alexandra's studio opened before Lilly reached it.

"Lilly Hawthorne?"

A woman Lilly had never seen swung the studio door open and Lilly walked through. She was taller than Lilly, and dressed in black cargos and a stretchy sleeveless camo top that showed off toned arms and restrained curves. It had the aura of a uniform, but there was no insignia anywhere. Her skin was a gorgeous coppery tan that made Lilly immediately envious. No spray tan here.

"For now," Lilly said, and watched the woman's brows furrow. Her eyes flicked to Fin, who had followed them inside.

He shrugged a response.

"I'm changing it soon," Lilly clarified.

"Good for you," the woman said after a beat. "Speaking of change, what do you think, Fin?" she said, touching her hair and turning her head.

The left side of her head was buzzed short, and the right side was long enough to curl past her chin. Deep red highlights sliced through dark amber, complimenting her skin color.

Fin scratched his chin for a moment, then shook his head. "Nope. I couldn't pull it off, Stone. Make me look too emo."

"It *would!*" the woman barked. They both laughed, and it was the first sign of personality Lilly had seen in Fin. Judgment was still out on Doug, who was parking the car. The small laugh lines at the corners of the woman's eyes pegged her near thirty.

"Sorry, Lilly, inside joke. I'm always trying to get Fin to loosen up, but it's hopeless." She held out her hand. "I'm Kris Stone. We're all part of Omron International, your security team."

Fin maintained a position by the front door as Kris accompanied Lilly to the locker room in back.

"You don't wear a jacket like the guys do?"

"Not right now. Alexandra wants me to work out with you."

"You know her?"

"I got some of my training from her," Kris nodded.

"So, you guys go way back as friends?" If Kris had known Alexandra for a long time, maybe she could dig up some background for Mike.

"Uh…no. We weren't exactly playing for the same team."

"What team?" Lilly asked, trying for that magical mix of innocence and determination that she'd practiced on her mother.

"Let's leave it that she's one of the best," Kris said. "Go ahead and get dressed and we'll begin." She took a seat on a bench by the lockers.

"How many of you are there? I mean on the security detail?" Lilly asked, deciding to let the obvious subject change stand—for now. She slipped out of her jeans and into stretch workout pants.

"Six total," Kris said, "but normally only four on duty at any one time, depending on how many directions your family is going on a given day. A new group of two rotates on every eight hours so we're always fresh. I think I'll be one of the two accompanying you to New York."

Six people paid to keep her from being killed by the vindictive Viera family. Even conservatively, it had to be costing her father thousands a day. That couldn't go on for long. Flying to New York and leaving the Vieras behind couldn't come soon enough.

As they walked out to the training floor, Lilly spotted Feral hunched in fighting position and firing hard rights into a hanging punching bag. With each mighty connection, she expected stuffing to fly out. Good thing he hadn't led with his right in the alley. She leaned close to Kris's ear. "Did Alexandra teach you about gouging the inside of an attacker's nose?"

Kris nodded. "Never had to use it." Then she followed Lilly's eyes to Feral, who was scowling at them, grunting and slugging the bag. She raised a brow.

Lilly sighed. "Let's just say that guy wishes my name was Everlast."

* * *

Lilly had used Kris as a buffer between her and Feral, though he'd kept a wary eye during their session. Kris thought the whole nose-gouging thing was hilarious and couldn't stop grinning at Feral. Lilly didn't think she'd ever seen a man turn that color of red.

Unfortunately for Mike—and for Lilly's own curiosity—Kris had successfully deflected all attempts to draw out more about

Alexandra's history. The Russian trainer remained as enigmatic as ever.

With the session finished, Kris released Lilly to Doug and Fin's care, and said she'd see Lilly at home after a shower and change at the team's hotel.

The twenty-minute-drive home took less than fifteen, and Lilly gripped the armrest the entire way, same as on the way to Alexandra's. Doug drove the armored Mercedes with a confidence that left her in awe and a little envious. Always several miles per hour above the speed limit, he handled the heavy vehicle smoothly. No squealing tires or weaving in and out of traffic. Although they didn't attract undue attention, it was like riding in the backseat of a Formula 1 race car.

"Do you guys have special classes that teach you how to drive like this?" she asked as he slowed in The Hills.

"We have refresher classes every year on evasive driving," Doug said, glancing at her in the rearview mirror.

Had that been a hint of a smile? Well, now she knew how to elicit a response from Doug—compliment his driving. Perhaps there was a real person under all that seriousness after all. If she asked nicely, maybe they'd give her a few driving pointers, take out her RAV4 and hit the Costco parking lot after hours.

Doug turned the corner onto her street and slowed even more. No one watching would notice anything unusual, but Doug's and Fin's heads never stopped moving, scouring every yard and car.

Fin spoke into his radio and it crackled back in response. "House is clear," he said to Doug.

* * *

Tommy had swapped his motorcycle for a white van with a well-known cable company logo on the side, and parked it several properties down from the house. Just another service van in a neighborhood where all kinds poured in each day: landscapers, pool cleaners, cooks, house cleaners, repairmen—and cable companies. It was perfect.

So that the van would appear empty to anyone walking by,

Tommy crouched on an upside down crate behind the driver's seat. The side mirror allowed a great view of the street behind him.

This was a nice change from the drudgery of distributing loads of marijuana around the state. The drug money was good, sure, but having to always work at night and in the cold was a pain. For him the whole idea of being a drug lord was using the money for good times. But Magda and Roberto were anything but a fun-loving family. Work, work, work…that's all they talked about. Growing the business. Developing new markets. At one of their last meetings, Magda challenged them all to shoot for better ROI—Return on Investment. Who talked like that? Tommy sometimes wondered if he'd been adopted. What was wrong with enjoying life? Hitting the beach and sucking down some margaritas?

Movement in the side mirror caught his attention, and he watched a black Mercedes SUV approach from the rear. Its deep-tinted back windows gave no clue as to occupants, but as it passed him, he caught a glimpse of one of the girl's bodyguards in the passenger seat.

Tommy lifted his two-way radio and keyed the button. "On my mark."

Two clicks from Ari signaled acknowledgement.

Tommy waited until the black SUV slowed to a stop before the opening gate, then keyed the radio. "Go, go, go!"

Thump, thump, thump.

Tommy's feet tap danced in anticipation.

Chapter 24

Lilly leaned forward, peeling her sweaty shirt off the leather seat. Her left leg was cramping from the workout, and she couldn't wait to strip off her damp workout clothes and dive into the pool.

Doug clicked the remote and the newly installed gate began opening as he stopped in the driveway entrance. Her dad was supremely unhappy with the gate's glacial crawl. A faster replacement was being installed tomorrow.

Through the right side window, Lilly saw three puffs of smoke shoot up from behind a house across the street. Three *thumps* followed. "What was—?"

"Code red! Code red!" Fin shouted into his radio. He hunched forward, craning his neck to see overhead. "Incoming!"

She was still looking at the house across the street when the left window lit up and the SUV rocked violently. Turning, Lilly saw the entry of her house exploding in fire and a rainstorm of debris.

Then another explosion erupted from the center of the house, sending a cloud of smoke and roof tiles into the sky.

"No!"

She threw the door open, instantly assailed by the violence that had been muted by the bulletproof window. Broken tile pieces smashed into the ground, cut through trees, and banged off the black Mercedes.

Lilly ripped off her seatbelt.

"Stay in the car!" Fin yelled, reaching through the seats for her.

* * *

Tommy stared, amazement turning into a wide grin as a giant fireball rose from the house. Auto and home security alarms blared up and down the street, and the leaves of all the trees vibrated like a giant hand had grasped their trunks and given them a good shake.

"Wow."

He dropped the radio and grabbed the controller for his remote controlled vehicle as a second explosion tore through the house. A push on the joystick shot the foot-long RC truck out from under the van and sent it racing down the street.

Two hundred feet.

The truck had big, fat tires, but its suspension was springy for off-road racing and jumping and wasn't designed to carry a load. The extra half-pound of C4 he'd added to the top at the last minute was playing havoc with the little truck's balance, and it weaved as Tommy fought the steering. It veered right, then left, leaning precariously. He slowed it down. Flipping wouldn't be good.

"No. No. No!" Tommy yelled as the left rear passenger door on the SUV opened and the girl jumped out.

A few more seconds. If he was lucky, the concussion might still get her. His finger hovered over the red button on the controller as the truck whined toward the Mercedes.

* * *

Lilly ran toward the house, covering her head with her arms as junk falling from above. A third explosion ripped through her father's office area, sending her cartwheeling over a waist-high hedge that bordered the driveway. She landed on the dry grass, struggling to comprehend the smoking chunks of her home raining down.

Ringing in her ears masked the sound of the chaos, but not the sight of the burning house. *Her* house.

It was just like before, when her mother died. But this time both her parents were inside.

She staggered to her feet on shaking legs, trying to decide how to get into the house before the next blast. She'd taken a step when Fin knocked her sideways. A refrigerator-size chunk of smoldering insulation landed where she'd been standing.

"Back in the car. Now!" Fin yelled in her ear and grabbed her arm. "We have to get you to safety."

"Let me go!" She fought against him, breaking his hold and backing away a few steps.

"Our priority is to keep you safe," Fin said, spreading his arms, blocking her from her objective. "We have to get you away from here."

The fire was spreading, licking through blown-out windows, roaring up the outside walls to the eaves. The kitchen was on the other side, facing the backyard patio. As far as she could tell, that part of the house hadn't sustained as much damage from the explosions. She could get in through there.

Lilly feinted right, then used her stronger right leg to dodge left, evading Fin's outstretched hand. She'd made a dozen steps when she heard Fin shouting. She glanced over her shoulder.

He was running toward the SUV, waving his arms. "Get out! Get out!"

Another explosion blasted the rear of the Mercedes into the air, engulfing it in an expanding ball of orange and black that scorched the air around her. The SUV teetered on its front end, then toppled over onto its roof. Fire covered the underbelly, now a tangled mess of wrenched metal bordering a gaping hole almost as big as the car.

Not far from her, Fin lay crumpled on the driveway. He wasn't burned, but he wasn't moving.

Lilly was torn. Should she help Fin and Doug, or get into the house? If she got Doug out, the men could help save her parents. Behind her, the fire roared louder with each passing second. By the time the men could help, the whole house would be engulfed. A second look at the car told her that Doug was beyond help.

Pull the trigger, Alexandra had emphasized. When confronted with a choice, decide immediately.

Lilly broke into a run—away from Fin, away from Doug in the burning SUV. She angled around the left of the house. The side gate was locked as part of the new security, and she was forced to climb over the six foot block wall beside it. A rosebush on the far side broke her fall, shredding her workout pants and carving long gouges in her legs and arms. She rolled off it and got to her feet.

The garden outside her dad's office was nearly unrecognizable. A camphor tree burned like a giant torch, the heat changing her route into a wide circle. Lush plants were burned to bare stems, and the fountain lay on its side, dribbling water from an exposed pipe. A heavy concrete bench right outside the French doors was cracked in two. Mounds of burning rubble made it difficult to tell where the inside and outside were once separated.

She tried not to look inside, but couldn't help it. Everything she could see was blackened or on fire. Paper from books and file cabinets flared in updrafts, then fell to the rubble pile as they were consumed.

Like my cardboard horses. Floating, burning, falling, until they landed in the tan dust of the trailer park in the Mojave Desert.

She shook off the memory and hurried toward the kitchen. The path was littered with roof tiles, glass, clumps of singed pink insulation, and chunks of charred smoking wood. She pulled her shirt up over her mouth and nose. It blocked some of the noxious smoke, but did nothing to protect her eyes.

Glass crunched under her tennis shoes as she stepped through the paned doors into the kitchen. Ignoring the smoke snaking across the ceiling, she started for her father's study. Ten feet into the hallway, a wall of collapsed ceiling beams blocked her progress. Fire surged through the timbers, pushing her back as it spread to the walls on this side. There was no way to get to her father's study.

Wracking coughs tore her throat, and each breath sucked in more of the poisonous air. She backed away from the burning wall, hands raised to ward off the searing heat. Outside was relatively cool, clean air. She could get her bearings and try again. But that would take time, something she didn't have.

Fully commit.

Once the decision is made, move ahead with 100% commitment.

Reversing, she doubled back through the kitchen to avoid the

152

fiery entryway and obliterated living room, and headed toward the bedroom wing. Though filled with smoke, there was no fire here. She dropped to her hands and knees where the air was clearer, and crawled, coughing and wiping her eyes. A wet trail streaked the once white carpet fibers, and her hand came up red and sticky. She hurried on.

A man lay outside the closed door of her parent's bedroom.

The blood trail stopped with him.

"Dad!"

Chapter 25

Lilly rolled the heavy body on its side. His eyes were open, staring vacantly into the roiling smoke. A splintered chunk of white pine a foot long protruded from his chest, its edges stained deep red where it entered the body.

It was one of the security guys. She recognized his face, but had never learned his name.

Relief washed over her. Then guilt that this wasn't her dad. Shouldn't she feel something? A man was dead. He might have a family. Kids. A pretty wife waiting for him to come home. Now he never would. Who decided which man survived? Was that God's job, or the devil's?

Tears and smoke blurred her eyes as she crawled to her parents' bedroom door. The lever twisted easily, but the door resisted. She shouldered it open a couple of inches.

"Mom?" she yelled into the crack. The door suddenly gave way and Lilly fell inside.

"Lilly!" her mom said, dragging her by the arm until she cleared the doorway. She fell to her knees beside Lilly. "Are you all right? When did you get here?"

As her mother checked her over, Lilly did the same. Blood smeared the left side of her mother's face. Her silk blouse and linen pants were blotched with soot and blood. She shut the door with shaking hands and re-stuffed a heavy robe against the bottom gap to keep the smoke out.

"Mom," Lilly got out between coughing fits. Even this room had a thick layer of smoke blanketing the ceiling. "Dad's office... It..." Even if she could make her lungs work, the words wouldn't come. How could she tell her mother—

"He's here, Lilly. I helped him here."

Lilly followed her mother's gaze across the large room to the king-size bed. From Lilly's position on the floor, she recognized her dad's hand hanging off the side of the bed. It was blackened and singed, but didn't appear badly burned. Blood dripped from one finger, creating a dark spot on the carpet. She turned back to her mom, saw the sadness, as if hope had drained away and left a hollow shell. *He's here.* But she didn't say *He's okay.*

"Dad!" Lilly lurched to her knees and crawled to the bed.

He lay on his back, slightly spread-eagled. He looked like he'd taken the blast face-on. His pants were all but missing, and his shirt was a shredded mess of red and black. The skin showing through was blackened with blood, embedded debris, and singed flesh. Thankfully, his face wasn't as bad.

"Dad." It was a hoarse whisper, a choking sob laced with loss. Then his chest rose and fell. "He's alive. Mom, he's alive!"

Her mother crawled up beside Lilly and put her arm around her shoulders. She nodded weakly. "I called 9-1-1. I... I don't know what happened—a gas leak maybe..." Her voice trailed off.

"We have to get Dad out of here." Lilly used the bed to pull herself up. She reached down to her mom.

"We shouldn't move him."

A crash in the hallway had them turning toward the sound.

"Mom, the whole house is burning down. We have to go." Another crash spurred her mom to action.

Working from the sides, they used the bedspread as a litter and pulled her dad onto the floor.

"You get his feet," Lilly said. From all the gym time, Lilly was stronger, and her dad was not a small man. She bunched the bedspread in her fists as her mom opened the doors leading out to their private patio.

"Okay," Mom said, picking up her end of the bedspread.

"Wait," Lilly said. "Where's your gun?"

"My gun? Why?" her mom said, clearly confused by the question.

Lilly quickly explained they were under attack. She didn't mention the burning SUV she'd been riding in minutes before, or the dead guard in the driver seat.

"Give it to me," Lilly said when her mom retrieved the gun from her purse. Fortunately, she didn't question the order. She knew of Lilly's training regimen. Lilly tucked the gun in her workout pants. The stretchy waist wasn't as secure as a holster, but she didn't have a choice.

They gathered the sides of the bedspread and began half-dragging her dad across the room. Lilly hacked and wheezed in the fouling atmosphere. She expected opening the outside door would bring in fresh air, but a blast of heat at her back engulfed them in thick smoke as it flowed out the opening. She hoped Mom knew where she was going, because suddenly Lilly could not even see her hands.

A *whump* came from behind, and fire spread across the ceiling overhead. Lilly ducked low as she caught the distinctive odor of singed hair.

Like Mojave. What color would her hair grow back this *time?*

Provided she survived.

Lilly felt her dad's body bump over what she hoped was the threshold; she stumbled over the ridge a second later, and they were outside.

Her mom's heel caught on the rough patio pavers, and she fell backward, dropping her end. Lilly nearly stumbled onto her dad's dead weight.

No, not dead!

Orange flared behind her, bathing her mom's strained face in a beautiful glow worthy of any movie set. But with the light came heat so intense at Lilly's back, she feared her clothes would combust any second.

"Keep pulling, Mom!"

Before the words were out, her mom was up. Lilly lifted, freeing the bedspread from the uneven stone.

She ignored the pain in her left arm as they scraped around the spa and through an opening that led to the backyard grass. The bedspread slid easier on the slight downhill of the lawn.

The smoke had released them, seeking its freedom in the open sky, but Lilly's lungs had trapped a ton of the evil stuff. Stinging tears blurred everything, and her head spun more with each breath. It was Mom's strength now that led them away from the destroyer behind, so she closed her eyes and staggered along.

Her tennis shoe caught on something, and she tumbled on top of her father. At the other end of the litter, her mom collapsed onto the grass.

Lilly still felt the heat on her back and legs. Were they far enough away?

* * *

Tommy might have been more impressed with the violence of the C-4 explosion if he could have watched. Instead, he was busy ducking as the shockwave shattered his van's windshield and sent beads of glass pinging off the steel inside walls.

He looked up in time to see the SUV rocking on its roof. Its interior was a mass of roiling black and red, each gaping window a view into hell itself. Fiery blobs began dripping onto the street as plastic trim melted.

"Wow!" Tommy grinned as he carefully shook glass off his clothes. "That is intense!"

For a moment, he missed having Ernesto with him to share it. This wasn't so unlike a couple of their exploits when they were young. His brother always loved a good explosion.

But Ernesto was dead. And today was about revenge.

Then a smile curved his mouth. "And money."

And to get that payoff, the girl had to die. He'd planned to blow her up in the SUV, but now she was loose on the grounds or in the house. She couldn't be allowed to come out front.

"Time for Plan B." He figured he had maybe five minutes tops until the cops and firemen arrived. That should be plenty of time. Get in, kill the girl, get out, collect his twenty grand.

"Don't even have to pass Go," he said, pushing open one of the van's rear doors. Glass sprinkled the pavement as he grabbed a pair of bolt cutters and stepped out.

He tugged his baseball cap low to frustrate any security cameras, then jogged across the street, following the sidewalk to the landscaper's access gate that led into the Hawthorne backyard. Even from here, the heat from the house was fierce. He cut the lock.

The gate opened without a squeak, and he almost laughed. Only in Beverly Hills. They had noise limits on everything here. He stepped through and dropped the lock and the cutters on the grass

Well, not today. Today was all about the boom. He drew his gun as he walked.

And the bang, bang, bang.

Chapter 26

"Well, well. The happy family all together. Isn't this nice."

Lilly rubbed her watery eyes, squinting at the man standing twenty feet away. He wore a baseball cap, but she'd know him anywhere by the red tattoo on the side of his neck. The man from the drug warehouse, the one arguing with Ernesto.

"Will you help us?" her mom asked him, then began coughing.

The man stared at her for a few seconds, then burst out laughing. "Oh, I'll help you all right. Right out of this world." He walked slowly toward Lilly. "This is for my brother. A little payback from the rest of the family." He held a gun in his right hand.

One of the Viera brothers. He'd come to kill her, for revenge. Instead, he'd probably killed her dad. Tried to kill them all.

Anger swelled in Lilly. Her right hand was trapped under her body, but it was near the gun. She had to stall him until she could get it out.

"I'll go with you," she said. "Anywhere you want. Just leave my mom and dad alone." Feeling a strong sense of déjà vu, she raised her left hand to show she was unarmed.

"No need," he said. "You're dying right here."

Sirens sounded in the distance, and the man's head turned slightly, as if gauging the time.

Her mother shrieked and crashed into the man's side. She strained for the weapon, but she was weak from the smoke. Viera clubbed her with the gun, sending her to the ground. He kicked her repeatedly with his boot.

Lilly used the diversion to do two quick rolls off her father's body, pulling the little .32 caliber from her waistband as she went.

Upside down, Lilly saw Viera aiming at her mother's limp form.

She brought her gun up and fired. Once, twice, hitting him somewhere in the upper body.

He staggered, firing wildly toward Lilly.

She rolled again, feeling the air concuss as his bullets whizzed by.

Her third shot caught the side of his neck, this one knocking him back as he fired again.

She squeezed the trigger for another shot. Nothing happened. No, no, no! Her mother must not have loaded the magazine to capacity.

Viera grabbed his neck, pressing against the wound. Blood ran between his fingers as he steadied himself and lifted the gun.

Not enough blood. She hadn't hit an artery or vein, and his chest wounds were barely bleeding.

He was ten feet away.

Distraction.

Lilly rolled again to gain a little distance and came up to a kneeling position. She cocked her arm and hurled the pistol at his head. Viera instinctively flinched, but she'd been off-balance and it bounced harmlessly off his chest.

He laughed at her puny effort, but it gave her a precious few seconds to gather her knees up for rushing him. She could see the dark hole of the muzzle lining up squarely at her.

There was nowhere to go. One twitch of his finger...

But even if he killed her, it might distract him long enough for help to arrive, for her parents to be safe.

Using all the strength in her legs, Lilly screamed as loud as she could and uncoiled like a striking rattlesnake. She didn't go for a low tackle, rather extended her arms and spread her fingers like talons on a straight line to his eyes.

She sensed his finger tightening, the trigger beginning its backward motion until—

A hole opened in Viera's forehead, and the top of his skull blew off at the same time Lilly collided with him. He toppled straight over backward, Lilly landing on his chest. She pushed away from his sightless eyes, from the ruined mass of his head.

Something jabbed her side, and she looked down. Viera's hand spasmed, poking her with the gun barrel.

Secure all weapons.

Lilly twisted the pistol loose. Compared to her gun, it was huge. How many times had he fired? She was tempted to empty it into Viera to make sure he was dead.

But she hadn't heard that last shot. Where had it come from? Someone else was here.

Scan for additional threats.

Damp grass scratched her face as she stayed low and panned the gun 360 degrees for more bad guys. Who had killed Viera?

She searched deeper into the yard, sweeping the pool, the seating area, the pool house, the—

Her eyes shifted back. Had something moved by the pool house? The way shadows danced on the walls as flames behind her crackled made it hard to tell. She blinked away smoke tears, squinting at the building.

"Lilly!"

She whipped around, taking up the trigger's slack as she leveled the sights on a man coming around the side of the house.

Fin. Running and two-handing his gun. She sighed in relief and lowered the weapon as he approached. He was all right.

He must have made that last shot, and she had been too focused to hear it. That could happen in combat situations when adrenaline flooded the system and the heart rate accelerated. Mike said hearing was the first thing to go, followed closely by peripheral vision. She took several deep breaths, slowing her pulse so she could think instead of react.

Fin bent and put his fingers to Viera's neck.

"Dead." He wiped his bloody hand on the man's shirt.

The man was dead and she felt nothing for him. It seemed odd. Had she grown objective about killing and death? She let out a breath. Maybe it was enough that she was really glad she couldn't see the missing part of his head.

"You okay, Lilly?" Fin asked, moving toward her.

"Dad and Mom need help."

Before she could check her parents, several police officers rushed into the backyard, guns drawn, and yelling multiple commands of "Drop your weapons!" and "Down on the ground!"

Fin complied and put his hands on his head. "I'm with Omron International, hired to protect this family," he shouted over and over as they manhandled and cuffed him.

Lilly tossed the gun aside and dashed toward her father. Before she reached him, someone kicked her legs from under her.

"That's my dad," she said as a hand shoved her face into the grass. She didn't resist. Alexandra had stressed over and over, never argue with a policeman. When they came upon a situation like this, they didn't know who was good and who was bad.

But she had to know if her dad was alive. She turned her head, trying to see his chest, but boots blocked her view. A knee in her back crushed the air from her lungs. "He needs help," she choked into the ground.

We all do.

The tears began, bursting like a failing dam.

We all need so much help.

Chapter 27

On the far side of the swimming pool, behind the pool house, Percy lowered his silenced pistol, and backed toward the property perimeter. He hadn't planned to use the gun. But everything was so screwed up now, what did it matter?

At least he'd killed the man who had shot at the girl.

He wanted to keep shooting, kill all the police who were interfering now. Kill the paramedics lugging their cases. Kill the men in suits arriving in twos and threes.

He took three deep breaths, but they did little to assuage the searing knot in his gut.

She was supposed to be *his!* He had a plan, a beautiful, perfect plan, and they had ruined it. All the work creating a diversion in Sacramento, planting clues to send the FBI team running in a dozen directions…

This was his day. The 21st. He'd been in place, waiting for her to come to the pool after her training session, come to him. The straight razor was honed to an edge so fine he doubted she'd even feel it parting her flesh.

The tiny camera was mounted on the pool house eave, recording even now. It would have been so beautiful. Her body floating face down in the pool, white hair spread in the still surface. Glorious red streams from her wrists staining the blue water, curling into beautiful patterns, draining her life away as the camera rolled.

So very Hollywood. Especially after he converted it to black and white, leaving only the blood in living color. Hollywood film noir with a tip to modern YouTube viewers. What a sensation it would have been! How many millions of views? Even if YouTube pulled it down, it would already be shared on dozens of other sites. His work would live forever.

But now it was lost. Ruined by this other man who had also come to kill.

The camera would record until its memory card filled, but instead of a beautiful death, it would capture an empty blue pool.

Firemen dragged hoses around the side of the house and began shooting streams of water on the roaring fire, further defiling his perfect scene.

Clouds of white steam rolled skyward as Percy slipped backwards through the wrought iron fence where he'd removed one of the vertical bars. Large shrubs on each side of the fence shielded the gap from view, and he paused behind the bush on the outside.

Who was the dead man? Percy had spotted him exiting a cable company van right after the SUV exploded, so it seemed likely he was responsible for that and bombing the house. Especially since he'd come straight for the girl. She'd clearly been his target.

Percy pulled a Dodgers cap from his pocket and put it on while he waited until the sidewalk cleared of pedestrians, then he stepped out and walked toward the crowd gathering across from the front of the house. Walking away from the scene too soon might arouse the suspicion of some nosy neighbor hurrying toward the excitement.

Flames and smoke rose above the rumbling fire trucks, which was about all the spectators could see from this distance.

Percy kept the cap's bill low, just another anonymous member of the crowd, but one out of view from any cell phone cameras. He'd wander away before the first news crews got their live feeds set up.

This was so unfair. He'd been cheated.

Percy paced back and forth at the rear of the growing assembly. He still had two more kill days before the month was lost. The house was a destroyed hulk, so the girl wouldn't be here. But he had several paparazzi on anonymous retainers. One of them should be able to find where she would be.

"Yes!"

Percy looked up, suddenly aware that others along the back of the crowd had turned and were staring at him. Quickly, he wiped the smile off his face, lowered his head, and coughed. He kept his head down until he sensed people turning back to the greater excitement across the street, then he walked to the other side of the throng.

Yes, he said, this time inside his head. He could save his plan. He'd have to think up another amazing, movie-worthy Hollywood death.

Five minutes later, Percy began backing away from the hundred or more people who had come to see the show. Others arrived every minute. Some watched in horror, others with gleeful interest.

As he turned the corner and made for his car, his cell phone rang. He pulled it out, groaning as he read the display. *Eve Nichols.*

"Mr. Maxwell. I regret I have some bad news."

* * *

"*What?*" Maggie shouted into her phone, stopping abruptly in the entrance to LAX's baggage claim. Kade stepped close, forcing other arriving passengers to flow around them. "When did this happen? Do they know who—"

Kade rubbed the weariness from his eyes...or tried to, at least. Their flight from Sacramento had been tossed all over the sky by coastal storms. The shiny floor beneath his feet still felt like it was undulating, and his scrambled inner ears weren't helping one bit.

He couldn't remember how many days they'd worked nearly straight through, and the schedule was taking its toll. He concentrated on not swaying while waiting to find out what was going on.

Part of him was interested—a tiny part. Mainly he wanted a shower and a bed. Any flat surface would do. He was coveting a deserted corner of the baggage claim area when Maggie pulled his arm.

"Come on, Kade, there's been an attack. One of our potentials this time."

"Who?" he asked, stumbling over the forgotten duffle at his feet.

He grabbed the straps and trotted after her. She was already out the door and shouting at the line of cabs, waving her FBI badge above her head.

Exhaust-choked air followed him into the backseat of the cab she'd entered. By the time he got the door closed, she'd already given the address to the cabbie, and they pulled into traffic.

"Who?" he asked again, situating himself and fastening his seatbelt.

She turned to him and paused. "Lilly Hawthorne." Her lips drew a grim line. "It's bad."

It was far worse than bad. From the cab window, it looked like an airplane had crashed in a residential neighborhood. Dark smoke covered the sky, lit by spotlights, red, white, and blue flashers, and at least three circling helicopters.

"Let us out here," Maggie ordered the cabbie. They were still more than two blocks from the scene, but the street ahead was clogged with vehicles. Maggie threw the driver some money and they got out.

A poisonous fog of charcoaled plastic, fabric, and insulation blanketed the area. It matched the fear that ate at his insides. There was a single question he wanted an answer to, but he was afraid to ask it. Voicing the words might confirm the worst.

He counted four news vans as they dragged their luggage between cars and people. There were probably more reporters on the far side of the blockade. Not even at the final shootout that Lilly was in had Kade seen so many flashing lights.

"Maggie! Kade!" Paul and Benny waved at them from behind the crime scene tape, and lifted it as they ducked under. They were still a block away from ground zero.

"This way," Paul said, taking the lead.

At first, Kade couldn't believe what he was seeing. Several emergency light stands were erected outside the dark hulk of the house, scalding some spots in brilliant white, while other areas were lost in black shadow.

They walked past a fire engine, its floodlights illuminating a charred, upside-down SUV in front of the driveway. Fire foam had formed pools around the wreck, and the stink of burned rubber choked him as they circled it. Blue body tarps were stuffed in all the windows to block camera views, meaning the body or bodies were still inside.

"Lilly and two security personnel were in the car," Paul said. "She and one of the guys got out." He turned up the driveway.

Relief washed over Kade until he got a clear view of the house. He stopped in his tracks. Maggie had told him there were explosions, but this...

Whole sections of the house looked like they'd been bombed in a war. Debris covered the front yard all the way to the street, a mash-up of roof tiles, insulation, drywall, splintered wood, carpeting, and unrecognizable chunks of furniture. Shattered glass lay everywhere, millions of glittering diamonds worth nothing at all. No one could have survived this.

"Based on testimony of a dog walker down the street," Benny said, "ATF and FBI located three mortar launchers behind the house across the street. They say it's US military, but from like forty years ago. Evidently commonly available all over South America."

"Three mortar shells did all this?" Kade said.

"Not the SUV in the street," Paul said. "ATF suspects C4, perhaps strapped to a remote controlled vehicle. They found a radio controller in a van down the street."

"This all happened when?" Maggie asked.

"Right before seven," Benny said. "Almost dark."

Kade checked his watch. The attack happened after their plane pushed back from the terminal in Sacramento. Their cell phones were turned off.

Benny led the way around the side and through a gate to the backyard. If Kade thought the front of the house a beehive of activity...

Across the yard, groups of two and three huddled over a dozen sites, measuring, photographing, collecting. Meanwhile, firemen stomped back and forth dragging their heavy hoses while the M.E. shouted complaints about ruining his crime scene.

What had once probably been a peaceful oasis now resembled the plane crash with a train derailment thrown in.

"What a zoo," Maggie said.

Kade had never seen this much concentrated activity, and the alphabet soup of agency windbreakers and jumpsuits was beyond his fatigued mind to process.

Four stand-mounted light banks flooded the scene, blasting every object in stark relief, and blinding anyone who accidentally looked into one of them—which Kade stupidly did. He blamed it on exhaustion, but it still took over a minute for the spots to go away so he could see again.

He kept his eyes on the ground immediately in front of him, while Benny described how Lilly and Ekaterina dragged the badly injured Nathan Hawthorne outside on a bedspread.

And then confronting a gunman.

"Was it JPK?" Kade asked.

"Unconfirmed," Benny said. "Today is the 21st, so it is one of JPK's kill days, but Lilly's initial statement indicates the perp who died back here was the brother of the guy who kidnapped her in July."

"One of the Vieras?"

Maggie turned to Kade, eyes narrowed. "How do you know that, Kade?"

He tried for a nonchalant shrug. "I stay up with the case. I was first on the scene with her back in July, you know. And the story of her kidnapping is why she's on our potential list."

"Umm," Maggie said, then turned to Benny. "How did this end?"

Kade couldn't wait any longer. "Is Lilly all right?"

Paul put his hand on Kade's shoulder. "She'll be fine. They've taken her to the hospital, but her injuries are minor."

Kade was aware of Maggie's scrutiny as Benny walked them through how Lilly used Ekaterina's gun to shoot the bad guy. "There's some discrepancy over whether it was Lilly who fired the killing shot or a surviving security guard. Police and local FBI are trying to sort it out."

"Lilly's parents weren't so lucky," Benny said. "Hawthorne got caught pretty bad by one of the blasts. He has second and third degree burns, numerous lacerations, and some deep shrapnel punctures. Lost a lot of blood. I got here when they were loading him for transport." Benny shook his head. "He was alive, but it doesn't look good."

"Ekaterina?" Kade asked.

"Head lacerations, concussion, bullet wound or wounds to"—he consulted his notebook—"I guess one to her torso. They weren't too specific. She's in surgery."

Maggie said to no one in particular, "So if this wasn't JPK—and we don't know that for sure yet—then she might still be his target."

Benny and Paul nodded. Paul said, "And one question is whether this news story tonight will make her even more attractive to him."

"Would he change targets mid-month?" Kade asked. No one had an answer. He was tempted to call a cab and head to the hospital to find Lilly. But they had work to do.

They spent another hour at the house, quizzing every investigator about jigsaw puzzle pieces and searching the shadow areas with flashlights. Even if the dead perp was Viera, Lilly was on JPK's list. And Kade had a bad feeling.

Chapter 28

October 28

"Are we boring you, Mr. Maxwell?"

Percy glanced up, stilling the staccato rhythm he was tapping on the legal pad with his pencil. The three large coffees were catching up with him. That, and he wanted to be in L.A., not New York.

Jonathan Fitzpatrick, chief operations officer of Maxwell Enterprises, stood at the other end of the conference table before a wall bright with four PowerPoint charts. His laser pointer had gone dark for the first time in forty-five minutes.

Bored? How could Percy not be bored? The entirety of yesterday's directors' meeting was swearing him in as the new CEO, then rewriting the company bylaws—a process that had been delayed for months due to his mother's illness—then introductions to dozens of department heads, tours of three of their facilities, and a meeting with representatives from two Chambers of Commerce.

Yesterday was particularly frustrating after being summoned for the meetings with the implied threat of action against him if he did not attend. He was the new CEO, after all, now that his mother was incapacitated. He'd been forced to catch a redeye out of LAX to make the meeting beginning "precisely at 8:00 a.m."

Today's gathering with the division vice presidents wasn't any better. The first two hours this morning was a review of old business, none of which interested Percy in the least. Then to listen to this pompous meeting instigator for nearly an hour spout drivel…

The timing—two days before his last October kill day—couldn't be worse.

He bit back a *yes* answer to Fitzpatrick's question. "Just contemplating my notes, Mr. Fitzpatrick," Percy smiled, tapping the pad again to annoy the man. "It's all a bit overwhelming."

"Yes, well, it would be easier if you'd shown an interest in our business enterprise before now. With Mrs. Maxwell gone, there is a lot more to cover, decisions to be made. I trust you can follow along?"

The others, seven men and one woman, shifted their gazes to assess Percy's reaction. A lesser man would bristle at Fitzpatrick's verbal jab, return fire. Percy simply smiled and motioned for the egotist to continue.

Fitzpatrick's condescending smile told Percy he'd said the right thing. It never hurt to have others underestimate him.

It was no secret Fitzpatrick felt the CEO position should be his now that Frances Maxwell suddenly resigned. Good thing Percy's mother still owned a 68 percent share in the company. She had secured Percy as her successor months ago.

As Fitzpatrick droned on regarding his plan to increase concrete and steel commitments, Percy noticed confused expressions around the table. They shuffled through their stacks of paper, glancing at each other and shrugging in response.

Ah. Fitzpatrick was making this more convoluted than necessary —for Percy's sake.

"That concludes my presentation," Fitzpatrick said, breaking into Percy's train of thought. "Mr. Maxwell, in your new position, I'm sure you would like to understand every aspect of our company as soon as possible so you can begin making informed decisions. Therefore, I've taken the liberty to schedule all-day briefing sessions for you tomorrow. I trust you have no objections?"

Percy smiled at the man. Fitzpatrick thought he was playing a clever hand that would end up with the board voting him in as CEO when Percy failed. Well, games were something he was very good at.

While pretending to pay attention, he sketched a stick figure holding a laser pointer. Tomorrow was the 29th. No, it simply wouldn't do to be in meetings all day. He had far too much to do in Los Angeles. But there was a way. According to Mother's new team of doctors at Cedars-Sinai, she had as little as two weeks before the cancer took her. She was his perfect excuse for rushing back to L.A. One fabricated phone call this afternoon and no one would question his need to speed to her bedside, especially now that her longtime assistant Eve Nichols had left suddenly for another position. No one would ever find that woman's body.

Percy shaded three, barely-visible concentric circles around the stick figure while a woman named Simmons launched into detailed earnings estimates for the next three quarters and how they would affect the company's long-range plan. All on an impossibly detailed spreadsheet.

How did his mother put up with this? The only good thing about his involvement in Maxwell Enterprises was it presented him as a legitimate businessman, a perfect cover for his more private business operations. And, of course, a great deal of money.

Eugene Barrow took over from Simmons and began discussions on the effect of predicted unseasonably cold weather on the curing times of concrete, which would delay the number of daily pours, thus affecting the quarterly profitability. Percy resisted the urge to scratch his ears out. Maybe he could achieve legitimacy in another business, one more in tune to his interests? That would require some thought.

When Frank "Bull" Everett rose and began expounding on new steel alloys, Percy tore off the top sheet of the legal pad and sketched a timeline for the next two days. Everett smiled, no doubt assuming the new CEO was taking notes on his presentation.

According to Percy's well-paid paparazzi informant, Lilly Hawthorne had moved into the family's house in Malibu. Enhanced security was a given. Percy's preference was to get the girl before sunrise on the 30th. And he *would* get her.

The following day would be October 31st. What would the headlines be? *Halloween Horror in Malibu*? He'd be more famous than

Charles Manson.

Percy rubbed his hands together as he reviewed the notes. This could be perfect. He would *make* it perfect. He was the Jigsaw Puzzle Killer, after all, and this would be his 22nd kill.

"Thank you, Mr. Maxwell," Bull Everett said, smiling from the front of the room. "I'm happy you're so enthusiastic about steel."

"You've made a *hard* subject interesting, Mr. Everett," Percy said.

Everyone in the room laughed—except Jonathan Fitzpatrick. The COO's lips were pressed in a cruel smile, perhaps contemplating tomorrow's further humiliation of Percy.

Well, unfortunately the COO wouldn't make any of tomorrow's meetings. Fitzpatrick wanted Percy to be the leader and make decisions? No problem.

I've made a decision about you, Mr. Fitzpatrick. See you tonight.

Too bad it would have to look like natural causes, but with a little time on the corporate computer this afternoon, Percy could make this personally satisfying.

* * *

Lilly sat under a white canopy at the gravesite. In the folding chair on her right was Dad's mother, Beverly Hawthorne. She had come all the way from Duluth, Minnesota, and was Lilly's only living grandparent, but they'd never met.

Dad had never taken her to visit her adoptive grandmother. His stock excuse was he and his mother were *"not very close."* With Lilly's biological mother dead and the man who fathered her a complete unknown, she couldn't understand how people let family slip away. Shortly after Lilly was adopted, she asked Ekaterina about Beverly. Lilly's new mom smiled and said something about Hollywood families being a little odd.

Now Lilly knew what Mom meant. Since Beverly's arrival two days ago, her singular topic of conversation was the early snows this year—how she needed to get back soon to stack firewood, insulate water pipes, and care for her twenty cows and dozen goats. Oh, and don't forget the chickens, barn cats, and three dogs. A neighbor was looking in on them daily, but Beverly didn't trust the old man to feed them right or make sure the stock was inside for the night.

The capper was tying the rope between the house and barn in case of whiteouts.

Lilly shook her head. No wonder Dad was reluctant to make a family visit. It was impossible to picture this woman raising Nathan Hawthorne, film producer. They were simply too radically different.

Mom's parents were long dead. Lilly sighed at the losses, of people living unconnected to the previous generations. That was not what she wanted for her future.

Yet as odd as Beverly was, she provided a welcome diversion from the oppressing weight crushing Lilly's chest.

A faint buzz sent Sylvia Straasberg rising from the chair on Lilly's left. The woman touched the Bluetooth receiver permanently attached to her ear, and began talking as she walked a short distance away.

Syl had functioned as Ekaterina's agent for several years before switching to a publicist role that served Nathan too. Her job was to keep them in the press, both individually and as a couple and family. She was one of the first people Lilly met upon moving into the Hawthorne household five years ago.

The first call Lilly made from the hospital after the attack last week was to Syl. She was the one to contact Beverly and manage the unenviable job of today's arrangements. Although they'd never been friends, Lilly admired the woman's ability to pull off the impossible —on short notice. She was a godsend.

Lilly glanced at her. She was probably arranging details for the public memorial service set for the weekend before Thanksgiving.

A hand squeezed Lilly's shoulder, and she looked back. Kris stood behind her chair, eyes sad but watchful under the canopy.

"You need anything?" Kris asked.

Lilly shook her head, welcoming the warmth of the touch. She also noted it was Kris's left hand, opposite of where she carried her weapon on her right hip.

The Viera threat remained, perhaps stronger than ever after Special Agent Blake confirmed the dead man was Tommy Viera. With

Ernesto and now Tommy dead, that left Magda and the remaining brother, Roberto. Blake was at the hospital when Lilly received a small bouquet delivery with a two-word note attached:

You're dead.

Were they here today, ready to strike?

She swiveled left and right, searching the low, grassy mounds, the stately trees. The tombstones.

So many people had put their lives in jeopardy or died guarding her. Doug in the car. The other Omron guard in the house's hallway —she'd never learned his name. She wanted to write letters to their families, but what would she say? That she understood? She didn't. Nothing made sense because, as even the entertainment reporters got right for once, this was *senseless violence.*

Fin could have died too, but he was here today, standing watch somewhere.

"It's okay, Lilly," Kris said reading her mind. "We've got it covered."

At least thirty cops and other authorities surrounded the cemetery. They arrived in a caravan of SUVs and vans, lights flashing silently to let the bad guys know to stay away. The air space overhead was restricted for the afternoon. Even distant rooftops were checked. There was nothing else to be done.

Except worry.

A cold wind sent oak leaves tumbling, their spiky tips catching on blades of the freshly mown grass. Forecasters predicted the first rain of the season to hit this afternoon, and the dark gray sky was heavy with promise. She tucked her skirt under her legs, already missing summer, missing boating on Santa Monica Bay with Chad and Pana. Even Mickey Cain. Not long ago, everything was bright, hot, and normal—her biggest worry whether Chad had too many beers.

"We'll get you back to the farm where you'll be safe," Beverly said, patting Lilly's knee. "There's lot's to be done. Feeding the animals, mucking out the barn—because I'm sure old man Walters won't do it while I'm gone. And don't let me forget to give the dogs their worm medicine when we get back."

Lilly sagged in the chair, unsure she could survive the next hour, let alone the next several months snowbound with Grandmother Hawthorne. The farm was evidently a hundred miles northwest of Duluth, and proudly in the middle of nowhere. It was Special Agent Blake's idea of the perfect hiding place while the authorities searched for the remaining Vieras.

The fact that Lilly had turned eighteen ten days ago may not have deterred him, but it meant she could do what *she* thought best. She wasn't going. Period.

But none of that mattered right now. Today was about letting go of the future as she had imagined it, as her parents had promised it. This was about saying good-bye while wishing it could all be different.

She had hoped today would be private, but that—according to Syl —wasn't possible. Seventy-five yards ahead and off to the right, a forest of matte black tripods sprouted from a small mound, each topped with a camera and telephoto lens. A necessary concession to the media.

Lilly's wide-brimmed hat and large sunglasses gave the illusion of protection, but in reality they made her the photographers' focal point, and she imagined them zooming in on the pores on her nose. They could—she knew from experience. *"Either hold your head high and look them straight in the eye, or duck,"* Syl always said. Today, Lilly chose the latter. That didn't mean her image wasn't being captured hundreds of times a minute. Any one of those could, and would, show up in tomorrow's press.

Not that it mattered much. Dozens of photos of her and her parents graced every supermarket tabloid the last few days, the stories speculating on everything from ancient family curses to connections with drug lords. They didn't know how close that last guess was.

Although the details of Lilly's life growing up with her new parents had mostly been kept private, her image had not. From day one she'd been photographed with one or both parents. Her role in the family was a part of their image, part of "the sell."

She hadn't resented it then. In fact, when Lilly first joined her new family, Ekaterina coached her how to "act" through it, make it a game. They had fun practicing in front of Mom's mirrored closet doors. Her mother loved the attention. Her dad used it. Lilly tolerated it.

Today she wished it would all go away.

Syl took her seat, and Kris's hand tightened on Lilly's shoulder as the minister, robe flapping in the building storm, took his place at the front of the gathering. He carefully hit his mark so as not to block the press's view angle. Lilly covered Kris's hand with her own, aware reporters were probably already researching the *mysterious woman giving comfort to the grieving teen.*

Mike and Alexandra sat a couple of rows back, Alexandra completely unrecognizable in a bobbed blond wig, rectangular red-framed glasses, and all exposed skin expertly tinted a deep mocha.

Lilly wished her mom had spent time with Alexandra. Ekaterina would have picked up the Russian's accent immediately, and probably cast her in an upcoming thriller. They would have made quite a pair. But that would never happen now.

Syl glanced sideways at Lilly, pursed her lips, then discretely pressed something into Lilly's hand.

Mom's favorite ring lay on her palm, a jade and silver beauty crafted by a Parisian designer as a gift from Dad on their tenth anniversary. She'd worn it to dozens of premiers and parties.

Oh, Mom. A tightly-held shudder escaped, followed by tears and a growing ache that threatened to consume. In a blur, she slipped the ring onto her finger. The metal was warm, probably from Syl's pocket. To Lilly, it felt as if her mother was with her.

The minister welcomed everyone and began speaking. All the right words that should be said, must be said. Lenses pushed in for close-ups, and shutters snapped on a hundred cameras. Satellite trucks broadcast video across the globe. Lilly kept her head down.

Ekaterina Orlov was now part of Hollywood history, someone who was, but is no more. A photo on all the coming New Year's shows looking back on 2010. Perhaps a special feature at next year's

Academy Awards show. *In Remembrance.*

Beverly captured Lilly's right hand, and Lilly drew strength from her grandmother's rough grip. Years of hard labor in middle-of-nowhere Minnesota would be fair trade if Lilly could only turn back time, skip that boat ride, the kidnapping, and have her mom back.

Did God honor bargains like that?

Chapter 29

"Why is he waiting to the last minute?" Kade asked. He was huddled inside a Starbucks with Maggie and Paul, sipping an espresso-laced concoction he didn't remember ordering.

They'd been split up guarding the people on the potentials list on both the 24th and yesterday, the 27th. No one had gotten much sleep, in between or since. One more kill day. The 30th.

"So it's possible the Sacramento murders were it and he's moved on," Paul said without conviction.

Cold wet air swirled around Kade's legs each time the door opened. Less than a half-inch of rain had fallen in the last twenty-four hours, but all of L.A. was on *Storm Watch* again today. Weather forecasters were positively giddy with the series of fronts feeding from the Pacific, something to report beside the endless sameness of SoCal days. Desperately needed moisture or not, the question leading every newscast was, *When will the rain stop?*

It certainly had been a miserable morning for a graveside service. He hoped Lilly was somewhere warm and dry now.

"We know three things," Maggie said, setting her cup down and ticking off the points on her fingers. "One, there wasn't one puzzle piece found at the Hawthorne house, so it doesn't appear JPK was involved there. Two, Tommy Viera led that attack. And now we know there was...is...a price on Lilly's head. And three..." She scrunched up her brow and turned to Paul. "What was three again?"

"Days of the month," Paul mumbled, barely rousing from his slouch.

"Oh, yeah," Maggie nodded, "multiples of 3. Sacramento was the 18th, one of the kill days. So that means it *could* have been him up there."

"But the attack on the Hawthorne house was also a kill day," Kade said. "The 21st. JPK could have been at both."

She folded her arms on the table and dropped her head. "I've never been this tired. I don't even remember if I brushed my teeth this morning."

"Another thing," Kade said. "If it *was* JPK that killed those people in Sacramento, why the extra puzzle pieces?"

Paul leaned forward. "Do you think he's purposefully changing things up? Making a new pattern?"

Organized serial killers were often predictable, but the more the team learned about JPK, the more it felt like a game to Kade. The puzzle pieces fit that theory. A big question was whether some insane killing lust drove JPK, or whether the game did.

"I know you're convinced Lilly Hawthorne was the target," Paul said shaking his head, "except there's no evidence JPK was involved at her house. We can only be sure that she is one of the names on the potential list and was unlucky enough to have someone else try to kill her."

"I think the Sacramento murders were a diversion, drawing us away from his intended target," Kade said, liking the idea more as he spoke it aloud. Larry and his team had reached the same conclusion. "The media's been reporting that we're figuring him out little by little. California was the first time we knew the state where he was going to strike."

"So perhaps that shook him and he decided to do something different to keep us off-guard," Paul said.

Kade nodded. "The Sacramento murders split up our team for four days, and shifted Larry's focus to sifting hundreds of data points for these new people, trying to find a connection. That's a huge distraction."

Paul lifted his hands in concession and shrugged. "There's just no evidence JPK was involved with the attack on Lilly Hawthorne."

Regardless, Kade's gut told him Lilly was JPK's target. But Kade wasn't objective about her, couldn't be now, not after seeing her picture on every newscast. They were file photos from months and years past, but even then her eyes reflected a depth and mystery. He felt her pull, her invisible gravitational field that urged him closer. If she was the target, JPK wouldn't give up.

The police, local FBI, and a private company were handling her security. And while Kade was assigned elsewhere on the 24th and 27th, he planned to be with her for the entire twenty-four hours of the 30th.

The door opened breaking his thoughts. Three moms and several kids blew in, a tangle of cats, vampires, pirates, and ballerinas, all ready for a pre-Halloween party. It was a time for costumes, parties, and candy.

It reminded him how he and his sister used to canvas their neighborhood. Families should be together, carving jack-o-lanterns, stringing spiderwebs across porches, and passing out treats. Instead, he and two colleagues were discussing murder, motives, kill days, and whether a serial killer was organized or disorganized. Ironically appropriate for Halloween.

Kade was sick of this whole business. How had Maggie, Paul, and the others managed this for so many months before he joined them? If they didn't catch JPK now, November was Indiana, then Mississippi in December. Christmas. The holidays. Peace on Earth.

Maggie's phone vibrated on the table. He and Paul stared at it, waiting until she reluctantly lifted her head and answered. After listening for a few seconds, she sat up straight. "Don't touch it. We're there in fifteen."

* * *

"This is a crime scene," Maggie said to the local FBI agent named Ron Blake. "Why was the pool guy even here?"

That was Kade's thought too as they entered the side gate of the Hawthorne backyard.

"Hawthorne had a new pool heater installed last week so Lilly could continue swimming as part of her recovery," Blake said, leading them around a burned sofa as they navigated the backyard. Low, scuttling dark clouds hastened the imminent dusk. "Kind of a rush job to get it up and working, and they were short a few parts. They came back today to finish up. It was already paid for, so they skirted the tape and went ahead."

Maggie voiced a few choice words about idiots who ignored crime scenes, but the truth was the crime lab was finished gathering everything and anything. Removing the tape was simply a formality.

Although the rain had washed away the gray dust, the grass was flattened by thousands of footsteps, and most of the flowering plants and shrubs were severely damaged by flying debris or emergency personnel. It would take a team of gardeners a week or two to set it right.

Of course, the house would have to be rebuilt first. Most of the structure still stood, but great gaps revealed the blackened interior. Where the fire hadn't actually burned, soot covered everything, and the astringent stink of burned fibers clung to the air molecules. Kade wondered if it wouldn't be better to start over.

The swimming pool and adjacent small pool house were about the only things not severely impacted by the bombings and fire. Yellow tape still ringed the blast perimeter, but the back of the pool house where the equipment was located was outside the area. They found two men in blue pool company shirts and dark pants talking to a man and woman. Blake introduced the man as a police detective, the woman as Blake's FBI partner, April Evans.

"The pumps, lighting, and waterfall can be controlled from the house by remote," the older pool guy explained, "but the system is several years old, so there was no way to integrate this new heater into the old control unit. Different frequency. The easiest way is to add a second remote. They're all wireless now, you know."

Paul was shaking his head, and Kade caught the hint of a smirk on Evans' face. Another case of a guy doing his job without logical thought that the old controller was a melted hunk of slag on the kitchen wall. Of course, the contractor wouldn't know whether someone might want to continue using the pool while the house was repaired. In this neighborhood, people expected work to be completed promptly.

"Because of the distance from the house, we needed to mount a long-range antenna on the roof." The man led them around the side of the pool house, pointing to a wire stapled under the eaves. At the front of the building, the wire hung free, the installation unfinished. "That's when we found this."

Kade, Maggie, and Paul joined him, backs flattened against the wall so they could see up under the eave. A rectangular object about two inches by one inch was fastened with tan-colored tape to the underside of the roof overhang. A thin wire disappeared through the two-by-eight fascia board.

"Comes out here," the man said, leading them away from the building so they could see the front of the trim. "Had to get a ladder to find it. Looks like a tiny lens, right up there by the tile."

The man pointed, but it still took Kade several seconds to locate the spot, a nearly invisible smudge tucked up against the bottom edge of the overhanging red roof tile. He switched on a penlight he kept on his keychain.

"It's definitely a camera. Spy grade unit a few years old. Available online," Blake said. "And we examined the edge of the hole where the wire goes through. It appears freshly drilled."

Maggie turned toward the house, and Kade followed her gaze to the hulking destruction. "Doesn't seem consistent with the Viera attack," she said, stating the obvious. "They're all about brute force."

Kade traced the angle of the camera. "It points toward the pool. If not the Vieras, who mounted this camera? And what were they recording?"

Paul joined them. "Well, since Lilly is on the potential list, and since she was attacked by Viera, I suppose it would be too much to believe there is yet a third someone besides JPK targeting or at least interested in her."

"Unless some paparazzi set it up," Maggie said.

"They're always trying stunts like this," Blake shrugged.

Kade didn't believe that for a minute.

"The question is," she said, "what do we do about it?"

Chapter 30

"I still cannot believe he is gone." Magda sank into the desk chair and put her head in her hands. She and Roberto had proceeded with a private memorial for Tommy this morning, knowing it might be weeks before an untraceable "distant relative" from Mexico could claim his body for a proper burial.

The service was a mere fifteen minutes, Magda, Roberto, and their friend Evie Mendez the only guests. The priest did not know them, informed only that their brother was lost in an overseas private plane crash, his body never recovered. The Viera name was not mentioned, nor Tommy's real first name. Evie had shed silent tears over that.

The Mendez family had lived next door to the Vieras while Magda, Roberto, Ernesto, and Tommy were growing up. Evie was the same age as Tommy, and Magda's parents took pity on the half-starved waif, inviting her into their household for meals and, eventually, a safe place to sleep. When the Viera business grew and money flowed in, they moved to a better neighborhood and took Evie with them. The girl's parents did not follow or complain.

At the time, Magda wondered if her own parents paid off the Mendezes. One day about a year after their move, Evie's father showed up at the Viera house, demanding his daughter back. Four days later, Magda learned Mr. and Mrs. Mendez had been killed in a home invasion robbery. The fact they had little to be robbed of made no difference to the investigating authorities. Case closed. That day,

Evie became family to the Vieras.

Today, the priest spoke of peace and comfort, the hope in life eternal.

But for Magda, the familiar religious platitudes lacked one thing she demanded: justice. Her peace and comfort would come after Tommy's killer paid—with her life.

"You're the one that enticed him to go after that girl," Roberto said, striding to the credenza and pouring two fingers of scotch into a glass.

The comment cut deep because it was true. She had not realized how inept Tommy had become in things like this, and she was at fault for tempting him with the extra money. She sent their brother to his death.

After emptying his glass, Roberto poured a larger portion and downed half in one swallow. "We're going to have to bring in someone else for the business."

Magda shook her head. "This is family run. Always it has been that—"

"You sound like Grandfather."

"And Father," she shot back.

"So because it's how we've always done it, that's what we're stuck with? That's stupid, Magda. Times have changed. And now there are only two of us."

His face, so handsome on most days that he could be on a Telemundo soap opera, was twisted in hate. For her? No. There was something else there. Anger. Fear.

"What is it, Roberto?" she said, rising and walking around the desk. She put her hand on his arm. "Something has happened."

"Besides Tommy's death?" He laughed and poured more scotch. "Emilio Sanchez and his boys tried to kill me this morning."

"But…but he is one of your—"

"Yes, Magda, one of my trusted men." He took another large swallow. "Not anymore. He's dead, along with his two sons. I sensed he was planning something days ago. Don't worry, no one heard. Their bodies are halfway to Catalina by now, and will soon be on the bottom of the ocean."

"He will be hard to replace."

Roberto laughed, shaking his head, the alcohol already altering his mood. "He was a shark. Flat eyes. He smelled blood in the water. *Our* blood, Magda."

Regardless of the internal betrayal, she was impressed with Roberto's quick action. For years he had let others do the dirty work, particularly Ernesto and Tommy. Even herself. Now that his men had turned on him, perhaps the old Roberto, the brother she loved, had resurfaced.

And he finally knew what she had been saying all along was correct: if their competitors or underlings sensed weakness, they would not hesitate.

"We need to take out the girl," Roberto said.

She nodded. The girl was connected to both her brothers' deaths. "I will put out the word we are raising the—"

"No," he said, slamming down his glass. Scotch dripped down the wall behind the credenza. "No more rewards. I still say we need to bring in more help to run the business, but we can argue about that later." He rose and paced the length of the room and back. "*We* do this with the girl, Magda. Like the old days before we grew lazy and dependent on those outside the family. You and me." He threw back the last of his drink.

"I have dreamed of this day, Roberto," she said, stroking his ego, feeling the heat rising within. It was long since they battled a common enemy. "But do you not think we need more men for this? There will be guards—"

"I've already made calls. We go tonight. The two of us."

"So soon?" A bubble of anxiety rose up in her breast. In general, Roberto handled the legal details, payments, or acted through others. Could he truly be the old Roberto once more?

"The weather forecasters are warning of heavy fog." He moved to the window with its view toward the coast, and pointed. "Look. It's already thick and moving in, and it's not even noon. The girl will die tonight in the dark and wet."

She smiled at him. Her Roberto was back.

Two of their family were dead, and the priest's words were useless. It was time to bring their own form of comfort. Revenge.

Chapter 31

"I need another gun," Lilly said to Special Agent Ron Blake.

She tucked her bare feet under a fleece throw on the leather sofa.

Her parent's second home in Malibu overlooked the Pacific Ocean and had a spectacular view. Built in the 1940s, the following decades had worn the structure down, like a pair of shoes now relegated to gardening, old and comfortable but no longer appropriate for dress-up. Lilly loved it. Because of the kidnapping and chaos that followed, she missed the whole rest of the warm summer here. It seemed odd this was now her full-time home.

Briny air swam through the sliding door that opened onto the deck. Although refreshing, it carried a chill missing earlier when she wandered out to the living room at dawn to watch the sun ignite the tips of the waves. When here as a family, Mom often joined her while Dad slept in. They would wrap themselves in blankets and sit outside on the deck loungers. Fortified with coffee or hot chocolate, they watched lines of pelicans heading out on fishing trips. It was Lilly's special time with her mom.

Agent Blake was shaking his head. "That's impossible, Miss Hawthorne, you're under twenty-one. You can't own a handgun."

A particularly soggy gust shoved into the room as Lilly met Blake's disapproving gaze. She pulled the fleece tighter and glanced at the clock: 10:02 a.m. Dawn was hours ago, and now the sun hid behind a gray wall that moved onshore with Blake's arrival. Coincidence?

The police had confiscated her mother's pistol as evidence in the investigation. She didn't tell them her own gun was lost in the SUV fire. If anyone found it, they probably assumed it was a backup piece for one of the Omron team.

"Your best hope is to leave as soon as possible, join your grandmother in Minnesota."

"Yes, and put her in danger from the remaining Vieras," Lilly countered.

Blake, perched on the edge of a matching white leather chair, shook his head. His pants had ridden up above his socks, exposing a band of flakey white skin. "They won't follow you that far."

Lilly was tired of the failed logic. "They bombed our house with military mortars; blew up the SUV with C4 explosive; killed…" She took a breath. "You told me yourself they have millions of dollars in resources and a network that spans the Southwest and all of Mexico. Yet you think if I run off to an unprotected farm with an old lady, they won't be able to find me?"

The front door opened, and Kris Stone entered. She was dressed in a long sleeve black polo, black cargo pants, and no-nonsense boots.

"Everything's fine," Kris said, coming to stand behind Lilly and the sofa. "Three assets around the perimeter, plus me inside. Same as we've been doing."

Special Agent Blake frowned at the report. He'd made it clear he wasn't a fan of private security of any kind. "I suggest you seriously consider the option of leaving town, Miss Hawthorne," he said, rising. "There's still time for a flight out today."

"That's not going to happen, Special Agent Blake." Lilly rose and faced him.

The agent pursed his lips, then said, "By staying here, you're putting yourself and others"—he glanced pointedly at Kris—"in danger."

"Our team is quite capable, Special Agent Blake, but is there something we don't know about?" Kris asked, her eyes narrowing as she came alongside Lilly. "Something that makes today likely for an attack from the Vieras?"

Blake shook his head. "We've heard nothing about the Vieras." He looked down and away.

Lilly had seen the classic "tell" hundreds of times in movies after her father pointed it out. Maybe not a lie, but... Before Lilly could probe deeper, Blake abruptly excused himself, claiming pressing duties elsewhere.

"And here I thought all government people were good liars," Kris deadpanned after the door closed.

Lilly held back a laugh, afraid if she started she wouldn't stop. Even with the exhausting rehab and training, sleep didn't come easy these nights. Not since the bombing. She folded the fleece and closed the slider against the increasing wind, staring out as a few raindrops sprinkled the glass. The sea was the color of gray slate, pressed flat by the lowering clouds. Like her soul.

"But he's right, you know," Kris said, joining her at the window. "The part about leaving town, not the part about staying with your grandmother."

Beverly Hawthorne's three-day visit ended soon after the gravesite service yesterday, when Lilly announced she wasn't accompanying her back to Minnesota. While Beverly's visit had been awkward, she surprised Lilly by enveloping her in a tight hug when saying good-bye. She made Lilly promise to take care of "her boy," stay safe, and come see her sometime. Lilly liked the woman better after that. Maybe a short trip to nowhere Minnesota wouldn't be so bad—after the snow melted.

Lilly didn't answer Kris. While leaving might be the sensible thing to do, nothing felt right about it. Her dad was still in the hospital—he couldn't be moved. And her mom was...

There were no answers in the oncoming weather front, so Lilly turned away from the view. "I want to go see Alexandra, then my mom and dad. Will you take me?"

Kris eyed the drops smacking the windows with sudden force. "This weather is only going to get worse. Sure you don't want to wait until tomorrow?"

"I need..." Her breath came in hard gasps, but she couldn't form the words. How did she explain to this woman who lived pragmatic reality and logistics that she *felt* an oncoming storm far worse than a few raindrops? Blake's evasive answer deepened the instinct already clawing up from her insides.

The explosion of her bio mom's trailer in Mojave had caught her younger self completely by surprise. And, although she trained in personal defense this summer, the attack on the Beverly Hills house was beyond anything in her preparation, or even her imagination. In both cases, she hadn't thought big enough. Wasn't that what Mike said? *"You train for the worst case. It's easy to pull back if warranted."*

Regardless of all the training, she hadn't been prepared for the worst. That had to change, because down deep she knew the Vieras wouldn't stop. Ever.

There must have been something in her expression that communicated her transitioning emotions. Kris's brows raised, then she gave a decisive nod.

"Give us five minutes." Kris walked away and spoke into her radio.

* * *

Alexandra hugged Lilly hard, hanging on while she whispered in her ear. "I am sorry, Lilly."

The training center was empty this morning. There was no danger of Alexandra revealing her softer side to anyone other than Lilly.

"Life's not fair," Lilly replied, pulling back. They held each other at arm's length. Alexandra's disguised skin tone from yesterday was back to normal. Hair too.

"No," Alexandra agreed, then looked Lilly over, head to toe. "You are strong. A survivor."

"I had a good teacher."

"*Have.* I am still here." Alexandra smiled. "And Mike."

"We can start up again whenever you're ready," Mike said, rolling forward.

They talked for a few minutes. She promised to get back into a training routine soon, but with the ongoing threat from the Vieras, she had no idea when that would be. Every friend and acquaintance was in danger whenever Lilly was close.

"I have to go," she said, explaining about visiting the cemetery and hospital. She turned to Alexandra. "But I need to ask you for a favor. It's kind of an emergency, and I don't—"

"Anything."

Lilly told her what she needed. From the look in Alexandra's eyes, Lilly wondered if her dad should have hired *her* for security.

* * *

Even at the lunch hour, traffic was surprisingly light on the way to the cemetery. Maybe the rain had scared off some motorists who didn't want to deal with the hundred or two accidents that always occurred on L.A. freeways whenever they got damp.

"We're here," Kris said, stirring Lilly from her thoughts. "Park over there, Dave."

The driver pulled to the edge of the cemetery's curving interior road.

"Want an umbrella?" Kris offered.

Lilly shook her head and pulled up her hoodie. Although the sky was nearly as dark as night, the rain had stopped for now. "I won't be long."

The cemetery was soggy and sink-to-the-bone cold, somehow both fitting and horrifying at the same time as she made her way across the grounds to her destination.

The gravesite smelled of raw earth, and the knees of her jeans soaked through the instant she knelt in the grass.

"Hi, Mom." A few raindrops tapped her hood, growing more frequent with each passing second. "I just wanted to come see you, let you know I'm okay. Dad's… Well, he's a little better. Maybe you already know that."

Thick slabs of turf were laid over the slight mound. With this rain, the ground would sink and level out. Except for words carved on a future headstone, no one would know someone was under here, someone who had influenced people all over the world through her performances. But Ekaterina Orlov was so much more than that. She was Lilly's mom.

Rain matched the tears, falling faster than Lilly could swipe away with her wet sleeves. Sobs wracked her body, and an eerie wail rose up as she imagined all their future times together so ruthlessly ripped away by an uncaring thug.

"I'm sorry!" she screamed. "I'm sorry I didn't save you. I should have."

She tried to get words of love out, but her throat no longer worked.

From their first days as a family, Ekaterina talked about Lilly's future graduations, and how on one special day she would be the most beautiful woman in the room: her wedding day. Although Ekaterina refused to consider herself as a grandmother—it wouldn't fit her image—she thought Lilly should have several children. They had laughed so often, anticipating the future.

The gravesite had become as blurry as her thoughts, and she fell forward, curled in a ball on the sopping earth. She spread one hand flat against the mound—as close to her mother as she'd ever be again.

Lilly no longer tried to wipe away the rain, instead she clung to the best image she had of Ekaterina Orlov. Not the glamorous, red carpet movie star. Not the woman who spent entirely too much time in front of her makeup mirror. Not even the wife who stood beside her handsome husband while thousands of shutters captured images.

No, the image Lilly held tight was her mom tackling Tommy Viera, straining for his gun. That was her love, in action. Sacrificial love for her family.

This was the true Ekaterina Orlov, the woman Lilly had known for only five years.

This was her mom.

And this mound was her grave.

Lilly wasn't sure how much time passed, but the rain suddenly stopped peppering the side of her face. She opened her eyes. Kris knelt beside her, shielding both of them with a wide umbrella.

"My cousin died a couple of years ago," Kris said, staring at the grave. "Not the same, I know, but she was only four years older than me, and we were like sisters.

"I was on assignment in North Carolina, part of a security team for a federal judge whose family was receiving threats. It was after 11:00 p.m., and we'd had a difficult day of shuttling here and there. Important stuff at the time, but I can't even remember what it was now. I'd been up since before dawn. When Dad called, my entire focus shifted in a second. The judge and his family were suddenly the furthest things from my mind."

Lilly sat up and wrapped her arms around her knees to stop the shivers.

"Within two hours, I was on a plane to California." Kris shook her head. "Completely irrational when I look back. I mean, Jen was already gone. She'd been sick for months with leukemia, and the treatment wasn't working. We all feared it was coming."

Emotion flickered across her face, a spread of sorrow, loss, regret.

"It's just... Well, I thought there would be more time. I had two weeks' vacation scheduled for the next month, and I planned to spend it with her. But time ran out." Kris sighed, her exhale a foggy plume in the heavy air. "There was nothing I could do by rushing to the airport in the middle of the night, but I had to."

Rain rapped on the stretched umbrella skin, falling in earnest as black clouds swept in low. Kris's eyes were dark with intensity, as if she was seeing more than the grave and a wet, huddled high school girl.

"But the most important thing—against all reason—was that I get to her. See her one more time. Be home with family."

Wind shook giant droplets from trees above and twisted the rain sideways. Kris angled the umbrella.

Lilly wiped her face. "They said Mom's injuries weren't critical. She wasn't supposed to die." Mom had gone into immediate surgery for the bullet wound from one of Tommy Viera's wild shots. Lilly curled up in the waiting room, praying for news about her father. "Then this doctor I'd never seen came in." Her mom had gone into cardiac arrest on the operating table. Bleeding on the brain from the assault was the determined cause.

"I know," Kris said.

"She just…" Lilly sighed. It was a whole-body shudder, but the gut-wrenching sobs had ebbed, leaving her with an achy emptiness in her heart.

"Left," Kris finished.

Lilly nodded. Her father was the severely injured one. He was the one in intensive care, the one with multiple surgeries, the one everyone was most concerned about. But it was Mom who went suddenly while Dad fought on. Lilly never got to see her.

It wasn't fair. But the other way, Dad dying while Mom lived, wouldn't be fair either, and Lilly felt guilty for even the thought of such a swap.

"None of this makes sense," Kris said, "and it won't make sense in ten years, either. But I promise you, it will get easier." Kris rose. "Let's get you home and dry."

A weight far beyond her wet and weary body pinned Lilly to the earth. It called her to despair. And even though she wanted to get up, she didn't have the strength—or the will.

"*The Lord is my shepherd; I shall not want. He makes me to lie down in green pastures.*"

Lilly looked up. As Kris spoke, she was standing tall and straight, staring across the cemetery, across the cold, wet, landscape of rocky headstones and memorials to the dead. There was nothing green pasture about it.

"*He leads me beside the still waters. He restores my soul.*"

Kris extended her dripping hand. Lilly gripped it, holding tight as she rose. Her left leg protested after so long in one position, but the discomfort faded with the calming words.

"*He leads me in the paths of righteousness for His name's sake.*" Kris began leading Lilly toward the waiting vehicle.

"*Yea, though I walk through the valley of the shadow of death…*"

Lilly inhaled deeply, drawing in air washed clean of the city's grime, and taking for her own the strength and confidence of the woman beside her.

"...*I will fear no evil; for You are with me*." Kris fell into silence as they reached the road a short ways behind the vehicle. Gravel crunched under their soles as they headed toward it.

"I didn't know you were religious."

"I'm not." Kris put her arm around Lilly's shoulders and smiled. "But I have faith. Without it, this job is too big for me."

Chapter 32

Percy woke in his hotel after a very short night. The flight from New York had landed in L.A. in the wee hours, but Fitzpatrick's kill left him restless, and sleep hadn't come.

So, he'd risen and driven his rental car to Malibu well before dawn, and walked the beach below the Hawthorne house.

The photos of the house from his contact were good, but observing it firsthand, even in the dark, was far better. The homes along that half-mile section of the coast were built on a steep bluff that rose fifty or sixty feet above a strip of sand that was often covered by tides. Fortunately for the wealthy owners who desired privacy above all else, it wasn't a desirable section of beach, the rocky gravel a poor spot for sunbathing.

Unlike the rest of the cliff that rose up sharply and obscured the homes set back from the crumbling edge, the wall below the Hawthorne house had broken down sometime in ages past, creating a jagged ravine that led up to the dwelling. Percy thought he might approach that way, but decided he'd rather go in from above.

Ramshackle and slightly misshapen, the house appeared as if a giant had wedged it into the soft dirt until the rear was half buried. Only the double-level decks, barely visible in the pre-dawn light, showed signs of being newer construction.

Nathan Hawthorne had money. He should be ashamed for allowing his daughter to live in such a shoddy dwelling.

Percy yawned again, swinging his legs out of the bed. A few wake-up slaps helped get him going. Midnight tonight was the beginning of his last kill day, and he needed to be seen at the hospital visiting his mother until late. Three or four trips in and out of her floor would get him noticed and firmly establish his alibi. The staff would swear he was there the whole time.

"And then the fun begins."

* * *

Two cars made up Lilly's caravan going to the hospital, plus another chase vehicle that hung back a couple of hundred yards, ready to intervene in case of an emergency. Before the attack, she would have thought it over the top.

Lilly rode in the second vehicle, driven by a taciturn Canadian woman named Yvette who had joined the team an hour ago. Lilly grabbed the armrest as the cars swerved onto the freeway exit at the last second. At the bottom of the ramp, they took a sharp right turn, then zigzagged across the city in the afternoon gloom at ten over the limit.

After the cemetery, Kris ordered Lilly back to the house to shower and change. It had taken all the hot water to eradicate the chill, and deep down, Lilly wondered if she'd ever be warm again.

By the time they headed for the hospital, the rainy skies had given way to an arctic front carried south by the jet stream. It sent temperatures tumbling and created a menacing fog that enveloped the city and triggered streetlight sensors well before dark.

The whole scenario of loading the vehicles in the swirling soup, headlights haloing in fog, then zipping across the half-paralyzed city was like a scene from a spy movie or political thriller. Only the reality of the Vieras trying to kill her kept it out of the Twilight Zone.

A few minutes later, Yvette pulled into the Cedars-Sinai entrance, took a short road around the side of the building, and parked at an unmarked door. The Omron guard in the passenger seat, a man named Reed, got out and joined those from the other vehicle. Lilly didn't know if Reed was his first name or last. She made no effort to know the new team. If they got hurt while protecting her…if she knew nothing about them or their families… Well, it was better not to get too close to these new ones.

After the agents checked the area, Lilly was hustled through the doors and into a private lobby where they were met by two men, a hospital Patient Relations staffer and a security officer. Her guards showed credentials, and the security man unlocked a door leading to elevators. Less than thirty seconds after exiting the car, they were moving upward.

Although she'd been through all this multiple times, nothing was routine, as if each trip was created from scratch. Even the hospital entry they came in was different than last time.

The doors opened to a hallway, quiet except for the occasional chirp of crepe soles on highly-polished floors and a pervasive beeping of machinery. A man Lilly had seen at the Malibu house met Reed and led the group to the ICU waiting room. Reed and the other guards stayed there while the man led Lilly down a short hall to a door where yet another security man stood outside. He nodded to her escort and she entered the room.

She wished Kris was with her, anyone other than impersonal security team members, but Kris was catching up on sleep for tonight. Not that Kris's job was any different than these guys. It wasn't her job to be a mom-substitute to a teenager.

Buck up, Lilly. You're on your own here.

The curtain was partially closed around the single bed, providing patient privacy. It gave Lilly a minute to take a breath—which may have been a mistake given how her stomach flipped at the antiseptic smells. The memories of her own wounds were a little too close.

She took another breath. Her dad had been beside her the moment she woke in the hospital after the kidnapping, and his presence assured her she wasn't alone. Right now, though, she'd never felt more alone in her life. She stepped around the end of the curtain.

Each time she visited, her dad looked smaller than she remembered, especially with the IV stand with its tubes and the beeping monitors mounted overhead stringing wires to various sensors. Powerful Nathan Hawthorne had vanished. Brown scabs peppered his face, and gauze covered burn spots on his scalp. Both arms were bandaged from shoulder to fingertips. His legs and chest were no doubt similarly dressed, though they were hidden under a sheet.

She touched the fingertips of his right hand. Warm. Alive.

Content with that simple truth, she sank into the side chair and sent tiny pressures from the pads of her fingers to his. Not enough to disturb him as he slept, but enough, perhaps, to let him know she was here.

"Hi, Daddy." She didn't tell him his Ekaterina was gone. Beverly hadn't told him, either. He'd been awake for only a few brief minutes since the attack; the doctor's thought it best to keep him sedated through his body's initial healing.

"I've been thinking a lot about school—after I finish high school with the tutors, of course." She talked how she'd grown in the last few months, how her life had moved beyond academic education. The traditional college he and Mom planned no longer appealed to her.

He gave no indication he heard or approved, but she kept going. And as she talked with him, the raw ideas coalesced into solid plans.

"I want to study art."

Two hours later, she left convinced her father's fingers had twitched several times as she enthused about color, form, and texture. He would understand. After all, movies were all about expression through art. He told her once that a great film could tell its story through pictures alone, and then screened a couple of silent films as proof.

Four security guys waited for her in the hallway outside her dad's door. As her mini entourage approached the elevator, a man came out of a side hall and stepped inside. He turned as they entered and faced her group.

Lilly smiled at him, but instead of smiling back, his eyes widened, and he pushed back against the wall.

At first she thought it was because of the four menacing men flanking her, but then she realized he wasn't looking at them, only at her. Had he recognized her from television reports?

"Hi," she said, hoping to ease his obvious tension. He was an inch or so shorter than Lilly, had mousey brown hair and a slender build. His face was shaped like a V. Large forehead with wide-set, slightly bulging eyes, narrowing to a small mouth above a pointed chin.

Her first thought was *praying mantis,* dramatically reinforced when he suddenly cocked his head sideways and continued to stare.

She turned, facing the front of the elevator car like everyone was supposed to, but hairs on her neck raised, and she fought the urge to smooth them. It was like turning her back on a giant insect stalking its prey, one slow-moving creepy step at a time.

When the doors opened, she pushed between the guards and rushed out, knowing they would close ranks behind her. She couldn't wait to get into the car and shut the door.

* * *

Percy didn't move, and shortly the elevator doors slid closed, blocking off the view of four men and one young woman hurrying away. Only then did he sink back against the waist rail.

Lilly Hawthorne. Right here within arm's reach. What were the odds? The girl's mother was dead, so she had to be visiting her father. Like everyone, Percy knew Nathan Hawthorne was in a hospital somewhere in L.A., but Hawthorne's P.R. people had done a masterful job keeping the press guessing as to which one. Cedars-Sinai made sense. It was notorious for its privacy.

The elevator car began ascending, and he quickly punched the button for the third floor, the floor he and Lilly Hawthorne had just left. Presumably Nathan Hawthorne's floor. Interesting.

With travels to New York and back, he'd had little time to do anything but solidify his presence here where his mother was under care. He'd talked with nurses at their station, the cafeteria workers, the business office, and the security people. Together, they would attest he'd been around the entire day and well into the night. No one could fault him for frequent visits to his dying mother. A perfect alibi.

The elevator stopped and he stepped out. The doors slid shut behind him, cutting off a guitar rendition of "The Girl from Ipanema."

He'd been heading out for a break and early dinner when the girl and her guards had stepped into the elevator. Perhaps instead he should scout around for Hawthorne's room?

* * *

While Larry and his team at MIT were working through how the murders in Sacramento might fit JPK's pattern, Kade used a couple hours of personal time and drove to Cedars-Sinai. It was late by the time he arrived. His FBI credentials got him past the guard.

The head nurse was a tougher sell than the guard, but finally agreed Kade could have a few minutes with Nathan. "You just missed his daughter. Such a nice girl." She shook her head. "So much tragedy in her family."

As Kade walked to Nathan Hawthorne's room, he swore he felt Lilly's essence, and he wished he'd been here earlier.

Nathan had more tubes and wires running to him than Kade had ever seen outside movies or television. But according to the nurse, he was stable.

Kade approached the bed. "I don't know if you can hear me, Nathan, but I want you to know, we're doing everything we can to protect Lilly. She's...become very important to me," he said, hoping it didn't sound completely inappropriate.

"I know you'd rather be with her right now." He sank into the visitor chair. Lilly had probably sat in it earlier. It was weird how he seemed to be getting closer and closer to her, but not quite connecting. Maybe tonight.

"I'm sorry you're in here, Nathan."

He let his mind drift, pondering the reversal of events. A little more than three months ago, it was Lilly lying in a hospital bed like this, fighting for life. Now her mother was dead and her father was the one in danger of dying. The one constant was Lilly was still under attack.

Hawthorne was a strong man, and the doctors were optimistic. That was the best part. The unknown was how he'd react to his wife's murder and the continuing threat to Lilly.

Kade's phone dinged, and he checked the screen. A text from

Maggie to the team:

Larry's conclusion - Sacto murders are not part of the sequence or a new sequence. Could still be JPK, but not his primary target. Diversion? Let's gather at 8:30 p.m. for assignments.

Kade was now fully convinced Lilly's threat was from two fronts: the Vieras and the Jigsaw Puzzle Killer.

The hidden video camera suggested a party other than the Vieras. And until they could talk to Hawthorne, they couldn't even rule out that he'd put it up himself for some reason. Benny still thought Tommy might have set it up, but Kade had argued again that Tommy used mortars and C4 explosives. Subtle spy hardware didn't fit his style.

And then Special Agent Blake had come by this morning and told them Lilly hadn't killed Tommy Viera. Her statement said she thought her bodyguard, Fin Silvan, had made the final headshot, while Silvan's statement pointed to Lilly as making all the shots before he'd come into view of the scene. That left the killing shot to a third party who hadn't come forward, perhaps the same person who installed the spy camera.

Kade theorized the only person it could be was JPK, protecting his target, Lilly, so *he* could kill her.

Blake had recommended, again, that Lilly leave town immediately, but Kade didn't think she'd do that, not with her father in ICU. He wished he could talk to her. Would she remember him? But there wasn't time. They were scrambling to come up with JPK's next move.

Kade stood to leave. "If I can, I'll stop by day after tomorrow. Hang in there, Nathan." He walked out the door without getting a response.

The guard lifted a hand as Kade left the room and headed toward the elevator. Halfway there, a man came alongside him.

"Visiting a friend?" the man asked, giving a friendly smile.

"Acquaintance," Kade said.

"Saw you talking with the guard. Your friend must be someone important to warrant that kind of security."

Kade remained silent, unsure where this was going. The man moved with precise, slightly robotic motions. Odd.

"Cedars has over a hundred security people," the man said, leaning closer to Kade as if speaking in confidence. "That's why my mother is here. Frances Maxwell. Perhaps you've heard of Maxwell Enterprises?"

Kade nodded, relaxing a little. Maxwell Enterprises was well known. It seemed the guy had a legitimate reason for being here.

"I'm Percy Maxwell," the man said as they reached the elevator, "head of the company now that my mother is near passing."

"I'm sorry to hear that, Mr. Maxwell," Kade said, waving the man inside. Kade pushed the button for the ground floor, then extended his hand. "I'm Kaden Hunt."

Maxwell's hand was strong and damp. "Glad to meet you, Mr. Hunt." But he didn't appear glad at all.

They both exited on the ground floor, and Kade proceeded to the main hospital exit. Thick fog funneled in through the automatic doors, as if planning to blanket the entire lobby. He stopped to zip up his jacket, casually glancing over his shoulder. Percy Maxwell still stood near the elevator, frozen in place. His head was cocked sideways, and he was staring straight at Kade with his unusually large and flat eyes.

Kade suppressed a shudder that didn't come from the night air, and hurried to his car. His first inclination was to call Maggie and have her run a check on Percy Maxwell, but she'd ask for a reason, and "the guy made me uneasy" didn't sound very convincing.

As he drove out of the parking structure, he shook off the weirdness of the encounter. Midnight tonight was the beginning of the final kill day for October, and it was going to be a long one.

The good part was being closer to Lilly.

Chapter 33

After the cemetery and hospital, Lilly wanted coffee, food, and twenty hours sleep. She squirmed against the hard cushions of the SUV's rear seat as she stared out the window at rows of cars. The lighter traffic from noon was no more, replaced by everyone in L.A. picking the Pacific Coast Highway as their evening escape route out of the city, and they were all crawling through soupy fog.

Up front, Yvette hunched over the steering wheel, gesturing and muttering in French at other drivers. She wasn't opposed to frequent use of the horn, either. Lilly understood none of the phrases, but they weren't expressions of love and goodwill. The woman tossed a few at Reed whenever he laughed at her.

The tinted side windows revealed nothing except the lights of other cars as they crept forward or fell back, jockeying for the slightest advantage. If it hadn't been for the optimistic woman in the dash GPS, Lilly would have missed the turnoff to her own house.

After dropping her off, the caravan teams left for the night, disappearing into the fog before they reached the end of the driveway. Lilly hoped their lodging was nearby.

Her stomach growled as she opened the front door and turned toward the kitchen. It wasn't to be. Abigail Coddington was waiting for her in the living room. Abigail was their family's main liaison to a law firm made up of a couple of Coddingtons, a Smith, a Bickers, and two or three other names. Lilly could never remember the exact order.

"Lilly," Abigail said, opening her arms awkwardly for a hug as

Lilly came through the door. The woman had never been a hugger. In fact she had essentially ignored Lilly the few times she came to the house, so this embrace felt as sincere as one from Faye Dunaway playing Joan Crawford in *Mommie Dearest*. But at least the woman appeared to be trying. She'd also come to the cemetery service.

Lilly pulled away as soon as appropriate, establishing a little distance, and choosing a modern, white vinyl chair set at a ninety degree angle instead of side by side on the sofa where Abigail had set up some paperwork. She reminded herself that—although the attorney was on the odd side—this was the firm her parents had chosen. They trusted Abigail to know what she was doing. Still, it was strange to suddenly be the center of her attention. Was the firm worried about losing the Hawthorne business?

Abigail sighed, then said, "I didn't want to intrude until after Ekaterina's service, but we have some things to discuss."

The first was a trust fund for Lilly that Ekaterina had set up in case of her "untimely death." Abigail's words. They might describe the practical reality—and maybe lawyers were immune, since they used them daily—but they were a hot knife straight through Lilly's heart. She'd trade all the money in the world to have one more day with her mom.

"It's a substantial amount," Abigail said, "and I recommend leaving it under our management. I brought forms for setting up a checking account as well as debit and credit cards to access your funds. A notary from our office will arrive in fifteen minutes."

Lilly nodded that she understood. From the volume of papers on the table, this could take a while.

"Of course your mother's half of the marital assets pass to your father."

A band constricted Lilly's chest. *Life must go on* might be true, but it sucked.

"We're also handling the insurance claim on the Beverly Hills house. We arranged for initial cleanup and making it safe. Those are complete. We'll wait until your father is better, of course, before starting any rebuilding plans, but I wanted to assure you how it all works."

"Dad's office…" All the awards, vintage movie posters, scripts, files. She'd never again sit with him on that soft leather couch and watch movies.

"I'm sorry, but it's all gone," the attorney said. "I loved that office." There was true regret in her tone. "Mr. Bickers heads up our entertainment division. He's brought in another producer to sort out the status of Nathan's current projects with the studios and keep things moving."

"What about paying the bills," Lilly asked, "like the mortgage and utilities?" She didn't even know if her parents had a mortgage on this house. Lilly's regular checking account had about three thousand dollars in it. That wouldn't go far.

"This house is free of a mortgage, but your parents have other commercial investment properties scattered across the country."

Lilly had never heard about those. Although now eighteen, she realized how little she understood about the practical aspects of owning and running a simple household, let alone a complex portfolio involving multiple properties and investments. She was more familiar with movie production budgets from all the time she'd spent in Dad's office as he talked on the phone.

"Everything except minor payments are already administered through our office," Abigail said. "If anyone comes to you, direct them to me and we'll take care of it." She handed Lilly a small stack of business cards.

Lilly relaxed into the chair, thankful there were competent people handling these things. They didn't teach this stuff in high school.

"Your parents' cars were destroyed in the garage by falling timbers. We've filed insurance claims for those. Your car received substantial damage, but can be repaired within a few weeks. Would you like to proceed with that?"

The damage to her red Toyota felt more personal than the house destruction. She'd spent a lot of time in the little car the eighteen months she'd had it, shopping and the beach with Pana, hanging out at their favorite coffee shops, cruising PCH. Even taking it to school that final time had felt like an adventure. Now it was another reminder of aching loss. Even fixed up, driving it would never be the same.

"Sell it," she said, shaking her head. It wasn't like she would be driving around on her own soon—not in anything less than a tank.

Abigail lifted an eyebrow, then nodded. "You can buy something else when you're ready."

The notary arrived, a stubby, efficient woman who spent the next several minutes arranging the trust forms.

Then, before signing, Lilly asked Abigail for a private moment. The notary stepped outside.

"I suppose you knew Mom and I were planning a trip to New York?"

Abigail nodded. "A film project. We contacted the producer immediately, of course."

"She was going to call your office about a name change. Did she?"

"She wanted to change her name?" Abigail's brows knit together.

"For me," Lilly said. "We talked about it for a while, and well…" She didn't want to sound as if she were removing herself from the family, or come across as disloyal, especially now. But she also didn't want to get into all the whys with the attorney. She opted for how her mother would approach it: direct and to the point. "With these attacks, we thought it might be a good time to do it. It would have to be kept secret. In case I need to disappear."

"Ah." Abigail nodded in understanding, then indicated the pen in Lilly's hand. "Go ahead and sign using your current name. I'll get someone working on the name change."

"No one can know," Lilly prodded, meeting the woman's eyes.

"Then I'll take care of it myself," Abigail said.

They invited the notary back in, and Lilly signed her name in all the places indicated, wondering if this was the last time she'd write *Lilly Hawthorne*.

The notary left for another appointment, and Lilly stood as the attorney divided up the forms, one pile going into her satchel, the rest to Lilly. She'd have to buy a small filing cabinet and folders to keep track of everything. She'd also have to buy more clothes, shoes, and a bunch of other stuff to replace everything lost.

But not everything could be replaced. The lung-crushing band tightened again. Her mother should be alive, filming in New York, her dad juggling four or five production projects. A dozen people had told her it wasn't her fault, but it sort of was. She was the target. They'd been coming for her.

She inhaled deeply. From the first day she came to live with Nathan Hawthorne and Ekaterina Orlov, they told her she was Strong, Savvy, and a Survivor. *"The three S's," Ekaterina said. "Without them, this town will eat you alive."* She repeated them to Lilly every time they were about to meet a group of people. Her dad had his own set of words, cruder ones he and Lilly laughed over in his office. His were the words Lilly thought of when she had to "perform" in public. They kept her smiling.

From the beginning, her parents taught her how to make decisions, and then made her choose—everything from clothes, to decorating her room, to what classes she took.

Right now she needed all three S's in spades.

"Unless you have any other questions, I think that's everything," Abigail said, hoisting the satchel.

As they walked to the front door, Lilly asked, "How much is the trust fund?"

"There's a consolidated statement in your papers." Abigail paused for several beats, then said, "It's a little over seven million dollars."

"Oh, my…"

"As I suggested," Abigail said, dropping her voice and leaning close as the door opened and Fin stepped inside, "it's best if we continue to manage it for you. We're very good at what we do." She left before Lilly could think of a response.

"A package arrived addressed to you, Lilly," Fin said. "Kris has it isolated up on the driveway."

"Why?"

"We want to make sure it doesn't contain anything to harm you."

Oh.

He held up his cell phone. "Here's a photo of the shipping label. Are you expecting books?"

She stared blindly at the photo for a minute, still reeling from the trust fund news.

"We can send it out for X-ray if you're not sure."

"Oh, uh…" She focused on the shippers address. *Kaleidoscope Gallery Books.* Books? Then she noticed that the first letter of each word was bolded and larger. *KGB.* That brought a smile.

"No, it's mine. I just didn't expect it so soon."

Fin returned with the box a few minutes later. Lilly juggled the awkward load, which was heavier on one side.

"Want me to open it for you?"

"Thanks, Fin, but I'll get it."

Alexandra had come through.

* * *

The meeting with Abigail had consumed an hour, but at least it left Lilly more awake. She set the box on the coffee table, and was pulling at a flap and cursing the fiber-laced tape when a man spoke.

"Here." Special Agent Ron Blake held an open penknife out to her, butt first.

When had he come in? A second man stood by the front door.

"Special Agent Blake," she said, sliding the box to the side. She fought the urge to hide it under the couch. "Nothing important. I'll get it later. I didn't expect you back today."

Blake paused a moment before pocketing the knife. The way he stared at the box, she wondered if he had X-ray vision or a sixth sense. But then he motioned toward a chair. She nodded with relief, and they sat down.

Without preamble he said, "Miss Hawthorne, the Coast Guard intercepted a boat earlier today a few miles out of San Pedro. It wasn't a fishing boat, and it had come to a stop, so they approached to see if help was needed. The lone crewman was dragging the last of three bundles up from below. They were wrapped in tarps and heavy chains. Didn't have to be rocket scientists to know what they were seeing."

Lilly wasn't sure how to respond, but didn't have to. Blake was on a roll.

"Three men, dead. I won't get into the details, but they didn't die peacefully." He leaned forward, elbows on his knees. "The *good* news is that the boat driver has a history and, depending on final charges, is facing way more than his third felony. They had to sweat him awhile, but he finally agreed to a deal. He was hired by Roberto Viera to dispose of the bodies."

Lilly's breath caught, the image of the boat, bodies, and chains spinning in her head. Were they innocent victims? Before her imagination could go too far, Blake continued.

"This isn't the first time this man worked for Viera. He knows quite a bit about the family: some of their connections to Mexico and Central America, and the location of some of the warehouses where they package drugs for shipment."

Like the one where Ernesto had taken Pana, Chad, and herself. Cold, dirty, deadly. Where she'd first seen Tommy Viera. An involuntary shiver crawled across her shoulders.

The agent looked at his watch. "I have to get going. We're hitting all known locations simultaneously in two hours. Not ideal timing. Normally we'd wait until early morning, but we don't want to risk losing them."

She knew exactly what the raids would be like: flash grenades, tear gas, explosions, gunfire. People dying. She hoped there would be no car chases and shootouts on the streets.

He rose and looked down at her. "I won't promise we'll catch them and this will all be over, but...well, it's possible." He smiled sympathetically, the first time he'd broken his stern demeanor. "I'll call or come by with a report as soon as we sort it all out, but it will be at least tomorrow. Multiple agencies, you know."

She didn't, but walked him to the door without comment.

Kris entered as Blake left. "News on the Vieras?"

Lilly filled her in about the bodies and the pending raids.

Kris nodded to the box on the table. "School books?" She covered a yawn.

"I thought you were off for a few more hours," Lilly said. "Did you get any sleep at all?"

"Enough."

Lilly picked up the package. "Come on." She headed toward her room in case any more law enforcement people dropped by unannounced.

Except for a mounted mirror and several pieces of Lilly's artwork, the room walls were bare. The retro boy-band posters Pana had pinned up three years ago were gone. Lilly and her mom had planned to repaint this summer.

While they only came to the house on weekends or to entertain friends and enjoy the ocean sunset, its simplicity felt more comfortable than Beverly Hills ever had. And the memories here were all good ones, not tainted by recent horror.

She placed the box on her small study desk and cut the tape with scissors.

The first wrapped package was a black nylon purse, complete with over-the-head strap and side pocket. The next was a large plastic bag filled with a dozen yellow ear plugs and a pair of safety glasses.

"Interesting," Kris said.

Then Lilly removed a small box and lifted the lid.

Inside, on a bed of gray egg crate foam, lay a .32 caliber Seecamp semi-automatic pistol, an exact match to the one destroyed in the SUV blast that had killed Kris's colleague, Doug.

"I didn't know it was Christmas," Kris said.

Three spare magazines and a thousand rounds of hollow point ammo rested in the bottom corner of the box, as well as an assortment of pocket and belt holsters and magazine retainers.

"I detect Alexandra's touch," Kris said.

"The woman's a miracle worker."

Lilly dropped the pistol's magazine and checked the chamber. She loaded one magazine, racked a round into the gun's chamber, then topped off the magazine. She tossed everything except the purse back into the box. "Follow me."

"Yes, ma'am," Kris said. "Anything for the lady with the loaded gun."

They detoured to the kitchen for peanut butter and jelly sandwiches, potato chips, and sodas, then descended the stairs to the lower level. Kris and the Omron team had searched out every corner of the house, of course, so they all knew about the downstairs room.

The lower level was about forty feet wide and sixty feet long, with the front leading out onto the lower deck with a view of the ocean. It had been a moldy unfinished space when her parents bought the house.

Going to public or even many private shooting ranges wasn't practical for Hollywood stars, so her father had the back portion partitioned off into a ten by fifty shooting range. Outside the entrance to the room sat a massive antique safe Dad used for a couple of shotguns and boxes of ammunition.

Kris opened the padded door to the range and swung it open while Lilly unlocked the safe. "9mm, right?"

"Yep," Kris said.

The right wall of the range was built into the cliff rock, and the remainder of the room was lined with a protective barrier and sound-deadening materials. Dual overhead cables for targets ran the length. Lilly set her box on a folding table and passed two boxes of 9mm cartridges to Kris.

"You using that peashooter?" Kris smirked, drawing her weapon and placing it on the table. "That's good for what, five feet?"

"Watch and learn," Lilly said, putting on eye and ear protection. She clipped a target to the cable and ran it out to the thirty foot marker. Then she focused, calming her breathing, relaxing her shoulders, widening her stance.

The first shot was always a slight surprise—exactly as it should be. *"If it surprises you, you do not have time to flinch,"* Alexandra had said during her instruction.

At the end of an hour, Lilly reeled in the fourth set of targets. They'd shot nearly a hundred rounds each, and her target's center was a riddled mess. She'd practiced shooting from the floor, lying upside down, and left handed. There were several outliers marking the edges, but overall she was happy with it.

Kris's grouping was much tighter, with almost every shot landing inside a three inch circle that was completely obliterated.

"I think you missed a bunch," Lilly kidded. "There's only one hole."

"Nothing but air." Kris said. "You want to try mine?" She held out her Glock.

"Nope. It might throw me off."

"Probably smart," Kris said. "Honestly, Lilly, I'm surprised at your accuracy. That mouse gun doesn't even have sights. How do you do that?"

Lilly raised a brow.

"Ah, of course," Kris said. "The miracle worker." She holstered her weapon and cleaned up the empty ammo boxes.

"Mike helped a lot too," Lilly said as she packed up the shipping box. "Alexandra taught the basics, but Mike ran me through dozens of practical situation scenarios."

Kris didn't respond, and Lilly became aware of the woman's eyes on her. She turned, leaned against the table, and crossed her arms. "What is it?"

Kris took a breath. "We'll do everything we can to keep you out of danger. I hope you know that."

"Are you worried about me being armed? That I'll accidentally shoot one of your team?"

Kris glanced at the targets on the table and shook her head. "Nope. I'm worried you'll have to shoot anyone at all."

"Already done that," Lilly said, remembering the way thirteen ounces of steel felt bucking in her hand as she aimed at Tommy Viera and squeezed the trigger. How she'd wished that magazine had been fully loaded.

"And you don't want to do it again," Kris said. "Did you know for most of our assignments we aren't even armed? Our visible presence keeps the bad guys away."

Lilly countered, "Even when a psycho drug family has your client in their crosshairs?" The anger she'd held in check these last days grew hot inside. "When they've already killed your client's mom and blown up her dad?"

Kris started to reply, but Lilly cut her off. "You think I should leave town, huh?"

"That would be the smart thing to do," Kris said.

"You forget…I'm a high school dropout."

"Doesn't make you dumb."

"I'm not leaving my dad," Lilly shot back.

"Lilly, I didn't—"

Lilly held up her hand and shook her head. Even with the humming exhaust fan, the smell of gunpowder hung heavy in the air. It had become as familiar to her as the smell of peanut butter. That couldn't be normal. Maybe there was something wrong with her. Something broken inside.

"Sorry," Lilly said. She didn't have the luxury of contemplating her own craziness right now. And she didn't blame Kris for suggesting escaping this madness. It's what everyone thought she should do.

Kris nodded, but didn't say anything.

"It's just… You weren't there in that van, Kris. You didn't see Ernesto after he'd shot Pana. Dead eyes—that's what I remember when I fall asleep. Then, when he escaped, he dragged me along with him like I meant nothing, less than a dog. He was in three shootouts with cops, Kris, shot up, yet he still got away. I've been trying to figure him out, you know? Come up with words to describe him, like cold, merciless. But most of all, he was determined. He never gave up.

"And when his brother pistol-whipped Mom in the backyard…" She shuddered at the memory. "He was going to shoot her, then me and probably my dad. He was grinning, Kris, enjoying it. Right up until my first bullet hit him. But even then, he still kept coming."

"We can protect you—"

Lilly shook her head. "If the other Vieras are anything like Ernesto and Tommy, they won't stop, ever. That's why I don't want to go to

Minnesota. No matter where I go, they'll keep coming, and coming, and coming." She dug her fist into her stomach. "I can feel it right here."

Kris eyed her for a moment, mouth in a tight line. "They killed cops, Lilly. LAPD wants them bad. They will get them."

Lilly met her eyes. "Maybe. But will the Vieras get me first?"

Chapter 34

"Okay, let's get to it, everyone," Maggie said, coming into the cramped conference room. She went to the head of the table, while Kade took a seat at the opposite end. The surface between them was overloaded with laptops, desk phones, radios, and two special systems with fast-scrolling GPS maps of the state. Larry scrambled to get his laptop connected to the proper cable.

For the first time in two days, all the team was together. Midnight tonight was the beginning of October 30th, the last kill day for the month if JPK kept to his pattern.

"Larry, do we have assignments on everyone?"

"Yes, I... Hold on a second." Even though sitting, Larry swayed like a drunk at last call, punching at and missing the button to turn on the projector.

The rest of the crew wasn't in any better shape. Benny's eyes were bloodshot and watery, Paul's skin tone had turned ashen, and Maggie appeared to have aged ten years in the few weeks since Kade met her.

Kade knew he looked no better. One more 24-hour period to survive...and then they would begin all over again in Indiana.

Larry got the projector on and the potentials list filled the wall. Kade tried to make sense of the names, but none were familiar. The total at the top said 174, far more than—

"Sorry," Larry said. "That's Indiana." He clicked his mouse and a new list came up, this one clearly labeled Mississippi, with 1,352 names.

Kade was so concentrated on California, he'd forgotten Larry and his team were working multiple future states all at the same time. The first kill day in Indiana was in only four days.

"Here we are." A simple table showed each potential's name on the left, with the assigned protective agency and name of the law enforcement lead on the right.

Everyone on the team had manned the phones, calling in every favor they could from local police and sheriffs' departments as well as FBI to cover the potential list for the last few kill days. When nothing happened, some departments were skeptical of tying up their resources again and again. And now, most departments were saving manpower for Halloween night. Asking them for special coverage for the entire 24 hours the day before was a stretch. Unlike previous kill days, some potentials had only one person assigned for tonight. Kade hoped it was enough.

The door rattled, and two additional FBI agents, a man and woman, filed in. Maggie introduced them all around as Kendra and Josh.

"They'll be manning the laptops and open phone lines with our field contacts tonight," Maggie said.

Maggie had surmised that if Sacramento was indeed a diversion, then the true target would probably be in the Southland. Benny countered it could easily go the other way, and JPK could pick someone in the North. The hard reality was no one knew.

That led to the next controversial piece of the equation: the potentials hadn't been notified of their possible danger. Every meeting before a kill day, Kade and Benny argued for informing them, but Maggie and Paul took the opposing view. Since each would be covered by law enforcement, they didn't want to unnecessarily alarm people.

However, the press had gotten wind that the FBI had a shortlist of likely targets, and every television commentator and talk radio host was demanding release of the names, citing the public's right to know.

Gun stores—regardless of California's ten-day waiting period and mandated handgun safety test—had lines out the doors, and sporting goods stores and specialty shops were selling out of stun guns, pepper spray, bear spray, and even long-distance wasp spray. Baseball bat sales had never been higher.

So far the public didn't know that JPK had only killed on days that were multiples of 3, so Halloween would be safe. Regardless, Kade knew the few parents brave enough to take their kids trick-or-treating this year were going to be armed to the teeth. The rest would be home with their weapons. Emergency rooms, typically already busy on Halloween, were adding even more staff.

Kade scanned the wall until he found Lilly's name. Beside it was *Ron Blake, FBI*, and a second line noted private security because of the Vieras. He shook his head. How had one eighteen-year-old girl become the target of multiple killers?

"Larry and I will be here from midnight to midnight, but you three"—she met eyes with Paul, Benny, and Kade—"will help cover the locals."

Larry typed in Paul's name next to the potential in Burbank, and Benny's name for the one in Riverside. Then he replaced Ron Blake's name with Kade's. *Lilly Hawthorne. Malibu.*

"Why is Special Agent Blake out of the picture?" Kade asked.

Maggie nodded. "Due to information from an arrest earlier today, they're hitting five Viera family locations simultaneously at about 10:30 tonight."

Kade checked his watch. It was 8:45 now.

"Why didn't we hear about this?" Paul asked, voicing Kade's thought. Five locations at once was a big operation.

"It's happening fast. They decided to keep it off the radar. I didn't even know until twenty minutes ago. But that takes Special Agent Blake out. So even though Lilly Hawthorne has private security, I'm putting you in his place, Kade."

Kade caught Paul's slight smile. His team member obviously had something to do with Kade's assignment. He nodded his thanks.

The good news was that the Vieras might be permanently out of the equation.

Kade might have lost the argument on notifying all the potentials, but he was going to be right where he wanted at midnight tonight.

* * *

"I want to assure you, Mr. Maxwell," the doctor said, coming out of Frances Maxwell's room after his examination, "we're keeping her comfortable. I'm afraid it's only a matter of hours now."

"She's lost her ability to speak?" Percy asked, repeating what he'd heard the nurse say a few minutes ago.

"Yes, it appears so. But she does respond, so I believe she will understand if you have some last words for her." The doctor placed his hand on Percy's shoulder. "I'm sorry."

"Thank you, doctor," Percy said, choosing the proper amount of somber concern and relief at the approaching end of a loved one's suffering.

He checked his watch as the doctor moved away. 11:45. He had to get ready for tonight. But the longer he was seen here at the hospital the better. He smiled. Perhaps one final visit.

Percy entered his mother's room. The head of her bed was littered with machinery, tubes, wires, and beeping monitors. Her face had softened to a sallow mask, no longer the demanding company head, nor the mother who controlled her son's life—or assumed she had.

Her chest rose slowly, straining for each breath. It was amazing how hard the human body fought to live. He'd seen it all in the last nearly two years.

Take Jonathan Fitzpatrick. Who knew the skinny Maxwell COO could thrash around like that? For a few seconds, anyway—until the succinylcholine paralyzed his muscles.

Fitzpatrick had been listening to Chopin and enjoying a glass of wine on the deck of his New York home last night where he lived by himself.

Far too narcissistic to share it with anyone, Percy thought, as the hypodermic slid easily into Fitzpatrick's neck.

They'd actually had an enjoyable conversation, particularly since Fitzpatrick couldn't talk back. While the drug spread through the man's system, Percy told him of the evidence he'd brought along that, when discovered, would hint Fitzpatrick had embezzled nearly a million dollars from Maxwell Enterprises. The money—not that there ever was any, of course—was gone now, untraceable.

"Such a bad boy, Fitz," Percy said, slapping the man on the knee. "Who knew you were capable of such treachery against the generous Maxwells? Of course I'll have to appoint a replacement for you—right after I return from Los Angeles where I'll be visiting my dying mother. Two tragedies for Maxwell Enterprises so close together." He tsk-tsked, a decent imitation of Fitzpatrick, he thought.

The once condescending would-be company head sagged further into the chaise, reduced to life through his eyes and minimally expanding chest. Percy leaned close, cocking his head and smiling as the man's chest exhaled one last time, watching the frightened eyes from inches away as the brain slowly starved from lack of oxygen. Then the light dimmed forever.

Percy let out his own breath and straightened. So satisfying.

He hummed along to one of Chopin's waltzes as he positioned Fitzpatrick's right hand, curling the fingers so they were clutching his upper left arm. Too bad the old boy suffered a heart attack. Corporate life was so very stressful.

After planting the incriminating evidence, Percy had headed for the airport to catch his flight to L.A.

The machines beeped. How long would his mother's chest continue to rise and fall? If she lasted through tomorrow, he could finish his work and still use her as an alibi.

"In some ways, I wish you knew all I've accomplished these last months while I've been *traveling*, Mother." He laughed aloud. If anyone poked their head in the door, he was a bereaved son sharing fond last memories with his mother.

Percy moved closer to the bed, reached out for his mother's hand. Dry, translucent skin revealed the underlying veins pulsing with blood. Not for much longer. He leaned close to her ear.

"I know you wouldn't approve, Mother, but you would be impressed by all I've accomplished these last months. You see, Mother, your son is the Jigsaw Puzzle Killer." Her fingers twitched against his own. "Ah, you've heard of me? Have you read about my ability to kill at will, leaving only a puzzle piece as a clue?"

Percy leaned back at his mother's moan. Her head shifted slightly, lips pressed in what might be a grimace, or perhaps an attempt at speech. When nothing resulted, he leaned close again.

"Twenty-one kills, not counting a few others along the way. You know," he said thoughtfully, index finger on his lips, "maybe I messed up. Should I have sent you pictures of the dead instead of waterfalls and mountains from my travels?"

His mother's hand recoiled from his, crawling toward the call button. Percy moved the device a tantalizing few inches away.

"Have I shocked you?" He chuckled and leaned in again. "Surely you sensed down deep I was capable of this?"

A moan escaped from her lips.

Regret? Horror? Acquiescence?

"I could take your life right now, Mother. Who would suspect foul play when you're hours away from dying?" Percy straightened, looking down on the skeletal woman who had birthed him. "Oh, and no need to thank me for taking care of that annoying Fitzpatrick. When he died, there were a number of crows in a tree by his deck. They're probably pecking his eyes out right now."

"Everything all right, Mr. Maxwell?" a nurse asked, brushing around the curtain. She checked the monitor readings, adjusted an IV flow, and patted his mother's shoulder.

"Yes. I was just telling Mother about some birds I observed when at home in New York. Mother loves birds." Percy sniffed, and dabbed his eyes with a tissue from the box beside the bed. "It's...such a difficult time."

"I'm sorry," the nurse said, turning back to his mother's inert form. "She's such a sweetheart, isn't she?"

Percy was aware Frances Maxwell the businesswoman always doubted his ability to carry on the family leadership in the company. But he had always counted on her long-suffering hope as a mother that he'd someday step up to the challenge. The little hints he'd fed her along the way had worked perfectly, for his mother's last will and testament left everything to him.

He returned the nurse's smile. "I couldn't agree more."

Chapter 35

October 30

Kade inched down the frontage road, the car's headlights dying in a white blur a foot beyond the front bumper. Cold, salty mist swirled in the lowered driver window as he searched for the centerline. Half of the time, he couldn't even see the pavement three feet below. The windshield wipers swiped away moisture, but didn't improve his view. If he met another car...

Weather forecasters had warned of dense coastal fog, and for once they'd gotten it right. LAX was diverting flights to Ontario, Palm Springs, and even Phoenix. Kade had hit a gray wall of the stuff a mile south of the office, and it had thickened more when he descended to the coast and crawled the five miles north on PCH until he finally found the turnoff for the frontage road.

He rolled his neck and checked the dash clock again: 12:02. The drive had taken him nearly three hours.

Even at this time of night, commuter traffic was still a snarled mess on the main road now fifty yards over, but you'd never know it. The thick atmosphere deadened all sound except the popping of gravel under his tires and the whir of the defroster fan.

Foggy summer mornings at the beach were one of his favorite times. Warm and intimate, the dense air magnified the thundering breakers, wrapping the beach in a comforting misty cocoon. The hotter the summer temperatures inland, the more fog got sucked in from the warm ocean, until it reluctantly burned away in late morning.

But tonight it was the plummeting fall temperatures that caused the condensation, coating everything with salty wet. He could almost hear metal rusting.

It was a miracle he noticed a post-mounted mailbox with the address in reflective letters on its side.

The driveway was a mixture of gravel and crushed shell of some kind, and the car tires made a racket. A man with a flashlight stepped out of the mist by Kade's driver window. He slowed to a stop.

"Are you lost, buddy?" the man said. He had on a short jacket, and his right hand was hidden behind his leg.

"I assume you're with Omron International?" Kade said.

"And you are?"

"Special Agent Kaden Hunt. FBI."

"ID, please," the man said, courteous, but his right hand still hidden.

Kade held up his badge. The beam illuminated it briefly, then pointed toward the ground. After the quiet clacking of the man's Kydex holster, he extended his right hand.

"I'm Fin Silvan, with O.I. Call me Fin. Sorry. Can't be too careful."

Kade shook his hand, then followed the flashlight to a spot beside a black SUV sitting alongside a freestanding garage. When he turned off the headlights, it got very dark. He grabbed his jacket and climbed out.

Fin had turned off his flashlight, but Kade's eyes gradually registered some slight diffused illumination from traffic, houses, and streetlights he couldn't see.

"We expected you sooner," Fin said.

"Me too." They stood in silence for a minute, adjusting to the ambient light. "You were at the house. I'm sorry about your coworkers."

"They were good guys," Fin said curtly.

"Not much you can do to prepare against incoming mortars."

Fin didn't respond.

"You've all been briefed about JPK and the 30th?"

The man sighed, the first sign of emotion. "It's bad enough having the Vieras after her, but this serial killer too? And I've got to say, I don't like keeping this from her."

"We're not 100 percent sure she's his target," Kade said. It was the official party line, but Kade didn't believe it.

"To answer your question, everyone here knows about JPK except Kris Stone. She's inside with Lilly. They've become quite close, and I didn't want to put her in an untenable situation, if you know what I mean."

"I understand." If Kade were to go inside, he'd end up telling Lilly about JPK himself. "Tell me about the others here tonight."

"We have four," Fin said.

He introduced Kade to Andy Rivera, a quiet man of slim build that reminded Kade of Paul.

"Andy will patrol up here, keep an eye on the driveway. If it's okay with you, I'll have you roam between Andy and where I'll be."

Kade agreed, and they began walking south along the back of the house, then made a right turn down some stone steps. About ten feet down, Fin stopped and indicated a dark door a few feet off the stairs.

"The house's main entrance is there. The stairs continue down to the lower deck. There's a sliding door entrance off the center of the deck. We keep that locked. It leads to the lower floor of the house, but all the main living space is upstairs." Then he pointed left into the darkness. "I've got a nice little spot behind some big rocks about thirty feet south. You can join me there."

Another O.I. guard named TT was down the ravine near the beach access.

Kade longed to see Lilly. Would she remember? Part of him still hoped she'd blocked out that terrible day. Car chases, explosions, multiple battles, and four gunshot wounds—her stress and physical shock must have been off the charts.

But if he was honest, another part of him wanted her to remember. The door to the house was only a few feet away. What if he knocked?

He shook it off. If he saw her now, he'd be even more distracted.

And what if she answered the door and said, *who are you again?*

No. His job was to get her safely through the next twenty-four hours, past JPK's last October kill day.

* * *

"We go in at 2:00," Roberto said, opening the car trunk. He switched on the second of two GPS units and checked its battery and settings. "It's 1:10 now."

They had parked at a popular surfer access spot about five miles south of the Hawthorne house. The rusty Honda, stolen earlier in the day, fit in with two other vehicles left overnight.

Magda frowned at the smell of alcohol on his breath as he lifted one of the two black duffels and shifted its strap across her shoulders to spread the weight.

"Is tonight the best time to be drinking?"

He retrieved the second duffel and closed the trunk of the car, extinguishing the reassuring light. "Let's go."

Magda stayed close as they moved away from the diffused streetlights, reaching with her ears for the sound of his footsteps. Soon her wetsuit booties sank into the soft sand at the beginning of the beach.

The swirling wet fog pressed from all sides and slid in and out of her lungs like cotton candy. Height, depth, and distance lost meaning in this muffled world where ocean sounds came from all sides. Except for her brother's footsteps, she could be lost in seconds.

The sand grew firm under her feet as they approached the waterline, and the sounds of lapping waves were louder. Another dozen paces had foamy water rushing around her ankles, and she nearly ran into Roberto when he stopped.

He spoke softly into a phone, and a moment later a red light created a glow three times off to their right. "There she is."

Evie Mendez was a black ghost in the night, her dark hair concealed under a skullcap, and her trim figure a blur. The tears that had stained her face at Tommy's memorial were replaced with deadly determination.

"Hello, Magda. Roberto."

228

Her brother grunted a greeting, then began loading the pontoon boat bobbing in the shallow waves. Even in the blackness, it looked too small to take on the open ocean. Fortunately, the night and water were calm, as if the weight of the fog pressed everything flat. However, that quiet would be a liability when they approached the house.

"Thank you, Evie," Magda said, handing off her bag to Roberto. Evie was the only person they could trust tonight.

"This is for Tommy," Evie said in a tone that could induce shivers in a battle veteran. No one who knew the successful realtor from Orange County would believe she had once been sweet on Tommy Viera, nor did they know she personally handled all the Viera property transactions through shell companies.

For the last two years, Magda had watched Evie's romantic interest shift to Roberto, but he was too blind to see the beautiful, loyal woman right in front of him, not even with Magda's hints. Men could be so dense.

"I should be going with you," Evie said, holding the line as Magda climbed into the eight-foot boat.

"Just be here when we return," Roberto ordered.

The hurt was clear on Evie's face, and Magda shook her head. The alcohol was talking.

Still, as she watched her brother settle at the stern and start the motor with a quick pull, she was proud of his leadership in this. It was good to see him take action rather than give assignments to others. And there was nothing impaired about the grim, determined look in his eyes. They would need all that determination and more if they were to be successful tonight.

The rubber boat bobbled. Never the strongest swimmer, Magda wondered if the rear-mounted motor was powerful enough. Roberto insisted a small boat would be less likely to be spotted, but with the fog hugging the water, they could have taken Magda's forty footer and no one would notice.

The boat reversed, and with a lift of her pale hand, Evie faded into the mist.

Magda held one of the GPS units as Roberto steered the boat north on the predetermined course. Moisture quickly coated her face and stung her eyes as the pontoons slapped the sea.

Chapter 36

"It's going on two o'clock. You should get some sleep," Kris said, entering the living room and plopping down in a chair. She was on her feet again pacing before Lilly had time to answer.

"Too much coffee?" Lilly asked.

Kris didn't know it, but earlier in the evening Lilly overheard Fin talking about a credible threat tonight. Lilly had asked several times if there was any word on the Viera raids, but the answer was always no.

It was the same answer as hers: *No way* was she sleeping in a back bedroom tonight while the Vieras attacked. The sofa she'd chosen faced the picture windows, and she was fully dressed beneath the fleece throw.

Kris stopped pacing and pivoted toward the big windows, her form a silhouette against the misty gray. The lights blinded them to anything beyond the cable railing.

There were fifteen more lights on the path leading down to the water. Lilly had helped Dad string them two years ago, right after he'd purchased the property from the estate of a woman whose husband had built it in the 1940s.

The house became Dad's personal project, as in *hands-on* personal. He declared it a good way to get some rare family time. On a break between movie shoots, Lilly and her mom had painted the kitchen and living room, while her father tried his hand at retiling one of the bathrooms.

Lilly quickly snapped off the table lamp, but not before Kris noticed her tears.

"Hey," Kris said, sitting down and pulling her close. They sat quietly for a moment, then Kris said, "Tell me."

Lilly took a shuddering breath, and explained about her dad's desire to keep them grounded by doing some of the house projects themselves instead of hiring contractors.

"I wish I could have been here," Kris said. "Ekaterina Orlov, movie star, convincing herself painting walls was good experience for an upcoming romantic comedy."

Lilly gave a weak laugh, glad it wasn't a sob. "She did hire a professional painter for an hour's instruction on the proper way to hold the paintbrush, and how to pour paint into a roller pan without making a mess. Mom was deliberate about role research."

"With your artistic talent, I bet you were a natural," Kris said. She'd commented on Lilly's drawings framed in the hallway.

Lilly nodded. "I was a pretty neat painter. But my mom… Well, by the end of the day, she had smears all over her clothes, arms, and face."

Lilly's smile widened as she remembered the look on her dad's face when he saw his wife looking totally innocent and hot in a *You've Got Mail* Meg Ryan sort of way.

Her parents had retired early that night, and her mother had never looked softer and more relaxed than she did the next morning.

"They were so in love." The tears came again, but they were mingled with happiness. She hoped she'd find that kind of love someday.

Lilly sagged against Kris, relishing the human contact.

* * *

Magda tried to relax as the inflatable motored through the mist, but it was impossible. Although the ocean was mercifully flat, she couldn't see more than a few feet past the bow.

The glow of the GPS indicated they were on course, but what stood between them and their destination? Rocks? Buoys? Another boat? She narrowed her eyes against the wet, bracing for a collision.

"Relax, Magda," Roberto said and cut the engine. "We're here."

Her brother turned the boat toward shore, and they used paddles to make their way through thankfully small wavelets and froth. A few minutes later, the bow shushed into wet gravel. Magda clambered over the rubber tube, relieved as her booted feet touched solid ground.

Within five minutes they had the boat staked to the beach, and had swapped their wetsuits for black cargo pants, long-sleeve pullovers, and lightweight boots. Robert unpacked their gear.

Magda had only practiced with an assault rifle a few times, preferring instead small caliber handguns. The AR-15s Roberto brought with the night scopes and suppressors weighed several pounds, and hers was going to feel like a sack of potatoes by the time they climbed to the house. But the full auto conversions would be worth it against the girl's guards. A pack around her waist held a dozen thirty-round .223 magazines. With the one already in the rifle, it gave them almost 400 rounds each, enough to take out a small army.

"Let's go," Roberto said, pulling down night vision goggles and walking up the sand.

Magda pulled her goggles down and followed, loving the way he was taking charge of this operation. If there was one thing good about their brothers' deaths, it was bringing back the old Roberto.

However, Magda would be watching him closely, prepared to step in if needed. She was the head of the family.

The path up from the beach was lit by a string of low voltage path lights. Although barely visible tonight to the naked eye, each shone as a brilliant greenish ball through the night vision goggles. The two decks of the house above had four lights each. Only the thick fog kept them from blinding her.

Roberto paused at the first path light at the bottom of the stairs. "Are you ready, Magda?" His voice was quiet and confident. Not a trace of nervousness.

"I am ready." She lifted her weapon.

Roberto threw a small blanket over the light. To anyone above, it would appear the bulb had burned out.

Magda pushed the goggles up and scanned the dark areas between the lights with her rifle scope. Roberto dug around the light fixture until he found the wiring. Using a pair of wire cutters, he snipped the two wires and connected an electrical device that would produce a pulse strong enough to blow the landscape transformer.

"Here we go." He pushed a button, and all the path lights and deck lights blinked out.

Chapter 37

"It's okay," Lilly said when Kris shot off the sofa in the sudden darkness. "The lights are on a timer. Dad programmed them to turn off around two o'clock. What time is it now?"

Kris checked her watch. "It's 1:50. They didn't turn off last night at this time. Or the night before."

"Really?" Lilly felt a little guilty for sleeping those nights while others guarded her. "Maybe the timer failed. It's just a cheap one plugged into the controller box. Dad talked about replacing it."

But Lilly was on her feet too, the awareness of the threat rumor amping up her energy level. The only light in the room came from a scattering of LEDs by the television and a nightlight plugged into a socket by the kitchen. That meant the house power was still on.

Kris frowned, her fingers twitching on the butt of her 9mm. "Where's the timer?"

"It's down on the outside wall at the end of the lower deck where the breaker box is." Lilly had showed its location to Fin when they first moved into the house. "I'll get the flashlight."

"No, you stay here." Kris reached for her radio. "Fin? The deck lights…"

Lilly waited as Kris listened to Fin on her earpiece.

"Right," Kris said. "Lilly says there's a wall-mounted timer by the main electrical panel near the lower deck?…Yeah. I'll go down and get them back on, then call you when I'm back inside," Kris said.

She clicked off the radio and turned to Lilly. "TT is down on the beach path. He called Fin when one of the path lights went out. Then they all went out. They could have shorted, but we don't know."

Lilly had met Terry "TT" Taylor this afternoon when they arrived. The man was a walking mountain. If anyone came up that path…

Kris pulled on a black windbreaker with the Omron logo on the left breast. Her right hand rested on her gun's grip as she opened the door and did a quick check outside. "Lock it after me."

Lilly did as instructed, then went to the kitchen where her purse was. She unzipped the side pocket and removed her .32 caliber and two extra magazines. Although she knew it had one round in the chamber and each magazine contained six, she checked anyway, the simple mechanical motions bringing reassurance and a sense of readiness. The gun went in her right back pocket, the extra mags in the left. She glanced at the windows, willing the lights to once again disclose safety beyond the cold wet glass.

Even with the dim nightlight and LEDs, she felt like a goldfish in a well-lit bowl. Tiny hairs on her neck stood at attention, and she shook off a prescient shiver that raced across her shoulders.

"It's only been a couple of minutes." In the quiet room, her voice didn't sound convincing.

Threat assessment.

Lilly ran through the facts. The bad was the Vieras were determined. They had killed Pana, Doug and the other guard at the house, her mom, and severely injured her dad. Although the address of this house wasn't generally known, it wasn't exactly a secret either. She imagined anyone could find it through public records.

She had a gun in her pocket but, as Kris joked, it really was a peashooter, designed for close-range personal defense against a single attacker, not fending off a coordinated attack. For that, she had armed guards outside.

But what if the Vieras got through the guards or around them? Lilly didn't want anyone else dying, and she wasn't willing to sit by if the worst happened. After a last glance at the dark windows, she dashed down the stairs to the lower level and went straight to the gun safe.

When she entered the combination and swung the door wide, the automatic light inside revealed her father's two Mossberg 12 gauge pump shotguns. She was comfortable with their weight and balance, having shot one of them last year when her father took her to a trap range. She'd missed almost every flying clay target, flinching at the massive recoil that turned her shoulder black and blue for a week. She'd sworn off shotguns forever.

But she couldn't argue with their power in a defensive situation. And after her weeks of training on all kinds of weapons with Alexandra and Mike, she now felt more comfortable with shotguns. These had the shorter of the two barrels they came with, designed specifically for home defense situations. The longer barrels used for hunting were in a case in the back of the safe.

She filled the magazine of one gun and pumped a shell into the chamber, then stashed the weapon behind the cushions of the sofa in the seating area for easy access. A sheathed hunting knife was too tempting to pass up, so it and the other shotgun came back upstairs with her. That gun received a similar hiding place in the couch. She placed a spare box of shells under the end table.

It wasn't that Kris or even Fin would give her grief about being armed, but some of the other Omron guys were kind of straight-arrow. Or maybe they were nervous about working with an armed teenage client.

Plus, Fin had mentioned to Kris that an FBI agent had arrived earlier. If it was Special Agent Ron Blake, she had no doubt he'd confiscate her guns if he saw them.

The windows were still dark. She picked up her phone. Fin answered on the first ring.

"What is it, Lilly?"

"Kris isn't back yet, and the lights are still off."

"I'm aware. We're checking it out."

"Call me." She hung up.

The hunting knife was ancient, its leather-wrapped handle blackened from usage and maybe other things she didn't want to think about. Unfortunately, the belt loop on the sheath had rotted long ago, leaving only stubs of papery leather. Lilly pulled the knife free and examined the blade. The steel was honed to a sharp edge, and glistened under the protection of a thin lubricant. There was a story behind why her father had it—and why he had old shotguns when he could afford new ones. The moment he came home, she'd ask him.

A skinny closet off the kitchen held the household supplies. She opened the door and breathed in the tangy flood of pine-scented cleaner, furniture wax, and dust that poured out. When the three of them first explored the newly purchased property, her mother had declared this tiny closet the heart beating under the surface of the home. This surprised Lilly, because at the other house her mother rarely did anything more than wipe down a kitchen counter. Yet here in their slightly shoddy house by the sea, Ekaterina Orlov put her hair up, donned yellow rubber gloves, and scrubbed floors and cabinets with pine cleaner like any other mom.

Lilly ached to move aside the vacuum and brooms, crawl into the narrow space, and close the door. It was crazy, but for a moment she felt her mom here picking out her favorite yellow gloves, a smile on her face so natural it could never be acting.

It was after Mom's comment about the closet that Lilly had fallen in love with this house, cherishing every minute she spent here with either or both parents. The worn edges lacked perfection, making it feel more like a home than a showplace.

And her dad. According to him, the two essentials for any house "with a history" were WD-40 and duct tape. Both were here. The blue and yellow can sat on a shelf, its thin, red nozzle sticking out at the ready. Below the shelf, someone had pounded in a row of large nails, rusty from years of salty humidity. Lilly removed the roll of duct tape from the nail it hung on.

She also grabbed the red plastic emergency flashlight and switched it on. An anemic yellow glow improved only slightly with successive slides of the switch. So much for emergency equipment. She returned it to the shelf and made a mental note to buy new batteries. Or maybe one of those blinding spotlights they advertised on late night TV, one that could light up a ship a quarter mile offshore.

Lilly ripped two long strips of the silver tape and secured the sheathed knife to her right leg at mid-thigh. Even Special Agent Blake couldn't complain about a simple knife. He didn't know she'd been trained in knife fighting. Throwing too, but she'd never practiced with this knife. Hitting flat or on its butt would do little good.

Using only the nightlight to guide her, Lilly went about emptying and rinsing the coffeemaker. The can of coffee was right there, but instead of refilling it and waiting for its snorting gurgles, she stilled, looking again for the missing deck lights. Kris wasn't back, Fin hadn't called, and the lights were still off.

Alexandra had told Lilly to trust her intuition, and her intuition was shouting something was wrong.

Keeping an eye on the windows, she bent down and unplugged the nightlight. Then she pulled the plug on the coffeemaker. Its green light went dark. She stayed low, listening to absolute quiet. No footsteps, no wind, no—

Lilly jumped and swore when the ice maker dumped a finished tray of cubes into the refrigerator's internal bin and began refilling automatically. The water shut off with a thwack that echoed in the still kitchen.

The .32 was in her hand. She didn't remember drawing it.

When her breathing calmed, she put the pistol back in her pocket, then moved to the living room. The only lights in the kitchen were the microwave and stove control panels. The entertainment center had flashing LEDs on the Internet router under the television. They lit the room with dim strobing. A digital clock on a bookcase shone the time in green numerals: "2:01." Kris had been gone about ten minutes.

Muffled thumps came from somewhere outside, and Lilly moved behind the sofa. Were the waves picking up? The sea had gone uncharacteristically flat this afternoon as the gray wall of fog rolled in like a ghost on a stealthy breeze. Sometimes if the waves rose to only a couple of feet, they could break with a thump magnified by the sides of the ravine until it sounded like boots on wooden stairs. Especially when deadened by thick fog.

Whatever the source, it sent shivers up her spine. She reached behind the cushions, her hand touching the stock of the shotgun.

Then a red laser dot jiggled across the ceiling and high on the back wall, and the front windows shattered.

Chapter 38

Percy had barely finished plugging the radio jammer into an outdoor electrical outlet and switching it on when the shooting started.

From his position beside the garage, it sounded like silenced weapons from somewhere down by the beach, answered by loud fire on the south side of the house.

"Fin! Kris!"

Percy jumped at the nearness of the voice and crouched low. A dark figure scuttled around the garage's front corner. His back was to Percy, no more than twelve feet away.

The shooting increased, concussive thumps that vibrated the foggy atmosphere.

"Fin, can you hear me?" the man said into his radio.

A new dark form joined the first man. "What's going on?"

"All hell's breaking loose and my radio's dead."

Percy smiled at the timing. The jammer knocked out all common channels for a quarter mile and disrupted cellular signals.

"You stay here," the new man said. "I'll go help Fin." With that, he vanished into the fog.

Keeping low, the guard shuffled two steps forward like he wanted to run toward the action. He swept the muzzle of his assault rifle back and forth across the parking area from house to driveway entrance, seeking a target.

Except Percy wasn't coming face on.

What opponent would make a frontal attack? Well, obviously

whoever was coming up the ravine on the other side of the house, for one. He shook his head. Those attackers were the opposite of subtle, but they provided a fantastic diversion for Percy's purpose tonight. They had to be connected with the man Percy had killed at Hawthorne's Beverly Hills house. This time it would be Percy who was the first one to the girl. And for that, he'd have to hurry.

He pried a softball-sized rock from the landscaping and hefted it in his right hand. Three pounds, give or take. He closed the distance to the man and slammed the mini boulder into the side of his head. He collapsed like a marionette with its strings severed. Percy dragged the body back along the garage wall and around the back, into the deepest shadow.

He reached into his pocket and pulled out a puzzle piece and tucked it under the body. "Now you'll be famous, because I killed you," he said, chuckling softly.

Moving swiftly, he stripped off the man's jacket and Kevlar vest. Percy donned the vest, then pulled the Omron jacket over it. "Now I'm official."

He picked up the man's rifle and slung its strap over his shoulder. "Always good to have a backup." His own pistol was in a holster strapped to his right leg Western style.

"Andy! Where are you?"

Percy backed away from the body. It was a woman's voice, and it came from somewhere in the dark yard. This place was like Grand Central. He couldn't see anyone, but her voice was older. Not Lilly. Probably looking for the dead guard. Perfect. She'd be busy up here while Percy was inside the house. He kept backing up.

Since all the action was coming from the left side of the house and down below, Percy scurried away from the garage and around the right corner of the rear of the house. There wasn't really a path down this side, so he carefully picked his way over jagged boulders and around cactus plants.

In a couple of minutes, he'd made it down the slope to the corner of the house. The lower deck extended about ten feet beyond the right edge of the house, and its top rail wrapped around the end of the deck and returned to the side of the house in front of him. Simple to climb over.

He'd just put his hand on the railing when bullets sprayed the deck and house. Percy jumped back, hugging the side wall and breathing hard. Some of those had come close. They were from a rifle or rifles with sound suppressors, but the slugs were every bit as deadly if they hit you.

"Hmm. What to do?" he whispered to himself.

* * *

Kade had made it into the brushy landscaping south of the house, directly upslope from Fin. It was even darker out here, and he was surrounded by three-foot shrubs that provided hiding places. He'd have to make his way down to Fin's position.

The breeze off the ocean picked up, dampening his clothing and coating his face and eyelashes. The heavy air shook with the muffled explosions and unmistakable clacking of silenced assault rifles cycling. Breaking glass and splintering wood followed each burst. Fin's answering fire was loud and rapid.

The bad guys definitely had the advantage. They were using illegal fully automatic rifles, whereas the Omron AR-15s were semi-automatics—legal, but not as good in a situation like this.

And Kade was stuck with only his 9mm pistol.

And where was Kris? Before Andy's radio crapped out, he told Kade she was going to check on the landscape lighting. If she hadn't been hit, she was probably back inside or pinned down somewhere.

The crack of overlapping gunfire came sharp and loud as Kade felt his way down the gravel slope. He wished he'd had time to get a better sense of the property layout. The dark and fog made it impossible to see more than a few feet. But that didn't prevent the occasional bullet from streaking by inches above his head.

He initially had his gun out, but finally stuffed it back in his holster, needing both hands to crawl and fend off the thorny shrubs. The firing got louder as the gravel transitioned to flat stone. He just had to make it across this flat area and he could drop down next to Fin.

He lifted his head. It wouldn't do to be mistaken for the enemy.

"Fin!" Kade said between firing. "It's Kade. I'm coming in."

A red laser dot speared the rock a few feet away and stitched a line of explosions toward him. Kade dove off the ledge and tumbled into the depression, coming to rest against a body.

"Get off me, you idiot!" Fin said.

"Sorry." Kade rolled off the man's legs and hunkered down.

On his knees, Fin fired several shots from his semi-automatic rifle, then ducked down. "My radio's out. Are Andy and Kris okay?"

Kade told him Andy's radio was out too. "They must be using a jammer. Andy's fine. Staying put. I thought Kris might be with you."

Bullets zinged off rocks. Through a crack between the boulders, Kade made out dim muzzle flashes below. They were probably using night vision scopes like Fin.

"Do you think Kris is back inside?" Kade asked, sparing a glance at the dark house. He hoped Lilly wasn't all alone in there.

"No idea. Last thing she said before the radio failed was the timer was toast. Said something about getting wire from the car to use as a jumper."

The assault was coming from the ravine leading up from the beach. Kade hadn't met TT, but there was no return fire down there. He asked Fin about him, but he didn't answer. Kade feared the man was out of the fight.

The sound suppressors the attackers used made it difficult to hear how many weapons were firing, especially with the loud returns from Fin.

"How many?" Kade asked.

"Two, I think." Fin showed his rifle to Kade. The front of its scope was peeled back in a jagged tear, split open by a bullet. "Lucky I wasn't sighting through this at the time."

That meant the Omron guard was shooting blind.

Fin dug into a duffle at his feet and pulled out two magazines. "There's a spare AR and ammo in the car. I'm gonna need it soon. Plus, we've got to get those lights on."

Kade rolled onto his back. Thirty feet to the house, then down the stairs to the lower level where the controller was. The ocean-side of the path to the house was lined with rocks the size of soccer balls. They would block the view from below if he stayed to the back edge of the path.

"Is there cover where the light controller is?"

"Maybe." Fin glanced at the house. "I'm not positive."

"I'll go."

"It's a shooting gallery out there."

"Cover me." He swiveled around on his belly until he was facing the house.

"Wait," Fin said. He let loose a short burst, then bent toward Kade. "The landscape light controller is on the lower corner of the house with three or four other boxes. The one you want is the farthest right. Maybe there's an override switch or something. If Kris went up to the car, she'll never make it back down the stairs with this incoming fire."

That Fin didn't say Kade wouldn't make it up and back either, didn't escape Kade. If he couldn't get the lights on, he might be stuck there. He had his pistol and six spare magazines. It wasn't much when facing down advancing automatic weapons.

"If you get the lights on, that'll kill their night vision for a few seconds. That might give you time to get up to the SUV and grab more ammo and the other AR."

Kade's heart was already threatening overload, and what vision he had narrowed in response to the flood of adrenaline.

Using only elbows, toes, and knees, he army-crawled along the gritty path. Fin laid down covering fire behind him, burning through copious quantities of ammo. Kade *had* to survive and make this work.

As he crawled, he began wondering if he'd hear the shot that killed him. He'd never know if Fin and the others overcame the enemy. Never know if Lilly was safe.

The shooting from below had stopped for the time being. Maybe Fin's last volley had done some damage. Grit cut into his elbows, and his pant legs were ripped at the knees by the time he reached the spot where the sheltering rocks ran out. Ahead was three or four feet of exposed path. He took two deep breaths, wondering again if he'd hear the final shot, then scrambled across the opening and onto the stairs.

The rock treads gouged his hands as he pulled himself headfirst down the stairs and onto a small concrete landing that abutted the lower deck. He wedged himself into the space where the house met the ground, making as small a target as possible.

Mounted on the wall above were the main electric panel, meter, and three weatherproof boxes. The fog must have thinned, because there was enough glow from overhead to make out the flat main panel, the glass electric meter, and three weather proof boxes to the meter's right.

The left of the three boxes had several thin wires trailing out the bottom and snaking into a plastic pipe at ground level. Probably a sprinkler controller. The middle box had wire feeding from the top. Maybe the telephone or cable television. The box on the right looked newer. Two thick, dark wires were stapled down the wall and disappeared into the sand, typical of low-voltage landscape lighting. Bingo. He scooted back until he was under that one.

He stretched his arm up, expecting bullets to rip his flesh any second. The box's cover was hanging partly open. He lifted it up higher and leaned back so he could peer inside. A white timer dial was blackened and partially melted on one side. He wiggled the timer until it came free from its socket and fell to the path. It emitted a pungent, burned electrical odor.

Now he could see the rest of the interior. There was a toggle switch in the upper right corner in the down position. He snapped it up, but nothing happened.

If the timer had shorted, it might have tripped a breaker. He felt along both sides of the box inside and out. Nothing on the bottom, either. The top of the box was out of reach.

Fin laid down a full magazine of fire, and Kade rose into a crouching position and slid his hand across the box's top. A button switch was popped up tight against its silicone cover. He pushed it down and lights bathed the deck in brilliant white.

He hoped Fin's assumption the attackers would be temporarily blinded was correct. Kade sprinted up the stairs as the shooting from below resumed.

"Andy, it's Kade Hunt!" he shouted when he reached cover at the top of the stairs. "Fin needs more ammo."

There was no answer, but with all the shooting, Kade wasn't certain Andy could hear him, especially if the man was patrolling out by the road. Kade's ears were still ringing from Fin's rifle fire.

Kade sprinted low across the yard, angling right of the garage to the cars. He expected Andy to pop out of hiding any second, and he hoped the guard wouldn't start shooting.

The SUV's interior lights were blinding when he opened the rear hatch, but he needed them to search through the several zippered black canvas bags. Two had spare vests and utility belts. He tossed those aside. Another contained a dozen or more boxes of 9mm cartridges and several preloaded handgun magazines. He slung the strap over his shoulder.

Hurrying, he ripped open the zippers on the remaining bags, stopping when he revealed an AR-15 with a night scope, several loaded magazines, and boxes of ammunition. Exactly what Fin needed.

Kade's vision was shot from the light, but he didn't dare take time for it to adjust. He retraced his path across the yard. The stairs weren't an option now, so he headed out into the scrubby landscape once again.

The attack from below was undoubtedly the Vieras, but he still expected JPK to put in an appearance sometime in the next twenty or so hours—whatever was left of the October 30th. Whether anyone else believed it or not, Kade had to be ready for him.

He wished he'd had time to reinforce that with Andy. And if he saw Kris, he'd definitely tell her. And Lilly too. Orders be damned.

First, they had to end this attack.

* * *

As soon as the bullets stopped hitting the living room ceiling and wall, Lilly reached over the back of the sofa and dragged the shotgun out. Shoving it along in front of her, she crawled toward the kitchen bar. The cabinets provided a lot better protection than stuffed furniture.

When she reached the end of the bar, she sat on her butt with her legs out straight, the shotgun across her thighs. It was then she remembered the box of shells under the end table. The open space between her and the table sparkled with glass. With the deck lights back on, she'd be like a target in a shooting gallery. She had six shells in the shotgun. That might have to do.

Or she could go downstairs and get several more boxes from the safe. Seeing the damage done by the bursts from the Vieras, she was going to need all the ammo she could get.

The stairs were between her and the back hallway, a shorter, safer route than across the living room floor.

A volley of shots outside provided the motivation needed. She shoved the shotgun toward the stairs and army-crawled after it.

Her elbows and forearms were bloodied with bits of glass by the time she covered the distance to the stairs, reminding her of the van, Ernesto, the broken windshield grinding into her back. If she could survive that, these little cuts were nothing, but she was getting damned tired of being sliced up due to the Vieras.

She slid halfway down the stairs on her belly before spinning around to her feet.

Once at the bottom, she propped the shotgun beside the safe and squatted down even with the numbered dial. A single nightlight lit the lower room. Even with the outside lights now back on, she needed every glimmer as she fiddled with the combination dial. It took three tries before the handle released and the heavy door swung open. At the same time, she heard a scraping behind her.

Lilly spun around, pressing her back against the open safe. A man stepped through a foot-wide opening in the sliding door from the deck. It had been locked. She'd checked it herself. The shotgun was out of reach behind the open safe door. Stupid.

Drop to the floor, tug the door closed, grab the shotgun, slide up the safety at the same time she aimed and pulled the trigger.

"Lilly? Are you all right?"

He was in silhouette, but the dim light revealed the white Omron lettering stitched above his left breast, and she exhaled her panic.

"I'm fine. Are you Andy?" He was the only one she hadn't met, and she was surprised how small he was. Most of the Omron guys were beefy ex-military. "I'm just getting more shotgun shells." She turned back to the safe and began grabbing 12 gauge boxes. A click sounded behind her.

"I wouldn't do that, if I were you."

Lilly turned. The assault rifle was leveled at her.

Chapter 39

A new volley of close hits sent Kade tumbling downhill through the scratching, poking branches. The metal-filled duffle bags struck him repeatedly, and he tucked his arms close and protected his face until he went airborne and slammed onto something flat and very hard.

"'Bout time," Fin said, helping untangle the straps from Kade's arms.

"You're welcome."

Fin pulled out the new rifle, switched on the scope, and pointed the weapon through a crack in the rocks. "I thought I saw someone shooting upslope not far below the house," he said, scanning the area. "They may be moving in."

"Kris?" Kade asked.

"Haven't seen her," Fin mumbled, his cheek against the weapon's stock. "Andy?"

"Didn't see him," Kade said.

"Where the hell—"

Bullets chipped off rock shards all around them, and they ducked for cover. It was an incredible fusillade, covering fire for something. But all they could do was keep their heads down for the moment.

All the while, Kade wondered if Lilly was safe and where JPK was.

* * *

"I don't understand, Andy" Lilly said. "What are you doing?"

He laughed, an unpleasant sound like hinges unoiled for decades.

"I'm not Andy. I'm the one who saved you in your backyard...when that man tried to kill you. Remember?"

"What are you talking about?" Hadn't Fin killed Tommy Viera?

"Now it's my turn," he said, taking a step forward.

"Turn for what?" She shifted the weight of the boxes to her left hand so her right would be free to draw the pistol in her pocket.

He took another step. "You're mine, now."

His head suddenly cocked sideways, like an insect inspecting its prey.

The movement sent a bolt of recognition up her spine. The man in the elevator.

Outside, a large figure that dwarfed the small man inside landed on the deck with a loud thump. He was dressed all in black. Even his rifle was dull black and oddly quiet as he swept the room left to right in a sustained burst.

The bullets weren't quiet, though, shattering the door glass, artwork, walls, and furniture. Lilly dropped, cowering against the safe. It was dark enough she wasn't sure the man could see her.

The little man inside dropped and rapid-fired the semi-automatic as he rolled. His bullets swept an arc up the big man's left leg, through his pelvis, stomach, chest, and finally across his face. The force of the hits carried the man backward, and his head exploded in a dark mist at the same time his back hit the railing. He teetered there for a second as the bullets punched him again and again. Then his feet came up and he toppled over.

The man inside got to his knees, ejected the spent magazine, and fumbled another into the rifle's receiver, slapping it home. He leveled it at her again.

Then the air split with bullets from outside. They tore up the deck rails, exploded through the remaining glass in the slider, and shredded the ceiling.

The little man was lying on the floor as the shooting stopped and dust rained down.

Lilly rose to a crouch. She didn't know who the man outside had been, but she knew the one inside wasn't from Omron. And he intended her harm.

Before he could rack another shell into the rifle's chamber, she had her pistol out and was firing. At twenty feet she didn't miss, but he didn't go down. Instead he brought the rifle around and clicked the trigger at the same time as her final pull.

Two clicks. Hers was empty. His was jammed.

He swore in the sudden silence and cleared the weapon. As he brought it up again, Lilly dove for the stairs, bullets tearing the air where she'd been, following her and chewing up the bottom part of the stairwell as she scrambled up and out of his line of sight.

* * *

Magda fired again and again at the two men behind the rocks. She could not get closer because of their fire, and she was unable to take them out because of their cover. But at least she could distract them long enough for Roberto to reach the lower deck.

Movement at the house drew her attention, and she saw her brother climb onto the deck. He opened fire into the sliding door.

Then Roberto staggered back, his body jerking.

"No!" Magda screamed. She watched in disbelief as he plunged onto rocks below. "Roberto."

The shooting had come from inside the house. From the girl.

Magda stood up and emptied a full magazine at the house.

* * *

Kade swiveled his head at the sound of silenced fire followed by a loud, semi-auto rifle. It was coming from the lower part of the house.

"They're inside! Cover me!" Kade shouted. But before he could sprint for the house, bullets peppered the rocks.

Fin returned fire, then tossed two empty mags to Kade. "Reload these, then I'll cover you."

Kade ground his teeth, but he had no choice. They were pinned down. He hoped Fin's scope would find a target soon.

Chapter 40

Lilly scrambled up the stairs and into the kitchen on hands and knees. She'd dropped her pistol somewhere on the stairs. The two spare magazines in her back pocket were of zero use now. And both shotguns were downstairs. Resting the shotgun behind the safe door had been supremely stupid.

The ringing in her ears was subsiding, and she heard grunting and thumping on the stairs. He was coming, and her options were limited. Hide somewhere in the house and hope the good guys beat the bad guys before one of them found her, or escape outside and hide in the dark.

She had seconds to decide.

Pull the trigger.

She gathered her feet under her for a sprint to the front door. She was almost past the end of the bar when a red laser tracked back and forth across the shattered living room. Lilly skidded to a stop and scrambled back to cover. The exit might as well be a hundred yards away. She'd never make it. And if she did, they'd cut her down the second she stepped outside.

The cleaning closet wasn't much of a sanctuary, but it was all she had. Lemon and pine. In the pitch black, she shoved the vacuum aside and crouched on her haunches at the back of the space. She felt for the hunting knife, but her fingers found only the crumbling leather and duct tape.

It must have slipped out of the sheath when she scrambled up the stairs escaping from... Who was that guy? If that was one of Vieras on the deck—and because of the silenced assault rifle, that made the most sense—who was the guy inside? He said he'd killed Tommy Viera. None of it made sense, except that he'd tried to kill her.

She shook her head. That wasn't going to happen. But she needed a weapon.

Closing her eyes, she visualized everything in the closet. Her dad had always been a MacGyver fan. Lilly hadn't cared for the show that much, but she'd sat through at least a dozen DVD episodes, happy to spend time with Dad between his projects. Now she wished she'd paid more attention.

The tools were out in the garage, so no screwdrivers, utility knives, or hammers. The flyswatter wouldn't do much good. Neither would the sponges, plastic buckets, or dust rags.

Lilly felt along the walls, going slowly so she wouldn't knock something over. Broom, mop, extension cord, toilet plunger. At least the plunger had a wooden handle. It was light weight, but might make a good club. She pulled it off the nail it hung on.

Nails!

Rusty metal bit into her hand as she wiggled one of the big spikes below the shelf. The first one broke off, too short to be any use. She gave up on the next two, which wouldn't budge. But the fourth one was loose, and a little tugging got it free. It was bigger and longer than the nail the plunger had been hanging on. She tried it in the hole on the wooden plunger handle. It was a tight fit. She pressed the nail's head against the floor until it was flush with the side of the round handle. The sharp end of the nail protruded out the other side about three inches. Perfect.

She unscrewed and set the bulbous plunger end aside. Her weak imitation of a gladiator's spiked club would have to do.

If the door opened—*when* the door opened—she'd have one chance to spring and fight.

Violence of action.

There would be no giving up. She'd hit with all she had, then keep going until he was dead. Or she was.

Total commitment.

She hated the thought of her dad being left alone. His recovery was already tough enough.

Even more, she hated that the Vieras might win.

Kris was out there somewhere. And Fin.

Lilly gripped the club tighter. This was where Kris would tell her how important faith was.

Yea, though I walk through the valley of the shadow of death…

Lilly checked the position of the nail in her club.

…I will fear no evil; for You are with me.

* * *

Percy left the assault rifle behind. He needed both hands to crawl up the stairs. Two holes in his left leg and one on the side of his neck were from the girl. The Kevlar vest had protected his torso. His wounds left a trail of blood behind as he ascended.

Normally he'd be more careful about leaving DNA at the scene, but it didn't matter. Not after he started the fire. Lilly Hawthorne had escaped for the last time.

His paused halfway up to rest. The puzzle pieces in his pocket called him, and he slipped his hand in. He'd brought six; used one. Should have tossed another after the guy on the deck.

When he began to crawl again, he touched something metallic and sharp. A knife about ten inches long, the blade half its length. Had Lilly dropped this? Was she planning to use it on him?

"So fitting, Lilly Hawthorne. This is what I'll use on you."

He wedged the blade into the thick vest and continued his climb.

At the top of the stairs, the carpet sparkled with glass, reflecting red LEDs from the entertainment center like a roomful of rubies.

He paused again to rest and listen. An apparition of fog floated through the shattered view-windows, ferrying odors of seaweed and rotting things. Or maybe that was from the blood running from his neck. Hot liquid soaked his pant leg, quickly becoming cold and stiff down to his ankle and boot.

Lilly Hawthorne was a worthy adversary.

Before this, he'd never considered his victims anything but just that: victims. But now he found one who fought back. Her little cap pistol had stung him.

She wasn't fighting fair, of course. Having a security team was hardly the same as one-on-one with him. Without them, she wouldn't stand a chance against his cunning. When he beat her, everyone would know JPK couldn't be stopped. He'd kill at will, always unexpected, and disappear without a trace, leaving only a puzzle piece behind. The world would live in fear.

Percy groaned as he put pressure on his leg, and leaned against the wall, panting while dizziness passed. He'd have to get to a doctor soon. And what doctor wouldn't believe Percy's story that he, head of Maxwell Enterprises, was mugged and shot by some thug with a small caliber weapon? He'd get the best of care while the police searched for the nonexistent thief. Later, he'd make a sizable contribution to the department for needed equipment or their police widows' fund. He couldn't stop a choking laugh.

"Lil-ly," he singsonged softly, hoping she could hear him, anticipate what was to come.

Where would she go to hide? Not outside. Too many bullets flying. Misty air brushed his cheek. In it he detected the faint smells of pine and lemon furniture polish.

Percy fingered the knife hilt. "Time to play."

Chapter 41

Kade heard the loud cracking of semi-auto fire below. "That sounds like—"

"TT," Fin said, the hope evident in his voice.

"Or someone with his gun," Kade cautioned. But the bullets were no longer hitting around them. Kade took that as a good sign.

More shooting came from below, a mix of silenced and non-silenced, the most intense exchange yet.

"It's got to be TT," Fin said. He was using the scope, trying to locate a target. "The fog's too thick at this distance. I can't see anything clearly. Sounds like the shooting is getting farther away."

He was right. The cracking wasn't as sharp, and they echoed more off the ravine's walls.

"I'm going," Kade said when everything remained quiet.

"No, I—" Fin began.

"You have the heavy firepower," Kade said to Fin. "Stay here in case I need cover." Before the man could object, Kade took off at a low sprint, pulling his gun as he went. No time for crawling.

The house wall gave him a modicum of protection as he peeked around the corner onto the lower deck where the shooting had been. Empty. The deck lights lit it up like a shooting gallery.

Kade held his breath and scampered along the deck, hugging the house until he reached a pile of glass and gaping hole where the sliding door used to be.

A single nightlight illuminated the room inside, but enough additional light filtered in from the deck to show the room was unoccupied. Kade hustled inside, veered right, and put the solid wall at his back.

Across the room, a gun safe stood open. A shotgun was propped behind the safe door. Kade kept to the room's perimeter until he reached the bottom of the stairs. Black streaks stained the light carpet on the steps.

Blood. He prayed it wasn't Lilly's.

Had one of the Vieras made it inside?

A quick check up the stairs showed them clear. Kade had taken one step up when a hand landed on his arm.

"Agent Hunt?"

The fact the harsh whisper was female was the only thing that kept him from dropping and firing. He spun around and slammed her against the wall.

"Who are you!" he hissed, pinning her arms.

"Kris Stone."

"Kris? Where have you been?" He backed up a few inches, and noticed the front of her jacket. It was glossy with fresh blood, and some had transferred to him. "Are you hurt?"

"No, I was helping Andy." She pulled him farther away from the open stairs. "He was… Someone bashed in his skull."

She sagged against the wall.

"I was up there a little while ago. I called out but didn't see either of you."

She gave a long sigh. "I didn't hear you. When I went up earlier, I heard a moan. I found him behind the garage in some bushes. I tried calling 9-1-1 but I couldn't get through." She looked at him. "I couldn't leave him. I held him until he died."

Kade gripped her arm. "You did the right thing."

A sob wracked her body.

"No one should be alone like that," Kade said. "But now we need to find Lilly."

Kris shook herself and wiped her eyes. Then she mentioned Andy's missing clothes. "Someone's trying to blend in. When I heard the shooting down here on the lower level, I circled down the far side of the house. What's going on?"

Kade gave her a ten-second briefing on JPK.

"Lilly's his target?"

"It's not certain, but the Vieras wouldn't take Andy's jacket."

Kade started up the stairs, but stopped midway. Something besides blood shined on the tread beside his shoe. He reached down and picked up the tiny object less than an inch square. It was a jigsaw puzzle piece. He held it up for Kris to see.

"JPK."

Upstairs, someone screamed.

Chapter 42

The closet door whipped open.

Lilly let loose a head-high blast of WD-40, then dropped the can and swung her makeshift spike club.

The man reared back, wiping his eyes. The nail missed his face and chest, plunging instead through the top of his boot. He screamed a high-pitched wail, but surprised her by lunging in and grabbing a fist-full of her hair.

Lilly drove forward, propelling them both across the room until his back cracked into the counter. She cocked her arm and punched him in the neck, then gouged at his eyes, missing as he ducked his chin and kneed her away.

She crouched, watching as he pulled a big knife—*her* knife. He rubbed his eyes, the lubricant shining on his face. The only light came from the low deck fixtures outside, casting shadows on the kitchen ceiling and bathing the room in surreal gray. But the glint off the five-inch blade was clear enough.

"Time for you to die," he croaked, holding his neck. Blood seeped between his fingers.

Her bullet had been close.

Long scarlet gouges appeared on his check from her fingernails, and his pant leg was slick with blood. The advantage was hers. As long as he held the knife, he couldn't go for the gun on his right hip. When he realized that…

"I don't think so," she taunted, feinting left. He lunged with the knife. Lilly dodged right and pulled four steak knives from the block next to the stove. Her first throw stuck in his left shoulder. He jerked in surprise, but didn't slow his advance.

She avoided a wild slash of the hunting blade, but he backhanded her across the face with his other hand, spinning her along the counter and sending her remaining knives flying.

The blow blurred her vision, and her ears rang worse than from the gunshots. Even injured, he moved like a cat. She focused on the knife point a yard away.

Sudden, blinding light from the overhead light fixture chased away the dark.

"Drop it!" a man shouted from behind her attacker.

He spun and threw the knife. The blade buried itself in the other man's gut, and he fell back into someone else, sending both to the floor.

But the attacker's spin had tangled the plunger handle between his legs. He stumbled while drawing his gun, waving it for balance.

Lilly screamed and leaped on his back, twisting her fingers into his hair for purchase. Bloody clumps pulled free as she rode him down and slammed his face into the floor.

The fall knocked the plunger spike free of his boot. Lilly scrambled off the man and brought the club down again and again, driving the spike as deep as she could in every vulnerable part of his neck, arms, torso, and legs.

Violence of action.

She straddled his prostrate body. Swing, wrench it free.

Overwhelm your opponent.

Swing, wrench it free. The wooden handle vibrated in her hands.

Unrelenting attack.

She swung again, unwilling to even think of him getting up...

"Lilly!"

...the murdering piece of—

"Lilly, stop!"

Lilly paused, her breath coming in rapid gasps. Sweat made the plunger handle slippery, but she kept it raised, ready to bring it down if the man under her so much as twitched.

"Kris! You're all right. I thought... You didn't come back."

Kris was bent over the other man, who was curled away in a fetal position and rocking in pain. White letters across the back of his jacket said FBI.

"Have you got something to tie him up?" Kris asked, nodding her head toward the attacker. She kept her hands buried in the agent's stomach. "I'm trying to stop the bleeding."

Secure the weapons. Secure the perp.

Lilly kicked the man hard in the side and got a weak moan in response. Keeping one foot on his back, she wrenched his right hand out from under him, bringing the gun with it. It was a Glock model she was familiar with. She checked the loads and slipped it into the back of her jeans.

An orange fifty-foot extension cord from the broom closet fit her need, and she used every inch, wrapping it under her attacker's limp body and securing the ends with duct tape. The man wouldn't get free without wire cutters.

Satisfied with the bindings, she ran to get some clean towels and came back to Kris.

"Is it agent Blake?" Lilly brushed the hair from the man's face. His eyes opened at her touch.

"It's not Blake," Kris said. "His name is—"

"Agent Gray Eyes," Lilly whispered.

"Palomino." His voice was hoarse with effort, eyes clinched in pain, but they stayed locked on hers.

"You two know each other?" Kris asked.

"No," they both said at the same time.

"Uh, huh," Kris said.

The wail of sirens floated through the shattered windows, growing louder and louder until the tone sharpened when they turned into the driveway and came toward the house.

"Finally," Kris said. "Lilly, can you keep pressure on his wound? The radios are still out, and I've got to find Fin and make sure it's safe for whoever is coming."

"I'm not going anywhere," Lilly said, kneeling. The agent groaned when she replaced Kris's hands with her own. Blood flowed through her fingers, hot and metallic.

Kris kept low going out the front door.

At some point, the shooting outside had stopped. And even with the kitchen lights on, it was still quiet.

Her hands trembled as she pressed her fingers tighter around the sharp steel.

Don't die. Please don't die.

So much blood.

God, don't let him die.

Outside, the siren stopped.

"Hang in there, Agent Gray Eyes. Help is on the way."

She was rewarded with a weak smile.

Chapter 43

Syl Straasberg arrived twenty minutes after the cops had disabled the signal jammer and Lilly was able to call her.

"Sorry it took so long," Syl said, coming into Lilly's bedroom in the back of the house. "Those line cops were harder to navigate than the fog."

"Thanks for coming."

"It's what I do," Syl said, slinging her purse onto Lilly's desk. "Did you call your attorney like I suggested?"

"She should be here any…"

Abigail Coddington swept into the bedroom with a sleep-deprived assistant in tow. "Talk to no one except me. Got it?" Abigail dragged her assistant out to survey the scene.

"The weather people are calling this the worst fog in recent memory," Syl said. "Even with that, there were two press vans setting up when I pulled in. I'd better go talk to them before they start making up stories."

Lilly sank onto the bed and leaned against the headboard. Syl would dribble out tidbits of information to keep the hungry reporters onsite as long as possible. Tomorrow would be a huge news day.

The police had already told Lilly the whole property from the beach to the frontage road was a crime scene. The street was cordoned off for blocks in each direction.

Lilly wrapped a down comforter around her shoulders, burrowing into its warmth. Now that the adrenaline had drained away, she shook with cold. No one dared turn on the heater until the gas company did a thorough inspection. The EMTs had cleaned and bandaged the glass cuts on her arms and legs, but she'd insisted she did not need to go to the hospital and refused everything except Tylenol.

Syl came back briefly and reported a turf war for control of the investigation was underway. So far, the FBI was winning.

Kris had been in earlier, the strain around her eyes evident. Andy's body had gone to the morgue. Between the Beverly Hills house and here, they'd lost three people. Her hands and clothes were stained with dried blood.

Lilly had scrubbed hers, but dark still showed under her fingernails. She'd walked with Kade Hunt as they carried him to the ambulance. It took all her strength to remain behind with Kris as it screamed away, lights flashing.

Fin stopped in to make sure she knew about Andy. "I knew you'd want to know."

Lilly appreciated being treated like an adult. She'd overheard two cops talking in the hall earlier, referring to her as "just a kid."

"TT was knocked out at the start of the shooting when he dove into some rocks," Fin said. "The rocks protected him. When he woke up, he engaged the last assailant, whom he was sure was a woman."

"Magda Viera," Lilly said. Cruelty evidently wasn't limited to one gender.

"Most likely." Fin shifted uncomfortably on Lilly's small desk chair, glancing up as Special Agent Ron Blake filled the doorway.

"Yes, we're pretty confident it was her," Blake said, stepping inside and bringing with him cold, wet air.

A specialty of his.

Lilly tucked the end of the comforter around her feet.

"We've identified the man who fell off the deck as her brother Roberto," Blake said.

Abigail returned and listened as Blake told them about tonight's simultaneous raids.

"We're guessing Roberto and Magda were out of reach by the time of the raids. Unfortunate. If they'd heard about the raids, they might not have proceeded with the attack. Our guys found blood in the sand as well as footprints and grooves at the waterline indicating a boat landing. The Coast Guard and every coastal group for fifty miles are searching for her."

"If it was Magda and Roberto," Lilly said, "who was—"

Blake put his hand to his ear radio for an incoming call. "Go ahead." He listened for a minute, then replied, "Is Special Agent Cartwright here yet? All right, don't touch the puzzle piece. She needs to see it before it's bagged. I'll be right there."

"What was that about?" Fin asked.

"The coroner found a jigsaw puzzle piece under your comrade's body," Blake said, his mouth a tight line. "Another one was on the inside stairs, stuck in blood."

"A puzzle piece?" Lilly said. "Like that serial killer, JPK?"

Blake nodded—somewhat reluctantly, Lilly thought.

"So Hunt was right about JPK targeting Lilly?" Fin asked.

"Wait a minute," Lilly said. "You mean the FBI knew I was JPK's next victim? That's why Hunt was here? Why didn't anyone tell me?"

"It's complicated," Blake deadpanned.

"Complicated?" Lilly yelled at the man. "Like in *no-one-thought-to-tell-me-there-was-another-nut-job-trying-to-kill-me* complicated?"

Blake grimaced. "Special Agent Margaret Cartwright will be here in a few minutes. She's in charge of the JPK investigation, and she'll answer all your questions."

And with that, he escaped, the coward.

Lilly sagged into her bed pillows, the weight of Blake's news sinking in.

Distantly, she heard Fin apologize and excuse himself—something about his boss at Omron calling, and if Fin didn't call him back immediately, he'd be looking for work. He closed the bedroom door on the way out.

She'd been wondering about the man she fought hand-to-hand. The local police assumed he was part of the Vieras, even when she insisted he shot Roberto Viera.

That little man who said, "You're mine, now," who screamed like a girl when she spiked him? That was the infamous Jigsaw Puzzle Killer?

She began to laugh. With the release came tears, followed by deeper sobs that wracked her body and soaked the pillow she clutched. She didn't even know what she was crying about. The escape from a threat she'd known nothing about? The defeat of one more Viera? No. They weren't worth tears. But Andy's death was. And Kade's injury.

Her tears ran dry, sheer weariness preventing a total breakdown. The clock on her nightstand read 5:07.

The table lamp cast a soft glow on the opposite wall. Over twenty drawings covered the space, some framed and hung, some thumbtacked to the drywall. A few were her earlier ones, crude sketches in pencil or charcoal as she learned the techniques.

The last two were award winners from an art fair held each year on the boardwalk at Venice Beach. Both were colored pencil drawings of horses running on the beach with surfers and sailboats in the background. Mom had liked them so much she'd arranged for a company to print copies for sale, and a dozen local galleries moved a few copies each month. It was Lilly's first foray into salable art, and she liked the feeling.

That all seemed part of another world, another life. A *normal* life, not her *Mission Impossible* franchise.

She snuggled down in the comforter, vaguely aware of Syl talking in the hall, shooing everyone away. With all that had happened tonight, sleep wouldn't come easy.

That was her last thought.

* * *

"Lilly. Wake up." Syl stood by Lilly's bed.

"What time is it?" Her voice cracked with fatigue, and her eyes were gritty. She rubbed feeling into her face.

"A little after 10:00 a.m. Sorry. I didn't want to wake you so soon, but the authorities are anxious to talk with you...get your take on what happened here."

"Fin and Kris?"

"Their interviews are complete. Fin insisted on doing them here because they are still on the job…"

Guarding her.

"…and the police won't let any relief Omron employees inside the crime zone."

Lilly crawled off the bed and nearly collapsed. Every muscle hurt or at least yelled out a noisy protest. She needed a hot tub.

"The police asked them to wait in their vehicles up on the driveway so they don't get in the way. "

At least Lilly got a few hours sleep. Fin and Kris must be dead on their feet.

"Also, we all have to vacate the house. I have workmen coming later to board up the windows so the police can seal it up for tonight."

Lilly hadn't thought about where she'd stay. Who had two houses destroyed in ten days? Even for Hollywood, that had to be a record.

Syl assured Lilly the house would be safe, guarded 24/7 by the same company watching the Beverly Hills house. And she had already arranged for a place to stay.

It took a while to sort out the logistics. Special Agent Blake insisted on driving her to his office on Wilshire Boulevard. The Omron replacements of Yvette, Reed, and two others drove separately, and Abigail followed in her car. Another attorney from her firm who specialized in criminal law met them at FBI headquarters.

"We don't want to give them any leverage," Abigail said to her in private. "Nothing that might make it difficult for you, your father, or Omron International."

They were all shown to a small conference room.

It turned out "talk" meant interrogation—or it felt that way after hours of going through the story again and again. The questions were all essentially the same, whether asked by the police or the FBI: What time did the attack start? Who fired first? Who killed Roberto

Viera? Did Lilly ever fire at the Vieras?

Special Agent Margaret Cartwright sat in for part of the time, quizzing Lilly about the Jigsaw Puzzle Killer. She wanted to know every movement he made and every word he spoke. Unfortunately, she left before Lilly had a chance to ask about Kade Hunt.

Lilly answered their questions truthfully—most of the time. She left out the part about Alexandra providing her replacement .32 caliber pistol. If the authorities assumed it was in the gun safe along with the shotguns?...well, she let them keep thinking that.

One thing she didn't have to hold back on was the fight with JPK. That was pure self-defense. She was fighting for her life, and expected him to turn the tables on her at any time. Every blow she struck was warranted. When she detailed the construction of the spike club out of a toilet plunger and rusty nail, a few of the men and women cracked brief smiles.

By the time everyone felt they had all they needed, it was late afternoon, and Lilly was yawning every ten seconds.

"I can't believe how tired I am," she said to Abigail, who also looked a bit ragged.

"It's the stress. You'll be better tomorrow after a good night's sleep."

Syl and the Omron team were waiting in the parking lot with Chinese takeout. Lilly finished hers and promptly fell asleep during the drive to what Syl described as a *little cottage.*

Lilly stumbled to her appointed bedroom and collapsed onto the bed fully clothed. The day was finally over.

Chapter 44

October 31

A long shower, clean clothes brought in by Syl, and more food had Lilly feeling human by noon.

Syl had worked one of her miracles. The house was on the property of a private villa in the hills above Pasadena. There were rooms for Kris, Fin, and two new rotating Omron staff. The "little cottage" was bigger than the Malibu house. The best part was the media had no idea where she'd gone since she left with Special Agent Blake yesterday.

Then she turned on the TV.

The news was even worse than she anticipated. Photos of her—everything from past years' photo shoots with her parents, to her mother's graveside service—were prominent on every news channel and daily newspaper. Several special edition tabloids were scheduled to hit supermarket stands this afternoon.

Now that the fog had dissipated, *TMZ* was filming live with telephoto lenses from the hillside above Pacific Coast Highway, and at least two helicopters circled the Malibu house, zooming in on investigators still combing the area for evidence.

And the headlines.

Serial Killer Targets Movie Star Heir!

Teen 'Nails' Jigsaw Puzzle Killer on Halloween Eve!

Her personal fav was *Teen Rambo Slaughters Drug Lords And Serial Killer!*

Speculation had begun about who would play her in several soon-to-be-made movies. Top mentions were Amanda Seyfried and Keira Knightley.

"I could live with that," Lilly mumbled as Kris came into the room "With what?"

"Who's going to play me onscreen."

Kris glanced at the TV, and switched it off. "Enough of that stuff. You need to get outside."

"Seriously?" Lilly said. "You've seen what it's like out there. I can't even go to see my dad since twenty media crews have Cedars staked out in case Supergirl makes an appearance."

"That's what they're calling you?" Kris asked, a wry smile on her face.

"People magazine came out with a special online edition; my head on Supergirl's body."

"Guess we should get you a cape. But you have to admit, it's better than Horse Girl, Miss *Palomino*." Kris pulled off a scratchy imitation of Special Agent Kade Hunt.

Lilly almost threw a pillow, but the strain around her friend's eyes stopped her. Kris was trying to cheer her up, but she had her own losses.

If Magda had died in the fight, there wouldn't be need for further protection. But Magda, probably wounded, was still out there. And if Ernesto's death was motivation enough to mount an all-out revenge war on Lilly, she couldn't imagine Magda now with all three brothers gone. Especially since there were several erroneous reports that Lilly had killed Roberto by *"cutting the drug lord nearly in half with a sub-machine gun."* Lilly rubbed her forehead.

At least the Jigsaw Puzzle Killer was locked up. Well, technically he was under guard in a secure hospital room. Doctors were "cautious" about his recovery. He'd lost a lot of blood from the gunshot wounds in the leg, but the deep nail holes with a rusty spike were their bigger concern. Two of them had gone in under the back of his skull. Half a dozen big name defense lawyers were jockeying for position if he survived.

She still couldn't believe she was the target of a serial killer. Wasn't one set of wackos enough? She should buy lottery tickets.

"By the way," Kris said, "I got word that Agent Hunt's surgery went well yesterday. He'll be in the hospital for another day or two. You should go see him."

When Lilly called the FBI office after the kidnapping in July, they told her he transferred to the East Coast. She hadn't expected to see the agent again. Then…was it only yesterday her hands were covered in his blood? She checked under her fingernails, then turned to Kris.

"Why didn't you just shoot JPK after he threw the knife at Agent Hunt?"

"With you jumping on his back and riding him like a *horse*?"

Lilly did throw the pillow this time.

Kris blocked it and tossed it to the other end of the sofa. "Honestly? After you slammed his face into the floor three times, I didn't think—"

"Three times? I thought I only did that once."

Kris shook her head and held up three fingers. "Girl, you didn't need any help." She came and sat on the footstool, her tone suddenly somber. "Though I did get a little worried when you wouldn't stop with the spiked club."

A vague recollection of Kris shouting at her bubbled to the surface. She shivered, aware of how focused she'd been on stopping the man—permanently.

"Are you sure you don't want to talk about it with someone?"

That was Kris's code for shrink, of course. But Lilly didn't need a therapist. If there was one thing she'd learned in the last three months, it was real life experience trumped academic theory. A professional might know the "why" of the brain reasoning behind her actions, but not the down deep gut mess of motivations that had her beating JPK nearly to death. She had wanted him dead. Not because she was afraid of him, but because she was afraid he might hurt Kris or someone else like he did Kade Hunt. In a strange way, JPK represented the Vieras and all those who hurt and threatened her friends and family. He had the misfortune to meet her face to face.

"Get your shoes on," Kris said, slapping her on the leg. "We're going out."

"Where?"

"Trust me. I know just what you need."

* * *

"Move feet!" Alexandra ordered, shoving Lilly off-balance so she *had* to move.

Sweat dripped off Lilly's nose as she jabbed the heavy bag twice with her left, followed by a hard right. After two hours of weight lifting and self-defense sparring, the previous fifteen minutes on the little speed bag had exhausted the last of her energy. Now the Everlast heavy bag was the last fifteen-minute segment—*if* she could lift her arms a few more times. Her legs felt as heavy as the bag she was pounding.

"Enough," her taskmaster finally said. "Off to shower." Like a usual day, Alexandra headed to her office.

"I'm too tired to shower," Lilly said to Kris, and fell onto a bench press seat. "A couple of weeks without training, and I'm a wimp again."

Kris laughed and continued punching her own heavy bag. Her skin glowed, not dripped like Lilly's.

She had to admit, though, taxing her body felt good, familiar. Especially without the threat of death. Although with Alexandra as her trainer…

And maybe the profuse sweat flushed away the last of the grimy coating of evil.

Strong, Savvy, Survivor. The three S's. Like Alexandra said in the alley, *"You fought, you won. That is what counts."*

"I've got what you wanted!" Syl called, coming through the front door of the training center. She carried a garment bag and large shopping sack with NORDSTROM on their sides. She brought the items straight to Kris, then wrinkled her nose at Lilly. "You need a shower."

"I need a spa," Lilly said, lying back on the vinyl. "And a

masseuse. I hope there's one in that bag."

"Up and at 'em, Supergirl," Kris said. "You have to get ready."

"No." If she kept her eyes closed, maybe they'd leave.

"Don't you want to go see your Secret Agent Man?"

Lilly cracked one eye as Syl unzipped the garment bag and lifted out a royal blue, off-the-shoulder fitted dress that could be at any red carpet event. "Wow." Her other eye opened.

"Shoes to match," Syl said, dangling a pair of pumps in her other hand. "And accessories." She dropped the shoes and lifted out a smaller bag. "Get crackin', girl."

Chapter 45

October 31

"Here he is, Kade." Maggie came into Kade's hospital room waving a photo. "JPK in glorious red, black, and blue. Just picked this up from a one-hour place down the street."

Kade took the eight-by-ten and studied the image. "Wow." White tape held the man's nose centered against purpling cheeks. His mouth and eyebrows were spliced together in several places with Steri-Strips, and it looked like a couple of the spike blows had dug into his right cheek at the jawline. Lilly had done a number on him.

"Never seen anything like it," Maggie said. "He looks like a porcupine got to him. A mean one wielding an ice pick."

Kade narrowed his gaze. The large forehead, wide-set eyes, narrow mouth above a pointed chin... Kade tried to sit up straighter and groaned with the consequence.

"And get this, Kade: twenty-one punctures. She stuck him once for each of the previous state's victims. Coincidence, of course. She couldn't have known about—"

"I've seen this guy!"

"What? Where?"

"At Cedars-Sinai when I visited Nathan Hawthorne." Maggie raised a brow at that, but Kade rushed on. "This guy was in the hallway."

"Ah. That makes sense. His mother is a patient there, dying from cancer."

Kade rubbed his forehead. "He asked if I was visiting a friend. Said his name was Max-something."

She nodded. "Percy Maxwell of Maxwell Enterprises. And here's an interesting coincidence: they found the chief operating officer of the company dead at his house this morning in New York. Thought it was a heart attack, but there was also evidence of embezzlement. Paul and Benny are in the air now to take a deeper look at it."

The eyes in the photo were nearly swollen shut, but malevolence poured through the slits so strongly Kade nearly dropped the paper. This was evil personified. He'd killed moms, dads, and grandmothers. He'd brutally murdered Tex and the toy company owners in Sacramento as mere diversions.

There were well-meaning people in the world who felt everyone, no matter how twisted, could be reasoned with. They hadn't stared into these eyes. Or if they had, they were lucky to still be alive.

Kade dropped the photo onto the blanket so he wouldn't have to touch it any longer, and was relieved when Maggie put it back in her folder.

"Now that we know JPK's identity, Larry's been on conference all day with his team at MIT. They're collecting the dates of every plane flight, phone call, and credit card charge and cross-checking with victim locations. He's already found evidence of at least one fake ID. We're going to nail this case up tight. Get it? Nail—"

"Got it, Maggie," Kade interrupted. After the months of strain, lack of sleep, and frustrating misses, it was good to see his boss happy. It looked good on her.

Margaret Cartwright practically danced out of the room a few minutes later, after promising Larry would stop in for a visit and update sometime this evening.

Unfortunately, her visit left Kade feeling a little sick. He could have arrested Percy Maxwell that day in the hospital and saved innocent lives. Saved Lilly from attack.

The nurse came in and gave him his next dose of pain medication. Maybe it would knock him out into a dreamless sleep.

The pill was beginning to kick in when the divider curtain

swished slightly. Kade turned, expecting to see another nurse or doctor.

A vision in deep blue stood before him. Her white hair glowed in the muted room lighting, falling past one bare shoulder like a silk curtain. Makeup didn't fully hide the dark bruising on her cheek and her split lip, and there were strain lines at the corners of her eyes usually reserved for someone older. But in this dress... Well, she looked nothing like a high school student.

"Palomino," he said.

She smiled. At him. "I can't believe you remembered that."

"And do I recall you calling me Agent Gray Eyes?"

She blushed and ducked her head, but the smile widened. "I may have been delirious...from pain, you know."

He tried to scoot higher in the bed and groaned. "Believe me, I *do* know."

"I guess we have that in common," she said, drawing still closer and gripping the bedrail hard enough her knuckles whitened. "You disappeared. When I was in the hospital, I mean."

Kade explained about his transfer to the East Coast, then his assignment to the Jigsaw Puzzle Killer team. A shudder rippled through her at the name.

"How are you feeling?" she asked, her brows gathered in concern.

"Peachy. Drugs are wonderful." He'd meant it to be funny, but she wasn't laughing, and the tension on her face deepened. No wonder after what she'd been through last night—the whole last month. On impulse, he reached out covered her hand on the bedrail. She turned her hand in his, giving a light squeeze. Not letting go.

"Really, I'll be fine," Kade assured her. "The surgeon said I got the male equivalent of a cesarean section, including the row of staples. But nothing major got punctured. I was lucky."

"Other people died." Her voice was thick, and her eyes glistened. "We didn't. And that's lucky?"

Kade had no answer. There wasn't one. He just knew they had survived.

"Now that this JPK is in custody, are you running off to Boston in the morning?" Her tone had lightened, and he liked the change.

"Depends," he said, hoping he wasn't being an idiot. But he wasn't willing to make the same mistake as last time. And she had come to him.

"On?"

"Where you'll be."

"Oh." Pink swept up her neck, and she was quiet for a long time. Kade held his breath.

Then she said, "I'll have to let you know."

He exhaled slowly, realizing that in spite of all her badass fighting and boldness walking in here in this dress, she was shy. He liked that.

"Meanwhile, maybe you can do me a favor," he said. Dad told him years ago the best way to win a friend was to ask for help.

One corner of her mouth lifted, and she leaned forward. Her hair slipped across one eye Hollywood style, and her voice dropped to a sultry Jersey alto. "Anything for a G-Man."

Maybe not so shy after all. For a moment, Kade had trouble remembering what he was going to say.

"I, uh… I had cream corn, about half an ounce of rubber chicken, and Jell-O for dinner tonight."

"So, copper, you want I should bring you somethin' more substantial tomorrow?"

"Please."

"Double-Double, chocolate shake, and fries from In-N-Out?"

"Oh, man," he groaned, dropping his head back on the pillow. He was in love.

She gave him a crooked smile. "I'll take that as a yes."

* * *

Lilly sat on a stool beside Kade's bed as he answered her questions about his parents, their move to Massachusetts, and his little sister, Rowan. She rubbed her thumb on the back of his hand, smiling as she imagined Pana's mouth a very round O if she saw Lilly doing that.

And really, Lilly was surprised at her own boldness. She'd never done anything like this, but it felt like the most natural thing in the world, like they'd known each other for months.

His voice softened as the painkillers worked their magic, and she was aware how his voice worked its own magic on her. This man had saved her once, then risked his life yesterday morning to do it again. And in a reverse of his actions on that July dawn, this time Lilly had felt his blood running through *her* fingers.

They hardly knew each other, but they were linked by blood—their own, and other people's.

She rested her head on her arm and listened to the soothing cadence of as he spoke, imagining them on the deck of the restored Malibu house, watching the sunset, slow-dancing to soft music from within.

Maybe it was too soon to hope for peace, for tranquility, but Kade's warm hand was a shield that pushed the news crews and tabloid paparazzi away. At least for now. For the first time in days, she allowed herself to relax and simply be.

The door to the hall opened behind her, and Lilly rolled her head so she could see over her shoulder.

A dark-haired woman in a white coat limped into the room. A stethoscope hung around her neck, and a name badge was pinned to her pocket.

It took Lilly a minute to register the deep red on the hem of the coat where it rubbed against black pants. The woman's left hand trailed a red smear on the wall as she braced herself.

Today was Halloween, but Lilly hadn't expected the hospital staff to dress so realistically. Or act so.

"You killed my family," the woman wheezed in a heavy Spanish accent. She raised an ugly knife and lunged.

Magda!

Lilly dodged, sending the stool flying. She banged her head on the bed frame as she fell, then whacked it again on the hard tile. Dizzying sparks colored her vision, and she fought the urge to vomit.

Above, Kade's hand shot out and caught Magda's arm, which was raised for another downward strike. Lilly's view was momentarily blocked by the woman's form as the two struggled, but large drops of hot blood splattered down. Monitor alarms beeped and chimed, and the IV stand crashed on top of her.

Kade.

Lilly looped her bleeding arm around the woman's ankle, trying in vain to pull her off balance. She got a kick to the ribs for her efforts.

Kade grunted, and Lilly envisioned Magda's knife plunging into him.

In desperation, Lilly rolled on her side next to Magda's shuffling feet. She opened her mouth and bit down on the back of a meaty calf.

Violence of action.

Her teeth pierced sinewy flesh and muscle, and the limb kicked in sync with high-pitched screaming. The salty, iron taste of blood filled Lilly's mouth, but she bit down harder, resisting the urge to pull away and gag.

The leg jerked free, and Magda fell on Lilly, crushing the air from her lungs. They were face to face, the knife in Magda's right hand huge, black, and deadly. She lifted it high.

"You killed my family."

Lilly spit blood and bits of flesh in the woman's face and grabbed her wrist. Magda was heavy, but she grimaced in pain from her wound. If Lilly hadn't used up her reserves at the gym…

Fully commit.

Lilly twisted the arm. Magda shifted her weight over it, pushing the vibrating blade closer to Lilly's heart. The tip slowly turned downward between them as Lilly wrenched Magda's brown flesh.

Then, over Magda's shoulder, Kade crawled onto the bedrail, trailing tubes and wires. The front of his hospital gown was red with fresh blood, and his eyes were clinched in pain.

"You killed my mom!" Lilly spat, and twisted the arm holding the knife with everything she had.

Kade landed on Magda's back, crushing her against Lilly and smashing the knife between them.

Pain stabbed Lilly's chest, worse than any of the gunshot wounds in the van. She swore her heart skipped a few beats.

The room door banged into the wall, followed by shouting, squeaking shoes, and crashes. The weight of the two bodies was lifted away, and Lilly rolled onto her side, gasping for air and spitting out more blood and flesh with each puny exhale. Shoes bumped her side and back.

The staccato pleas from alarms brought more hospital staff and clattering carts. Every sound was amplified like a bullhorn, blasting more searing spikes deep into Lilly's skull. She would have clamped her hands over her ears, but they were busy pressing against her chest where the knife dug deep. A male voice called Code Blue.

Someone bent over Lilly, flashing a penlight across her eyes, blinding her and triggering more pain so intense she thought her head would burst.

She asked about Kade, but no one answered. On a three count, she was lifted onto a gurney and rolled out of the room.

Behind, the chaos continued.

That was a good sign, wasn't it?

Epilogue

"I envy you," Dad said. "You'll be in Paris for springtime."

Lilly's two suitcases were packed, a paltry amount of belongings for a year or more in France, Italy, and other places throughout Europe. But as Mom always said, she could buy what she needed when there.

"Got your passport?"

Lilly pulled it out and showed it to him.

" 'Palomino Ekaterina Glass,' " he read aloud, then handed it back. "It's official. And I like it."

"It still sounds foreign to me." The picture staring back at her was the same. Nothing else was. No part of her life. She stuffed the passport into her bulging travel backpack.

"You'll get used to it, Mina," he said, already comfortable using his preferred nickname.

She liked it too. So much better than Lil.

He leaned on one of the leather chairs beside his desk in his rented house. The room featured mahogany wainscoting, but was devoid of the movie posters, awards, and film memorabilia that made his former office special. Whenever she closed her eyes and thought of her father, that was the room she pictured him in. Maybe someday.

Although the worst injuries from the explosion had long healed, the burn scars on his legs and torso still bothered him. But only in private. On the site of his projects, Nathan Hawthorne once again presented a commanding presence.

His face had been shielded and suffered less damage, and only a few minor discolorations reminded them of the horror of that day. Still, she worried about him. Some scars went deeper than skin and bone.

"I'm fine, Mina. Stop worrying."

She met his eyes again, then laughed. "You always know what I'm thinking."

"Not that hard. After all, you are your mother's daughter."

Lilly was Ekaterina Orlov's daughter for what she now knew was a heartbreakingly short five years. Was that enough to really *be* someone's child? To take on their traits, mannerisms, values, and become like them?

Yes, definitely.

She was glad he talked about Mom so often, though there was a sadness around his eyes when he thought no one was looking. In so many ways, it was impossible to think of Mom as gone, only away on some exotic film location. Her photos and film footage were everywhere, and would be for many years. But long after Ekaterina Orlov faded from the ever-changing daily entertainment news, she would still be Lilly's—and Mina's—mom. Her *real* mom in every way.

"Any word from Syl?" Lilly asked. Syl had hired an interior design firm for the Malibu house that specialized in maintaining the mid-century modern look yet bringing some futuristic technology and splashes that promised to wow. After all, Syl said, isn't that what mid-century modern was in the first place?

"All the permits are in," he said. "They're beginning construction at noon today. I'm meeting Syl there next week to check the progress."

"Text me lots of pictures. I want to make sure they don't ruin it."

"Yes, ma'am."

The remains of the Beverly Hills home would be scraped away

and the lot sold. Neither of them wanted those memories.

Lilly had also worked with three tutors and finished a grueling alternative high school program, successfully testing out of her remaining classes and earning her diploma. The pride on her dad's face when she showed him the paper was worth ten times the effort it took.

The Jigsaw Puzzle Killer's trial wouldn't be for a year or more. Lilly had given video depositions, but would undoubtedly be called back to testify. Defense attorneys had gone on record with Percy Maxwell's statement that he had no knowledge of JPK, that Percy was an innocent businessman, an acquaintance of Lilly Hawthorne's, and only in the house that night to protect her.

ABC's 20/20 was readying a series of shows that would follow the trial proceedings, and the *National Enquirer* had already published two issues with a Photoshopped pregnant Lilly on the cover, speculating she carried JPK's love child.

More than anything, Lilly worried about her father's safety. Threats directed at him had arrived from the me-too psychos that obsessed over entertainment celebs. There were probably more he hadn't mentioned. A big comfort was that Fin Silvan had resigned from Omron International and hired on as Dad's head of security. The taciturn guard was gradually loosening up, and was a hit on set among the beautiful starlets who were secretly placing bets on who could first get him to blush.

Lilly probably would have stayed in L.A. longer, but Special Agent Ron Blake's warning visit last month pushed her to a decision about the future. Magda and the rest of the Vieras were dead. The knife blade had sunk deep into Magda when Kade landed on her, piercing vital organs Lilly didn't want to know about. Lilly's only injury was a severely bruised sternum from the butt of the handle.

Yet even with Magda dead, someone had sent a one-page letter to FBI headquarters in L.A.

TELL LILLY HAWTHORNE TO LOOK OVER HER SHOULDER, I'M RIGHT BEHIND HER.

SHE IS A DEAD WOMAN.

Lilly's name change was finalized out of state and buried deep. Mina Glass would only become Lilly Hawthorne again when back in the city for the trial, and then only under heavy guard. Meanwhile, she'd see her dad on distant film locations whenever they deemed it safe.

The rest of the time, she'd be studying glass artistry with some of the European masters, including glass sculpture in Paris, and Venetian glass in Italy. It was time to leave L.A., and she couldn't wait to get started.

"Hey, kiddo," Kris said, poking her head in the doorway and tapping her wristwatch. "Transport's ready. Gotta bounce."

Kris was accompanying Lilly to Paris and helping her get settled in an apartment. Lilly hoped to convince her to stay for a week or two. Kris deserved a relaxing break before returning to the Omron headquarters in San Francisco for a new assignment.

"Straight to Paris?" her father asked, his face unreadable.

Lilly dipped her head and cut a sideways glance at Kris, who gave her a subtle nod. "Actually, I'm stopping in Boston for a couple of days...to get my hair cut. And..." How was she going to tell him—

"Tell your Secret Agent hello for me."

Lilly looked up and saw the wide grin on his face.

"Sheesh. Is nothing secret?" She glared at Kris, but the woman simply held up both palms and shook her head.

"Not as long as I'm your father," he said, laughing. "After all, you're *my* daughter too."

They held each other for a long time, silently remembering the good of the past, the all-too sharp pain of the present, and the promise of the future.

"I love you, Daddy," she said, kissing him on the cheek. She picked up her bags. "Stay safe. I'll see you soon."

"Good-bye, Supergirl. I'm proud of you."

As sad as it was to leave, Palomino Ekaterina Glass couldn't wait to land in Boston.

Agent Gray Eyes was waiting for her.

~ ~ ~

How you can help

First, please consider writing a review at your favorite retailer site. You can't imagine how much they help. Advertisers look for how many reviews a book has, and sometimes it's why they will accept a book in this competitive world.

Second, I'd love to hear from you. Tell me what you liked or <gasp!> didn't like, and why. Your feedback will make me a better writer.

Finally, I have a great team of test readers and editors, and we work hard to catch every error before my books are published. So, if you find one that slipped through, please let me know! Just send a short phrase I can search for in the master document.

rich@perilousfiction.com

A note to readers

Thanks for reading *Shattered Glass*!

Except for the Prologue, *Shattered Glass* is set around the same time as *Perilous Cove*, the first book in the Perilous Safety Series. However, *Shattered Glass* is not a prequel to that series, and therefore can be read anytime.

When I began writing *Shattered Glass,* I thought it would be current day. But this is Lilly's story, and she insisted it be told as she lived it. How do you argue with Supergirl?

But don't be surprised if next time Lilly "Palomino" Glass and Kris Stone show up at Storm Lake, right after the terrible incident at *Desperation Falls*.

See you at the lake!

Perilous Safety Series
Perilous Cove
Storm Song
Desperation Falls

Glass & Stone Series
Shattered Glass

Chronological Order of Books
Shattered Glass
Perilous Cove
Storm Song
Desperation Falls

Acknowledgements

Jan Scanlin from Jan Scanlin Glass gave me initial inspiration for Lilly and the career she continues in the next story. Until I met Jan, I knew little about glass art except glass blowers. I learned there is a whole lot more to it. You can find pictures of Jan's amazing creations and contact information at www.scanlinglass.com.

Robert Henslin Design for another amazing cover. Rob's cover art is often the push I need to finish a book. www.rhdcreative.com

Cade Courtley's *Seal Survival Guide* (I listened to the audio book) is a wealth of knowledge on how to deal with dangerous situations, everything from personal attacks to surviving natural disasters and nuclear blasts. Entertaining, educational, and it could save your life. I combined some of his principles with others I learned in self-defense training and used these for Lilly's instruction. And no, I didn't morph his name to Kade for the book. Kade Hunt already existed before I came across this resource.

Corey Hart spent two decades in hospital security and provided great inside information about how top hospitals protect the identities of their more famous patients.

My wife, Sheryl, who puts up with long absences as I lose myself in my characters and stories.

And finally my beta reading team: Nancy Bailey, Patricia Bossman, Carol Dickerson, Clayton Hutsler, Lisa Gregory, Sis Hammack, Jennifer Haynie, Hannah Prewett, and Jonelle Stevens. They read the draft of this book, and their feedback and suggestions were invaluable.

About Rich Bullock

Rich Bullock writes stories of ordinary people put in perilous situations, where lives are changed forever.

Fortunate to grow up in small-town San Luis Obispo, California, he developed an eye for settings that remind people of home. He now lives and writes in Redding, California, where on most days he sees Mount Lassen, Mount Shasta, and the inside of a coffee shop.

Connections
Web: www.perilousfiction.com
Facebook: /perilousfiction
Email: rich@perilousfiction.com